VALERIE FRENCH

VALERIE FRENCH

BY

DORNFORD YATES

WARD, LOCK & CO., LIMITED
LONDON AND MELBOURNE

Library Editions of " Valerie French "

First Published	.	.	1923
Reprinted	.	.	.	1925
Reprinted	.	.	.	1928
Reprinted	.	.	.	1929
Reprinted	.	.	.	1931
Reprinted	.	.	.	1934
Reprinted	.	.	.	1936
Reprinted	.	.	.	1940
Reprinted	.	.	.	1942
Reprinted	.	.	.	1943
Reprinted	.	.	.	1944
Reprinted	.	.	.	1945
Reprinted	.	.	.	1947

MADE IN ENGLAND
Printed in Great Britain by Butler & Tanner Ltd., Frome and London

To

THE ENGLISH

TO WHOM

TO LIVE, OR DIE, ACCORDING

TO THE BEST TRADITIONS

COMES NATURAL.

CONTENTS

CONTENTS

VALERIE FRENCH

CHAPTER I

A PILLAR OF SALT

THE fire was still raging.

For thirty-six hours, now, it had burned steadily, a firm east wind directing the work of destruction with the lightning precision of an overseer who knows his job. Of the five thousand acres of woodland, once so luxuriant, barely a tenth part was left.

For week after blazing week the proud estate had gone thirsty. No rain falling, the wind had made hay, literally, while the sun shone. Springs had dwindled and died : empty beds showed where the brooks had run : pools had disappeared. Even the lake itself, no longer fed, had shrunk to a dull pond, a widening belt of mud, seamed with innumerable cracks, about its sides. As for the trees, the source of sap failing, they were hard put to it to live. Without, at any rate, trunks, twigs and branches were dry as any bone.

Everything, then, was in train. . . .

Whose hand it was that touched off the piece will never be known, but word that Gramarye was on fire came to *The Rose* at Girdle by ten of a handsome morning in the last week of July.

The news spread but slowly. Nobody cared.
The park was deserted : its owner lay in a mad-
house : the house was tumbling. If the tidings
were greeted at all, they were greeted with approval.
The host of *The Rose* himself made no secret of his
persuasion.

" Bes' thing as could 'appen. No manner o' good
to man nor beas', that place was. They're payin'
fourpence a bucket at Beauty Cross, but if this 'ere
drort 's put ' paid ' to Gramarye . . ."

He sighed dramatically, raising his eyes to heaven,
and, after a decent interval, his tankard to his lips.

" Wot's the place done ? " said the Cockney, who
was taking a car to Wales.

" Done ? " said his host. " Well, it's sent three
men mad to my knowledge, and that's the gospel.
Livin' an' workin' there, as lanskip-gardeners. Got
'old o' their brains it did, an' who's to wonder ?
Lanskip ! " he added contemptuously. " 'Owlin' wilderness. Nothin' but woods an' woods. Miles of
'em. An' never nor beas' nor bird in all them acres."

" Go on," said the Cockney, staring.

The lord of *The Rose* did not appear to hear him.
He continued absently.

" An' now she's burnin'. . . . Well, well. . . .
Maybe it'll lif' the curse. Valuable buildin' land it'll
be . . . one day. . . ."

That evening some children had straggled up
Gallowstree Hill, to see what they could. This
was nothing at all, for the fire was below and beyond
a tremendous shoulder. They returned querulously
to Girdle and declared the report untrue. Keepers
of neighbouring property knew better, and kept
an eye on the wind : Sir Barnaby Linchpin. whose

land lay to leeward of Gramarye, held fifty beaters at hand for twenty-four hours : an evening paper announced that Sherwood Forest was in flames, and gave a *résumé* of the career of Robin Hood.

But that was all. And now thirty-six hours had gone by, and the fire was still raging.

From an odd chain of road, cut like a shelf upon a spur of the Cotswold Hills, a man looked down upon the holocaust.

From where he stood, this was indeed a stupendous spectacle. Distance and Night lent it a supernatural majesty. The one robbed the flames of their sting ; the other gave them their proper setting. The man found the sight fascinating. He did not, of course, care. Gramarye was nothing to him.

He must have stood gazing for half an hour, before a wandering breath of cool night air brought him to earth. With a shiver he turned away, making as though to button his coat about him. In the midst of the gesture he stopped and stared at his forearms. *He had no coat to button.*

The discovery clearly surprised him. After a moment he lifted his head and frowned into the starlight. Then he fell to inspecting his apparel, as well as he could. He had a shirt, certainly, and the wreck of a pair of trousers about his thighs, and there were shoes on his feet. The shirt was in tatters, the trousers ragged and foul. So much his fingers told him. The report his nose rendered was worse still. Both garments stank to glory.

The man exclaimed disgustedly, and his hands flew to his belt. It was in his mind, I fancy, to strip then and there. Reason, however, suggested that he must first find a change : he could not go naked.

Again he raised his head and blinked into the night. Mechanically he put up a hand to finger his chin. . . .

As he touched the bristles, he started violently. Till then he had had no idea he was wearing a beard. As in a dream he felt all over his head. He found it unkempt, beastly. His face, he noticed, was gaunt, the cheek-bones staring. . . . Here his stomach got in a hungry word. For the first time the man realized that he was starving. . . .

Instantly the craving for food overwhelmed all other inclinations. This was, of course, common sense. Filth and odours could wait : hunger such as this was in Death's service—a running footman, in fact. The man knew in a moment the dreadful livery.

At once he started to walk along the road, squaring his shoulders to cheat the sense which told him his strength was failing, and hoping hard for a sign-post to point him the nearest way—*whither ?*

The query occurring to him, the man stopped still.

He had no idea where he was. If it came to that, he had no idea, either, how he came to be in such a plight. His thoughts flew back desperately. He had met with an accident, of course. That went without saying. Foul play, perhaps. Hence his condition The last thing he remembered was—was——

For the third time he frowned into the night, rack-ing his brain.

This he did to no purpose at all.

For him there was no 'last thing.'

He could remember nothing.

*   *   *   *   *

When it dawned upon Lyveden that he had lost his memory, he became profoundly interested. So much so, that he forgot his hunger and sat himself down on a bank by the side of the road. After some meditation, he recited the Alphabet aloud. Pleased with this effort, he announced that London was the capital of England, and enumerated as many counties as he could think of. He was proceeding to another such exercise, when something touched him upon the calf of the leg.

Sitting at his feet was a small rough-haired dog. His eyes were dull, and he was very thin. His coat appeared to be grey, and there was a definite black patch upon his back. For a long moment the two regarded each other in silence. Then the dog rolled over and put his paws in the air.

Lyveden patted him kindly.

"Where have you come from?" he said. Then: "By Jove, poor fellow, you're thin. Which reminds me . . ." He got upon his feet. With a manifest effort, the dog followed his example. "It's obvious I must . . . have . . . food." He looked up the ghostly road, pursing his lips. "It must lead somewhere," he muttered, and started off. . . .

The first fifty paces bared an unpleasant truth—that to walk exhausted more quickly than to stay still. That Lyveden was heading for succour was practically certain. That every step brought him nearer the end of his tether was painfully evident. Which of these halts would come first, he had no idea. Lyveden set his teeth and hoped for the best. . . .

It was only ten minutes later that he remembered the dog.

Peering back into the darkness, he saw no sign

of him. He whistled and stood waiting, without
result. After a little hesitation, he began to retrace
his steps. . . .

What those two furlongs cost him I dare not think.
Perhaps Sir Philip Sidney walked at his elbow.

He found him at last, sitting miserably in the
middle of the road. The poor little vagabond could
go no farther. Lyveden picked him up gently and
put him under his arm.

" Buck up, old fellow," he said. " It won't be
long now—one way or the other."

The scrap put up its nose and licked his face.

*　　*　　*　　*　　*

Private Albert Rogers, of the R.A.S.C.(M.T.), was
bored stiff.

When he had been given his itinerary and told
that he was to take ' The Swine ' to Hounslow, he had
at once protested that she would never get there. The
wording of the sergeant-major's reply may be imagined,
but must not be here set out. Suffice it that that
authority had lamented the fact that there was no
Rolls-Royce available, had criminally libelled Private
Rogers's forebears and had prophesied, first, no good
concerning Private Rogers, but evil, and, secondly,
that ' The Swine ' would get there, even if Private
Rogers had to push her the whole of the way.

With burning ears and a full heart, Private Albert
Rogers had proceeded to pack his kit-bag. . . .

Quite early he had lost his itinerary, and somewhere about noon he had lost his way. It was when
he was hopelessly confounded, that ' The Swine,'
who had lived well up to her sobriquet ever since
she had started, had played her trump card. In

a word, with a diabolical scream she had spilled the contents of her gear-box upon the King's highway.

Private Albert Rogers had coaxed the lorry to the side of the road, shaken the sweat out of his eyes, and prayed for death. . . .

His comrade-in-arms, Private Hoskin, was less dejected. Gifted with an invulnerable sense of humour, he had found the journey diverting, and had sung most of the way. He had not, of course, been driving. As the stertorous breathing of 'The Swine's' engine subsided, he laid a hand upon his heart and commenced a tender rendering of 'Where my caravan 'as rested.'

This was too much for Private Rogers.

As his comrade's superior officer, he issued two orders. The first was that Private Hoskin should "for gauze sake give over." The second, that he should get upon his flat feet, fare to the nearest village, and report 'progress.' The first command was disregarded : the second was obeyed after much argument and a delay of more than two hours.

It proved subsequently to be just six miles to the village of Broad-i'-the-Beam, and as Private Hoskin did not march four miles to the hour, but rather two, by the time he arrived the Post Office was closed. Not so *The Black Goat*. . . . After his third 'bitter,' Private Hoskin decided that to return to the lorry that night would be the act of a fool.

All things, then, considered, it is not at all surprising that Private Albert Rogers was bored stiff. The lorry was empty : the two kit-bags offered a miserable couch : he had run out of cigarettes. . . .

For the hundredth time he was polishing the

apostrophe with which he would welcome his subordinate, when somebody rapped with his knuckles upon the side of the cab.

Rogers got upon his knees and thrust out his head.

A figure was leaning against the lorry's side, breathing distressfully.

" I say," said a voice faintly, " I'm—I'm rather done. . . . Could—could you spare me something to eat ? "

Private Rogers stepped on to the footboard and sprang down into the road. Then he lugged a lamp from its bracket and held it to illumine the speaker.

The white, pinched face, the sagging knees, told their own tale.

" 'Strewth ! " said Rogers, and slid a sinewy arm round Anthony Lyveden's back. . . .

It was a near thing.

Bully beef and warm water are simple fare, but Private Albert Rogers had a head upon his shoulders.

So soon as Lyveden was settled by the side of the road, his craving for food yielded to a frantic desire for sleep. This the soldier would not hear of. He fairly forced Lyveden to eat, feeding him with his fingers. He decanted the contents of the tin on to a newspaper, picked out the jelly with his knife, and watched his patient masticate every dram. When the latter had eaten perhaps a tablespoonful, he gave him water. Then he wrapped a greatcoat about him, and set a kit-bag under his head.

" Now you kin sleep, mate," he said, " for 'alf an hour. Then you'll 'ave to wake up an' 'ave some more grub."

Thankfully Lyveden closed his eyes.

The next moment he was propped on an elbow.

"The dog!" he cried. "I forgot. There was a dog with me."

"Now you lay down, mate," said Rogers. "The dorg's orright. 'E's 'avin' 'is whack now. 'Elp," he added, staring. "'E's pouched the lot. Never mind. There's more where that come from. But you didn't ought ter eat so fas', Toby; nor yet so much, neither." The dog wagged his tail and licked his lips. His host shook his head reprovingly. "Don't want to burst yerself," he added. "Now you wait there while I get my mug. Then you kin 'ave some water."

He turned to glance at Lyveden. He was asleep.

The soldier's idea of nursing was rough and ready, but it was very sound. Faithfully, three times in the night Anthony was awakened and given nourishment, and when Private Hoskin arrived at nine o'clock, he was sent pelting back to the village for eggs and milk. To give the rogue his due, he went gladly. He had a good heart.

By half-past two o'clock that same afternoon man and dog alike were changed beings. They were shaky enough, certainly, but they were not feeble. Beneath the care of Privates Rogers and Hoskin they put off their corruption.

Lyveden was assisted to remove his beard, and his hair was rudely cut with a pair of nail-scissors. The kit-bags were opened, and, after a heated discussion, a shirt, a cardigan, socks and an aged pair of slacks were selected and assigned to his use. Then a bucket was produced, and 'The Swine's' radiator used as a cistern. Anthony washed and was washed. The dog was cleansed also.

B

By the time assistance arrived, Lyveden was enjoying a cigarette. . . .

Even the two soldiers were surprised at the result of their handiwork. Out of their vile chrysales had emerged two thoroughbreds. There was no doubt about it. Thin as rails though they were, the thing stood out. Lyveden's fine, clean-cut face, his quiet air of dignity, his pleasant voice alone were evidence and to spare. As for the Sealyham, he was an attractive fellow. His pert tail was up, and there was a light in his eyes. He rested a lot, certainly, but when he was on his feet his carriage was bold, and he held his head high.

At last Relief came panting out of the distance. . . .

When 'The Swine' had been made fast to the new-comer, Rogers approached his patient and offered to take him as far as Broad-i'-the-Beam.

" You ain't fit, sir, for duty, an' there's a pub there, Ted says, where they'll look after you. If you git there, you kin write 'ome an' say where you are, like."

Gentlemen both, neither of his two hosts had asked questions.

" You're awfully kind," said Lyveden, rising and picking up the dog. " I suppose you realize that you've saved my life."

Private Rogers grinned.

" You was a bit queer las' night, sir," he said clumsily. " Firs' good turn the ole Swine's ever done, I reckon."

Half an hour later they stopped before *The Black Goat.*

Preceded by Hoskin, Lyveden and Rogers made their way into the inn. The landlord received them with a nod.

" This 'ere's the gent," said Hoskin, " as I was tellin' you of." The landlord bowed. " 'E ain't quite 'isself yet, 'e ain't, but I said as 'ow you'd give 'im a bed to-night, so's 'e kin write to 'is friends."

" 'Appy, I'm sure," said the landlord. " Sit down, sir. You've——"

" One minute," said Lyveden. " I have no friends to write to : I haven't a penny piece : and these two gentlemen here are the only beings I know."

The three stared at him.

Then—

" But you're a toff ! " cried Hoskin. " A proper toff. Them trousers was dandy once."

" S-sh ! " said the landlord. " I know a gent when I sees one. Look 'ere, sir, you've 'ad a tumble or somethin', an' if you'll give me your name——"

Anthony Lyveden started and clapped a hand to his head.

The three watched him curiously.

At last he looked round and smiled.

" Can't be done," he said quietly. " Not even that. You see, my memory's gone."

There was a long silence, broken only by the snuffs and blowings of the Sealyham, who was exploring the parlour and drawing the sweet sawdust into his nose.

" Well," said the landlord at length, " well, that's all—all right, sir. You . . . you . . ."

" If you'll give me shelter," said Lyveden, " just for a day or two, I'll pay you back. As soon as I can earn money, I'll——"

The host of the inn cut short his promises.

" 'Ave what you like, sir," he said, " an' settle the bill when you please."

"You're very good," said Lyveden, and called for drinks.

It was before these were finished that Rogers excused himself to Anthony and, promising indeed to return, haled his subordinate outside. After a minute or two they both reappeared—sheepishly. . . . Then Lyveden asked for paper and wrote down their names. When the time of parting came he walked with them to 'The Swine.'

"You know how it is with me," he said, "so I've little to say. If my memory ever comes back, you'll be the first to hear. One doesn't forget one's pals."

He shook hands with them, and they climbed confusedly on to the footboard.

A moment later 'The Swine' was under way.

Anthony watched it lurch round a corner.

Then came the sound of steps, and Rogers, red in the face, came running back.

"Quite forgot," he said jerkily. "Found this 'ere in your trousers, sir. In the 'ip-pocket. I 'ope perhaps the wordin' 'll 'elp your memory."

He thrust a slip of paper into the other's hand, took two paces backward, saluted, turned round and ran like mad.

As Lyveden unfolded the paper, there fell out two ten-shilling notes.

*　　*　　*　　*　　*

When Anthony Lyveden realized fully the state he was in—got, so to speak, the hang of his situation —he found it extremely good.

That he did not esteem it at once is not surprising. For one thing, the man was a wreck: for another, his loss was peculiar enough to bewilder a sage. It was not, in fact, until the fourth day of resting in and about *The Black Goat*, that the excellence of his lot presented itself to his mind in all its glory. Many minds would have seen no excellence, nor glory either. *Quot homines, tot sententiæ.* But Lyveden was a philosopher : also his sense of humour was fine and sturdily grown. It was, indeed, thanks to this sterling equipment that he had determined to make the best of a bad business, and, whistling an air, whose extraction he could not remember, climbed cheerfully into bed. He had his reward. Waking at seven o'clock of a fragrant morning, and lazily planning, while he lay, the execution of his recent resolve, Lyveden suddenly saw that his task was already done. He found, in a word, that the business, which he was to better, was not bad at all.

Anthony sat up in bed, his brain whirling.

Here was a man, he judged, some thirty years old, intelligent, healthy, and soon to be very strong, without a care in the world . . . without a care. . . . Actually in the prime of life, he had been miraculously flicked back to the threshold. He had been given that for which Piety and Wit knew that it was idle to ask. The Moving Finger had been lured back to cancel thirty pages.

Sirs, let us take this fortunate point of view, and, doing what Lyveden cannot do for himself, set it under a microscope. Two things stand out at once —a curious egoism, for one, a sense of relief, for another. Philosophy never wrought these. That relatives might be frantic, because he was out of their ken, never occurs to the man. Why ? The bare idea of security has made him throw up his hat. Why ? The reasons are plain. Lyveden's experience is at work—*behind the veil.* Again let us do as he cannot, and raise that veil. There is the truth, gentlemen, as clear as crystal. An orphan from birth, Anthony has no relations and next to no friends. As for his cares, he has of late been opposing a very sea of troubles. . . .

I have no wish, sirs, to labour this matter, but we are dealing with a man's mind now—always stuff of importance, but in this tale the very headstone of the corner. Here, once for all, if you will, let us examine its state, and then—the lesson over—pass out of the latticed chamber to look at the bowling-green. Brains are all very well, but the turf at the back of the inn is a very masterpiece. But then Nature has slaved at this diaper for more than three hundred years.

That Lyveden had lost his memory is a loose statement. He had lost part of it only. For him, his personal past was blotted out. He could remember nothing that he had ever done or ever suffered. He could remember no acquaintance, local or personal, animate or inanimate, which he had ever had. With these important exceptions, his memory was pretty sound. What general knowledge he had possessed was, more or less, at his disposal. Names that were household words he well remembered, and their associations also : only—from those associations were excluded himself and all his works. Oxford, for instance, he knew for a seat of learning. He could name most of its colleges. He recalled the look of the place—hazily. Whether he had been schooled within its grey walls he had no idea. The fact that he could name but five of the colleges of

Cambridge, and could not picture the town, *suggested* that he had favoured Oxford, but that was all. Again, he was clear that there had been a great war—most recently. Its cause, progress, and result, he perfectly remembered—particularly its progress. He dared not swear that he had soldiered. Later, his detailed recollection of the fighting *suggested* that he had served with the guns on more than one front, but that was all. He could not remember that he had ever dressed for dinner, but he knew that this thing was done. . . .

Here we are coming to Instinct. Lyveden's instinct was as sound as a bell. As such, it was a buckler worth having, for while a baby's instinct is above rubies, that of a man of thirty, who knows his world, cannot well be appraised. Moreover, between Experience and Instinct there is a positive liaison. . . .

The moment that Anthony Lyveden found his necessity virtuous, he became almost debonair. Curiosity would have been inconvenient—spoiled everything. But he was not curious. He had no desire to remember. If it was so ordained, he was quite ready to remember. Indeed, he was eager to see whether the faculty of recognition had gone the way of his memory. Until he recognized something, this question would remain unanswered. It occurred to him that he might be recognized . . . accosted. Then he would learn about himself. Without doubt, a rare entertainment awaited him. . . . Anthony began to like his reincarnation better than ever.

It was later upon that same morning that he addressed the Sealyham. The two were seated beside that elegant green, waiting for the church clock to give the word for their departure. A shabby haversack had been packed, farewells had been taken, compliments exchanged. Refreshed and grateful, man and dog were going to seek their fortune.

" It is clear, my fellow," said Lyveden, " that we cannot remain anonymous." The terrier moistened his lips. " Quite so. You see, it's not only unfashionable—it's inconvenient. That we have names already is a charming but futile reflection. Whatever they happen to be, they've served their turn. You see, I'm a brand-new broom, and you know what new brooms do. . . . Well, I don't know about dogs, but I have a sort of idea that a man may not be his own godfather. The cryptic phrase ' deed-poll ' seems to stick out of the mud at the back of my brain. Still, we must chance that. I propose to give names to us both— nice new names." The dog rolled over upon his back, and Lyveden patted him abstractedly. " The devil of it is, what to choose. They must be slap-up names. We shan't ever get such a chance again, you know, so we may as well do ourselves proud. Let's see . . ." For a moment he sat, knitting his brows, and stroking the dog's rough coat. Then his face lighted up. " ' Hamlet ' ! " he cried suddenly. " There's a name for a dog. ' Hamlet.' My son, you're lucky. That was a blinkin' brain-wave, that was. Good name to shout and everything. ' Hamlet.' Well, that's that. Now it's my turn. I think," he continued slowly, " I think I must be called ' Jonathan.' I like ' Jonathan.' I've always liked ' Jonathan.' At least, I suppose I have. At any rate, I like it now, and——"

Here the church clock began to strike nine leisurely. . . .

Two minutes later Hamlet and Jonathan emerged

from the kindly shelter of *The Black Goat* and, passing through Broad-i'-the-Beam, set their faces in the direction of the Oxford road.

*   *   *   *   *

Sitting in a very French room, overlooking an orchard, Lady Touchstone read through the letter which she had written

> *Villa Narcisse,*
> *Dinard.*
> *29th July.*

DEAR JOHN,

Letters from you suggest that we have been corresponding. I am glad to know it. The truth is that for the last six weeks I have done what I have done in a dream.

When Tragedy leaps from behind a curtain on to shoulders as old as mine—I feel four hundred—the effort requisite to deal at all reasonably with the event empties the brain. One's old wits fail. I cannot remember what I have said or done, or—worse still—whether I have said or done it. (I bought our tickets twice over—the same afternoon.) For the first time in my life I have a sound sympathy with those poor old people who, whenever you see them, tell you the same anecdotes. It is not their fault. Some effort has emptied their brains.

Poor Anthony Lyveden's body was found a fortnight ago—in a terrible state. The hot weather, of course. The clothes were gone. They say the left leg was broken. . . . We had him buried at Girdle. It seemed the best thing to do.

I notice I say 'we.' I should have said 'I.'

The moment the news came, Valerie threw down her cards. I tell you, it was like Bridge. Up to that moment she and I had been partners, and she'd been the one that mattered. Suddenly she became 'Dummy,' and I had to play the game. She's been 'Dummy' ever since. Wonderfully sweet and gentle, unnaturally calm, apparently perfectly content. But no initiative —no energy of mind—nothing. Every plan I make is 'admirable': every suggestion 'splendid.' She 'can't imagine how I think of it all.' But ask her opinion, and she'll smile and shrug her shoulders. She just doesn't care about anything, John. The frocks her maid puts out for her Valerie puts on. If she put out odd stockings, on to her feet they'd go.

I brought her here to get her out of herself.

To tell you the truth, I hoped and believed she'd kick. Do you understand? I wanted a sign of life. This agreeable apathy is frightening. A raging Valerie makes me tremulous, but Valerie meek and mild is shortening my life. I tell you I feel aged. . . .

Well, from that point of view, Dinard was such a failure that I was quite thankful I hadn't suggested Pekin. We should have had to go. This terrible approval of one's choice is far more compelling than any criticism.

I heard of a villa somehow, and here we are.

I have a good maître d'hôtel, who does everything. I think he is lining his pockets for years to come, but I would not part with him for a thousand pounds.

We eat, sleep, and are driven about the Department. We watch tennis; we hear music; we attend the Casino. We discuss—more or less cheerfully—the small things in Life. The world sees a silly old fool with a devoted niece. I tell you, John, the girl is sweetness itself.

*Her affection brings tears to my eyes. But she is just
' Dummy.' Her character has gone.*

*Pray for her. Pray for us both, because, for the
moment I am, I think, indispensable.*

Affectionately,

HARRIET TOUCHSTONE.

*P.S.—If only they had been married instead of be-
trothed. . . . I shall always say that wedlock would
have been proof against that influence. Valerie's arms
would have won. Of course you'll shake your head.
You must pretend disapproval, because you're a priest.
But you won't groan. I'll bet you don't groan.*

H. T.

Lady Touchstone addressed the letter with a sigh.

It was right that John Forest should know what
was going on. She had told him, therefore, what
she was telling herself. She did not tell him the
fear which knocked at her heart daily, insistently.
This was that Valerie French, that glorious, dazzling
creature, had gone the way of Lot's wife.

' She became a pillar of salt.'

A tall, graceful pillar—stricken, yet tearless—
heedless of pain or pleasure as the pitiful dead, Valerie
was warranting the comparison. Desire had failed.

Let us see for ourselves.

Upstairs, in a lavender wrap, hairbrush in hand,
Valerie sat in her chair and stared at her glass.

An Eve stared back.

A painter once said of Miss French that she had
never been born. He was meaning, I fancy, that
she had sprung, like Cytheræa, out of the loins of
Nature. Indeed, she did not look a daughter of
men : and if Cytheræa rose from the foam of the

sea, Valerie French came stepping out of the heart of a forest one sweet September morning, twenty-six years ago.

Nature's treasuries had been ransacked to make her lovely. The cool of the dawn lay in her finger-tips ; the breath of the mountains hung in her nostrils. Violets, dew, and stars went to the making of those wonderful eyes. Her skin was snowy, save where the great sun had kissed her—on either cheek ; her mouth was a red, red flower. Her voice was bird's music ; her dark hair, a cloud ; her carriage, that of a deer. As for her form, straight, clean-limbed, lithe, its beauty was old as the hills. In a word, Valerie French threw back to Eden.

Valerie gazed and gazed. . . .

After a long while—

" Not a grey hair," she said slowly. " Not one. By rights, my hair should be white. By rights, my eyes should be staring. . . . They're not even strained. I ought to be thin, pale as a ghost, with great rings under my eyes. . . . I looked a million times worse before—before it happened. . . . And now, when nothing matters, when everything's gone—smashed—finished, I look my best. . . . I suppose it's because I can't care . . . the power of caring is gone. I'ld give my life to cry, but it can't be done." Her gaze fell to the table. " First, the golden bowl ; then the cord—that beautiful, silver cord ; then the pitcher of life ; and now the wheel at the cistern. . . . Yes. The wheel's broken. I can't draw up any tears." She fell to brushing her hair absently. " We should have been married now, and he 'ld 've been dressing, too. The door 'ld 've been open, and he 'ld 've come walking in. Perhaps he 'ld 've played with my hair.

. . . bent back my head and kissed me . . . laid
his cheek against mine. . . . Instead, he's lying at
Girdle, under the ground. No one was there to
hold his head at the last . . . to give him water . . .
tell him it wouldn't be long. Perhaps the dog was
with him . . . whining . . . licking his face. I wonder what Patch did when—when it was all over. . . .
I'll bet *he* cared, poor scrap. But I, his queen . . .
no. I'm not allowed. The wheel's broken."

*   *   *   *   *

Three slow-treading hours had gone by since Valerie
looked at herself, and now Lady Touchstone and
she were listening to an admirable orchestra rendering
the duet from *Cavalleria Rusticana* with real emotion.

A silence had fallen upon the frivolous crowd.
Beneath the music's spell the hubbub of mirth and
chatter had sunk to a murmur of talk ; in turn the
murmur had died ; only one voice had survived, nasal
and drawling. . . . For a moment it seared the
music. . . . Then some one touched its owner upon
the shoulder. The drawl snapped off short.

Step by step the air climbed to the pinnacles of
Glistering Grief, trailing its audience behind. The
exquisite atmosphere became rarer, more difficult to
endure. A merciless fellowship of wizards, the band
slaved at its charm, sobering vanity, finding souls
in the soulless, plucking out hearts right and left
and clapping them upon sleeves. Lips began to
tremble, hands to be clenched ; eyes stared upon the
floor.

Lady Touchstone blinked back her tears.

Valerie sat still, watching a moth that was busy

about a lantern, and wondering where they would go when they left Dinard.

Suddenly, six feet away, a girl broke down.

Her chin on her fists, her elbows propped on a table, blowing furiously at a cigarette, she strove to carry it off. All the time tears coursed down her cheeks. The man beside her bent forward. . . . She shook him away fiercely. Her gleaming shoulders began to shake convulsively. A quivering sob fought its way out. . . .

The girl flung down her cigarette, buried her face in her hands, and bowed before the storm.

Perhaps five hundred eyes saw Valerie step to her side, put an arm about her, and lead her away. She went like a lamb. Lady Touchstone followed, snivelling and praising God. The gallant came last, feeling his position and savaging a young moustache. . . .

As they came to the doors—

" We'll take her home, Aunt Harriet. She says that she'ld like to come."

The car was sent for.

As the girl took her seat—

" Don't you come," she jerked out, addressing her squire. " Tell th' others I met some friends."

The youth uncovered relievedly. The last thing he wanted to do was to enter that car.

Then the door slammed, and he was left standing, headgear in hand.

He stared at his hat before replacing it.

" André ! " he said. " André of all women ! . . ." He sighed profoundly. " My word, what a show ! " He clapped his hat on his head and sought for a drink.

So far as that search was concerned, his lady beat him. While he was still wobbling between a vermouth, which he disliked, and a whiskey, which he mistrusted, she was seated in a salon of the Villa Narcisse, sipping a brandy-and-soda of a very fair strength.

The liquor steadied her nerves. After a minute or two she accepted a cigarette.

Once she began to stammer some gratitude.

Valerie checked her at once.

"We'll talk when you're better," she said.

Then she turned her back and picked up a book. . . .

André Strongi'th'arm was English and an attractive lady. Tears, of course, will make havoc of any countenance. They could not hide, however, her exquisite complexion, nor could they alter the shape of her maddening mouth. Pearls looked dull against the white of her throat, while her auburn hair alone made her remarkable. Enough and to spare for two women was crowning her pretty head. The lights that flashed from this glory beggar description. Her fine green frock became her mightily. This was none too long, but the shape of the slim silk stockings and little shining feet turned the shortcoming into a virtue.

Perhaps five minutes slipped by.

Then—

"You must think me a fool," faltered André. "A soppy, half-bred fool."

The other closed her book and rose to her feet, smiling.

"I don't at all," she said quickly, turning about. "As a matter of fact, I should think you could stand more than most people."

" I can," came the reply. " You're perfectly right. That music to-night caught me bending. I'd been thinking all day . . . thinking . . . letting myself remember . . . sticking a knife in my heart. Then that duet came along and drove it home." She snuffed out a sob with a laugh. " Serves me right," she added, " for being a fool."

" I wish," said Valerie French, " you'd teach me to cry."

The other stared at her.

" What on earth for ? " She gave a hard laugh. " ' Teach you to cry ? ' My dear, you wait. . . . Yes, and thank your stars. When your hour comes, you won't want any teaching."

"It's come," said Valerie. " It came a fortnight ago."

Miss Strongi'th'arm shook her bright head.

" No, it hasn't," she said. " Don't think I mean to be rude, but I know what I'm talking about. You think it has, but it hasn't. I know the symptoms too well."

" And I haven't got them ? " smiled Valerie. " I know. That's just my trouble. . . . Supposing you're deadly ill, with a temperature of a hundred and four. All the time you look perfectly well, and the thermo-meter says ' normal.' Yet the fever's there—raging. Raging all the more because it's suppressed. . . ."

" You'd die," said André.

" I don't," said Valerie. " I wish I could. But that's where the body's so much better off than the mind. Symptoms or none, it can take to its bed and die. The mind can't. It just carries on and on." She sat on the arm of a chair and crossed her knees. " Death and tears are denied me. What's worse, I can't even care."

" Then why on earth worry ? " said André bitterly.
" My God, I wish I couldn't ! "

" I don't worry," said Valerie, taking a cigarette.
" I tell you I can't. But you forget the fever . . .
the raging fever . . . raging to be expressed. You
see, the tears are there. They must be. I can't get
them out."

André Strongi'th'arm stared at this strange, quiet
girl who talked of death and tears as though they
were pens and ink. She began to realize that she was
in the presence of one whose acquaintance with Grief
was rather more intimate than she had believed.

At length—

" You ask me," she said slowly, " to teach you to
cry. Well, I'll tell you a tale. If that doesn't make
you weep, I shouldn't think anything would."

" Do," said Valerie French.

The other leaned back in her chair and covered her
eyes.

" I was engaged," she said, " to a king among men.
He looked like a god. He could have married anyone, and—he chose me. The trouble was, Life wasn't
big enough for him. He wanted worlds to conquer,
and there weren't any worlds going. He was like
Warwick the King-maker. If the earl was alive to-
day, I imagine he'd be out of a job. So was Richard.
Then some relative died, and he inherited. Hardly
any money, but an estate—a cursed horror of woodland
down in the Cotswold Hills." Valerie started violently. Her face went very white. The voice proceeded jerkily. " A place called Gramarye. Only
about forty minutes from where I live. . . . Well, the
estate was a wreck. A park had been made once—
cut out of a forest. Then it had been let go, and the

c

forest had gradually swallowed it up again. It was a pity, of course, but the damage was done. Any idea of restoration was fantastic . . . out of the question. Very good. So was any idea of building the Pyramids. . . .

" I said Richard wanted a world. Well, here was one for him to conquer. He set himself to restore this dreadful estate. It gave his ambition scope, his wonderful ' drive ' a field, his tremendous physical energy something to spend itself on. But the place was accursed. Soon it got into his blood. He could think of nothing else. Our marriage was postponed . . . postponed . . . postponed. . . . I hung on and hung on, watching Gramarye squeeze me out of his life and worm her way into his brain. . . .

" Then . . . some one else came along—more splendid than Richard. His name was Anthony. . . ."

The girl stifled a sob and bowed her head, pressing her pointed fingers against her temples till the blood ran back from the nails. Valerie French sat as though carved out of stone—or salt.

" He—was—the—most—perfect—thing. . . . I told you Richard was a king and looked like a god. Well, Anthony *was* a god and looked like a king. He was the handsomest man in mind and body anyone ever saw. Of course I went under at once—right under. I flung myself at his head. So would you. I dare say you think you wouldn't, but I tell you you would. I never even stopped to think—I'll tell you why. *This wonderful creature was sitting at Richard's feet . . . working at Gramarye, too . . . . wrapping her ghastly toils about his brain.* If I hadn't lost my head, I might have saved him. He might have listened to me if only I'd held myself in. I went to see him one night,

determined to open his eyes. I opened them wider
than I meant—and finished everything. I meant
him to turn down Gramarye. I only strengthened
her case and got turned down myself. . . .

"Well, Richard went mad. I knew he would.
He's in an asylum now. And, after a little, Anthony
went mad, too. Where he is, I don't know."

There was a long silence. Presently André's hands
slid into her lap.

"I think that's enough to bear," she continued
dully, "but there's some more to come—a sort of
aftermath. You see, my people don't know . . .
that there was somebody else. They know I'm
half off my head—all my friends do. *But they think
it's because of Richard*. They're sweet and kind
and gentle. They do all they can. Their interest's
amazing, their understanding marvellous. But all
the time *they're bathing the wrong leg*. Bathing and
rubbing and bandaging till I could scream." She
smote upon the arm of her chair. "I don't care a
damn about Richard. He's nothing to me. They
tell me the doctors' reports—break the bad ones
gently, and wave the good ones about as if they were
flags. All the time I don't care . . . I don't care.
I'm thankful he's out of my life. I've not a scrap
of compunction. I never meant anything to him.
He was too big. . . . When I say I don't care
—as I do—they think it's a phase of my grief. When
I say he means nothing, they soothe me and change
the subject. They've not the faintest idea that there's
anyone else. . . ."

She broke off and shrugged her white shoulders.

"Well, there you are. You're not crying, I see,
but then it's not your affair. Besides, I've told it

badly. But if you could have seen that glorious specimen of manhood—that great-hearted, clean-handed gentleman, quietly working out his own damnation with an eager, grateful heart . . . if you'd had a chance of stopping this hideous rot, and chucked it away . . . if he'd shown you out of his cottage as he'ld show out a wanton—so firmly, so sadly, so handsomely—with the kindest look that ever a man gave woman——"

André stopped short, and a finger flew to her lip.

The other's eyes were swimming . . .

A moment later Valerie French was weeping passionately.

* * * * *

Twelve more hours had gone by, and André Strongi'-th'arm was packing her trunk.

A sudden knock at her door preceded a page, bearing a telegram.

André ripped it open casually enough.

Most splendid news darling come home at once Gramarye caught fire and is burned out apparently as direct result of this Richard completely recovered wire where and when you arrive Mother.

The girl stared at the words.

These slid to and fro, making absurd combinations. Presently they became ridiculously minute.

The sheet slipped from her fingers, but she continued to stare blindly.

Behind her, the page, who was waiting to hear if she had any answer to send, began to fidget. After a little, he stood upon one leg. . . .

CHAPTER II

LEVIATHAN

THE man who had lost his memory was growing tired.

Fourteen miles he had come from the village of Broad-i'-the-Beam—he and Hamlet, his dog. So much a map would have told you. As a matter of fact, they had covered a good twenty. Ever since nine o'clock the two had gone as they pleased. Time was nothing to them, except an easy-going host. The clocks they saw and heard were jolly-faced, merry-tongued butlers, predicting meals and sleep. Did Jonathan like the look of that peeping church, the shrine had been visited. Did Hamlet, panting, declare this wood a rabbitry, the brake had been scoured. Somewhere about noon the gentle plash of water had attracted them both, and tacked a brace of miles on to their journey. The two had spent an hour beside the scrambling stream, looking for water-rats, unearthing brown pebbles, finding in ' flotsam and jetsam ' a gay significance which Blackstone seems to have missed. The burden of the day became a shuttlecock ; its heat, a cordial. Man and dog ' fleeted the time carelessly, as they did in the golden world.' What if they were making for Oxford, and Oxford was yet a score of miles away ?

Were they not Time's guests ? The city could wait. What if the two of them were growing tired ? They would sleep the sounder. What if they had but sixteen shillings in the world ? The morrow should take thought of itself. The past had done so—was doing so, and doing it devilish well.

The man who had lost his memory burst into song. . . .

It was at this musical juncture that the two wayfarers rounded a bend of the road to see a large brown limousine perhaps one hundred yards ahead. The car was standing idle under the grateful shadow of a convenient wood. Its back was towards them, and the business of a blue-suited chauffeur about the spare wheel behind was arguing the recent occurrence of a familiar mishap.

That there was something amiss, however, beside mere tire trouble soon became evident. Indeed, as the pair drew abreast of the workman, the latter raised his fists skywards and shook them in inarticulate fury.

Jonathan stopped still.

" What's the matter ? " he said.

The man started violently, looked the speaker up and down, and then put a finger to a coarse lip.

" Shut yer row," he whispered. He jerked his head at the car. " My bloke's asleep, 'e is. If you go an' wake 'im, there'll be the —— dooce."

" All right," said Jonathan quietly. " But what's the matter ? "

" Lef' me spanner be'ind," was the savage reply. " Firs' a —— puncture : then this 'ere's the wrong wheel : now the 'ub-cap won't move."

" But if the spare wheel's no use, what's the good of taking it down ? "

" So's I kin take it beck to the ——— 'ouse an' git the right one, smarty. 'Ere, jus' 'old this ——— catch in. Shove the ——— 'ome whiles I turn."

With a frown, Jonathan did as he was bid, and a moment later the refractory wheel-cap began to revolve.

The trick was done.

With a protruding tongue, the chauffeur lifted the wheel clear of its brackets. Then he turned to his ministrant.

" If you'll watch 'ere with the car, you kin give me a 'and, you kin—when I comes beck. An' if I puts in a word—why, my toff's good fer 'alf a dollar."

Jonathan hated the fellow, but two good shillings and sixpence were not to be sneezed at. Clearly the morrow was taking thought of itself. Not to encourage such initiative would be cavalier. He nodded agreement.

The other trundled the wheel down the road, and presently dived at right angles into a lane and out of sight.

Jonathan and Hamlet sat down in the shade of the trees by the side of the road. . .

Ten minutes, perhaps, had gone by, when somebody yawned.

Hamlet leaped to his feet and put his head on one side. . . . Nothing further occurring, the dog shot his smiling master a reproachful glance and once more laid himself down.

Another yawn was luxuriously expressed.

Again the terrier started to his feet and put his head on one side. . . . After a moment he approached the car gingerly, nosing the nearest running-board, as one who suspects a booby-trap. Venturing farther, he had placed two paws upon the step and was snuffing the sill of the door, when an explosion from within the limousine, in the shape of a violent inclination to sneeze violently indulged, at once confirmed his suspicions, cost him his balance, and sent him sprawling upon his back. . . .

Heedless of the contingent two shillings, Jonathan roared his pent-up merriment, while Hamlet, conscious of lost dignity, retreated to the bank and, apologetically wagging his tail, trumpeted a ridiculous defiance of his invisible discomfiter.

The face, however, presently thrust out of the limousine's window should have been sobering enough.

Large, round, red, transfigured with wrath and surmounted by a vast grey hat, it was filling most of the frame, and when a tremendous fist followed it, to be shaken furiously in Hamlet's direction, there was practically no room left. The puffed-out cheeks suggested Æolus at work, blasphemously ' potted ' by Aristophanes : the monstrous air, a pet of Rabelais'. Only the keen, blue eyes redeemed the countenance. By rights, these should have been flaming. That they were merely bright, argued the rage skin-deep.

But for Jonathan, Red Face and Hamlet might have exchanged threatenings for half an hour. The more the one bellowed, the more the other lifted up his voice. The dog had now just cause. The extraordinary picture clamoured for criticism.

His master called Hamlet to order and took off his hat.

" I'm very sorry, sir. The dog——"

" Venomous brute," raged Red Face.

" —didn't know you were there, and when you sneezed——"

" I didn't sneeze ! " shouted the other. " Where's my chauffeur ? "

Jonathan swallowed.

" I think he'll be here any minute, sir. The spare wheel was not satisfactory, and he's gone——"

" What d'you mean—'spare wheel'? What's the spare wheel got to do with it ? "

" You've got a puncture, sir, and——"

" You're drunk ! " roared Red Face. " Most beastly drunk. Where's the puncture ? "

Swiftly Jonathan perambulated the car. *Each tire was as sound as a bell.* He returned to the near-side door in some uneasiness.

" You're perfectly right, sir. I——"

" Of course I am."

" —I must have misunderstood. When I arrived, your chauffeur was having some difficulty with the spare wheel, and I helped him to——"

" You're a lying vagabond," said the other. " You did nothing of the kind. You're attempting to extort money."

" I tell you, sir——"

" You've never set eyes on my chauffeur. You've——"

" If it hadn't been for me," retorted Jonathan, " he'ld never 've had the spare wheel——"

" Goats and monkeys ! " yelled Red Face. " 'S the man mad ? " He wrenched at the door-handle. " Lemme get out, you fool." Jonathan opened the door, for a body and limbs proportionate to the face to be launched into the road. " Now, then, what the devil d'you mean by it ? Where's this spare wheel, you——"

" It's gone," said Jonathan. " The chauffeur's taken it away."

The simple announcement appeared to bereave
Red Face of the power of speech. Taking advantage
of the silence, Jonathan led the way to the rear of the
car and pointed to the empty brackets.

" You see ? " he said quietly. With bulging
eyes, the stranger regarded them. " I certainly
understood that you'd had a puncture, but, any
way, the chauffeur's taken it back to get another."

" ' Back ' ? " croaked Red Face. " ' Back,' you
gibbering fool ? Back where ? "

As he spoke, the beat of a coming engine made
itself heard, and, without waiting for an answer,
the giant stepped from behind the car to peer up the
road.

A moment later a Ford came to rest alongside,
and a spruce little man in fawn-coloured livery descended, filter in hand, and touched his hat.

" Where the devil have you been ? " demanded his
employer.

" Quick as I could, sir "—cheerfully.

" You lying hound," said the other. " You've
stopped at every pub for miles round. You know
you have. Where's the spare wheel ? "

The chauffeur stared at its room.

" It was there when I left, Sir Andrew."

" What ? "

Jonathan put in his oar.

" This isn't the chauffeur I helped," he said. There
was a dreadful silence. " In fact," he added stoutly,
" I'm afraid—I'm awfully sorry, but the more I think
of it, the more afraid I am that I've helped some
fellow or other to pinch your wheel."

The murder was out.

For a moment Jonathan thought the giant was going

to strike him. The chauffeur plainly was of the same
mind, for he made an obvious movement to catch his
master's arm.

But Sir Andrew never moved.

After a little while he took a deep breath.

" Did I call you a liar ? " he said.

" You did," said Jonathan.

" Well, I dare say you are. The world's full of 'em.
Still . . ."

It was a gruff ghost of an apology, yet the best
Sir Andrew Plague had made for twenty years. It
was not the man's fault that it was no better. His
pride's neck had grown stiff. As though to correct
the impression that it was at all flexible, he turned
upon his chauffeur with a quick roar.

" Move, you fool, move. Don't stand there drivel-
ling. Fill up, and send these thieves about their
business." A mechanic in the Ford shifted uneasily,
and his fellow let fall a can. " A-a-ah, you blundering
felon. . . ." He swung on his heel and called to
Jonathan. " Here."

The latter followed him, walking up the road.

" Never help anyone," said Sir Andrew. " If you
do, you'll regret it. If I'd caught you assisting to
steal my wheel, I'ld 've broken your back : and if my
chauffeur'd caught you, you'ld 've got twelve months
—if there's any law left in England. Never help
anyone." He turned abruptly, to make his way back to
the car. " Oh, and get rid of that dog," he added,
over his shoulder.

Jonathan watched him stop to curse his chauffeur
and shake a fist at the mechanics, before flinging open
the door and heaving himself out of sight. He was
sorry, to tell the truth, to see the last of him. . . .

He liked Sir Andrew Plague and admired him enor-
mously. For such admiration, he must himself be
admired. Worth knows worth in an instant, smother
it how you will. That which the mechanics reluctantly
respected, Jonathan found inspiring. Whensoever a
deep calls, the shallows tremble, but only a deep will
respond.

Jonathan saw in Plague a man born out of time.
He saw a man made of the Conqueror's stuff, cast in
the Norman mould, seized of that dukely 'drive,' in
mind, as body, towering above his fellow-men—to
his own hurt. He saw a giant stalking through pygmy-
land, chafing for company and finding none—a giant
whose lack of peers and vigorous mental fellowship
had spoiled his temper, who had come to say in his
haste, 'All men are fools.' Here was a lion, then—
flaunting a lion's faults—cloaking a lion's virtues.
All the time the lion's personality blazed. . .

Jonathan's estimate was very sound.

Sir Andrew Plague's nickname was 'The King of
Beasts.'

What Plague thought of Jonathan will presently
appear. Suffice it that the deeps were in touch.

" Hi ! "

The large red face was protruding from the limousine's window.

Jonathan hurried to the car.

The engine was running, and the chauffeur was in
his seat.

" What's your name ? "

The man who had lost his memory started. Then
he lifted his eyes and stared at the dust-laden trees.

" Wood," he said suddenly. " Wood. Jonathan
Wood."

" Mine's Plague," said the other roughly. " Andrew Plague. Want any help any time, I'm in the book. But don't telephone. Filthy instrument. Where's that brute of a dog ? "

Jonathan whistled, and Hamlet came running up. Sir Andrew blew through his nose. Then—

" Does he eat sausage ? " he asked.

" He will—gratefully."

" Ugly brute," said Sir Andrew. " Get rid of him." He turned to rave at his chauffeur. " Drive on, you fool, drive on. What the hell are you waiting for ? " He flung himself back on the seat and closed his eyes.

The chauffeur let in the clutch. . . .

Before the car was fifty paces away, something white came fluttering out of the window.

Upon examination it proved to be a confectioner's paper bag containing a sausage-roll.

* * * * *

Tall, grave-faced Jonah Mansel, of White Ladies, Hampshire, could tell a good tale. That which he told to his cousins, some five days after Hamlet had eaten the sausage-roll, was no exception. I will, if you please, set out his very own words.

" I'd meant to lunch at Oxford, but by the time I'd got there it was a quarter to one, so I thought I'd better push on to Ruby Green. I found it easily enough. Nice little place, smacking of peace and plenty. Obviously old as the hills, and, happily, off the map. Stocks, pound, etc., and a church you could get inside a furniture-van. We must go there one day. . . . Well, I found out where the Justice Room was, and then I made for the inn.

" To tell you the truth, I'd expected a royal welcome. You know. Genial host, scurrying maids, foaming tankards, venison pasty, raspberries and cream—and the rest. The place suggested it. I was never more mistaken. I got no welcome at all. The goods were there all right, but they weren't delivered. I couldn't get any attention. The host was—well, preoccupied and perspiring. The maids certainly scurried, but not for me. The tankard only foamed because I filled it myself. I actually had to force my way into the kitchen to get any food. . . . Anybody would have thought the devil was in the house. *As a matter of fact, he was.*

" D'you remember, when Dumas' Musketeers honoured a tavern in an ill humour, how they made things hum ? Well, there you are. Porthos was in the parlour and the deuce of a rage. Only one or other of that Big Four could possibly have raised such Cain—and got away with it. The house was bewitched . . . terrorized. The one idea of every soul in that inn was to gratify ' his ' desires the instant they were expressed—' lest a worse thing befall.' Did ' he ' want cream, there was a rush for the dairy. Did ' he ' want pepper, the boots was hounded to the grocer's. Did ' he ' want ale, the bar was stormed. And as ' he ' was never satisfied, it was a constant *Sauve qui peut.* All the time Porthos was bellowing like twenty bulls. The inn was no longer an inn, but Porthos' temple. All other custom went by the board. I could have eaten and drunk as much as I liked. As a matter of fact, I did—and put five bob in the till by way of payment. If I'd taken out ten, instead, it wouldn't have mattered. . . .

" Well, I was so much entertained—that's an

unhappy expression, but you can guess what I mean
—that I almost forgot about my summons. . . .
Some one was yelling 'Maunsel' as I came in.

"'Here,' said I. . . .

"There was a full Bench—I couldn't think why.
You know. The usual crowd : retired colonel, couple
of grocers, lord o' the manor, a carpet-knight or
two, and an earnest, throaty gent, wearing a pained
expression and a black bow-tie.

"The Clerk had just asked me whether I was
guilty of exceeding the speed limit or not, and I'd
just said 'No,' when there was what sounded like
a first-class row outside the Court, and the next
moment Porthos appeared—in the flesh.

"Sir Andrew Plague, K.C. ! I knew him at once.
Brought down specially to do some motor-car case
. . . a point of law, of course. If those seven magistrates had known him by anything but name—well,
the Bench wouldn't have been full.

"Of course, everything stopped dead. And old
Plague just flounced his way to the table like a great
sea-lion. Some wretched fellow's hat was on the
chair he chose—a bowler hat. When Plague got
up cursing, it looked more like a game. Plague
just snorted and pitched it over his shoulder. . . .
As for the Bench—well, Porthos had just changed
temples. That was all.

"They got back to me at last.

"As if I was going to 'plead' to sixty-five ! I
told you I knew the police had bungled the
thing.

"Well, I got up at once and asked that the witnesses might be out of Court. The Bench stared.
My presumption amazed them : clearly they thought

it bad form. They began to consider whether it would be decent to accede to my odious request.

" ' Put 'em out,' says Plague. ' You heard what he said. Put 'em out.'

" Those magistrates just collapsed. They sat like seven stuck pigs, while a solitary constable elbowed his way to the door.

" By way of attempting to save the situation—

" ' You ought to have been out of Court,' blustered the chairman.

" ' No, he oughtn't,' snaps Plague. ' Read your Manual.'

" Well, the case against me went bust.

" The first policeman described my car ; the second, some other fellow's. They gave different times. They lost their places in their notes. The Bench did their best to help them, but, when they saw it was hopeless, they lost their temper and tore the idiots up. I wasn't called upon.

" I could have gone, but I didn't. I had a stall for a show you can't pay to see. . . . It was worth waiting for.

" Some chap had left his car standing in the street, and had been summoned for obstruction. The A.A. had taken it up and briefed old Plague to go down and fight the case.

" My word, that man's a marvel. He never looked at a paper or made a note. When he was sitting down, his eyes were closed. But—when he got up . . . It's difficult to explain, but there were certain answers he wanted—meant to have. It was perfectly obvious. You could see them coming. The witnesses could, too. They didn't want to give them, but they just had to. With it all, he was as quiet as a lamb—

except once. The solicitor for the police interrupted.

" ' Silence ! ' says Plague, in a voice of thunder.

" The Bench just quivered, and the wretched solicitor crumpled like a wisp of foil on a red-hot plate. . . .

" Presently he—Plague—got up to speak.

" I'd always heard that he hated a country Bench, but . . . talk about Contempt of Court. . . . I could hardly believe my ears. As for those magistrates', they must be burning now.

" ' There's a Court up in London,' he said, ' called the Divisional Court. It's a pillory, where they set Country Justice by the ears. 'S often as not, I'm the hangman. I dare say you've been there before. You can go there now, if you like—and be hanged. I don't care. Or you can save your bacon. Understand this. You can convict—if you like : you can impose a fine—if you like : you can all sign the record, like so many sheep—if you like. But the conviction will be quashed : the fine will never be paid : the record will have to be corrected—by so many sheep as signed it. I know what I'm talking about. You can't touch this man because the law's against you—good, sound law, laid down by men who are dead, the more's the pity. For what it's worth, I'll try to make plain what it says . . .'

" He gave them those cases with a spoon, as you feed a baby. I understood every word. You couldn't miss it.

" When he'd finished, he chucked the last book down.

" ' And now,' he said, ' sit still, and continue to sit. Or go to the Court—and be hanged.'

" Yes, the summons was dismissed.

"Well, you might think that was enough for one afternoon. But not at all. The show was to come.

"You know the sort of upheaval that takes place in Court at the end of some *cause célèbre?* Well, that was in full blast. Everybody was either trying to get out, or passing somebody else, or changing his place : four of the justices were on their feet : a superintendent was leaning across the table talking to the Clerk : I was half-way to the door : Plague was demanding his hat, and a constable was yelling 'Silence!' In the middle of it all, a door was flung open, and some prisoner or other was hustled into the dock. As he stepped up, he looked round, and the moment I saw him I was certain I'd seen him before. Tall, good-looking chap : a bit on the thin side, and roughly dressed : obviously unfamiliar with docks and rather worried. Now, the dock was directly between me and where counsel had been sitting, and, as I was staring at his back, wondering what he was there for and where the deuce I'd seen the fellow before, I suddenly realized that I wasn't alone in my interest. *From the solicitors' table old Plague was gazing at that chap as if he'd seen an apparition.* His mouth was open, and he looked like a great red fish. . . .

"I heard the Clerk's voice—

"'. . . loitering upon enclosed premises, with intent to commit a felony. Are you guilty, or——'

"'I appear for the defence,' says Plague thickly. 'And I plead "Not guilty."' Then he turned to his solicitor and jerked his head at the dock. 'Take his instructions,' he said.

"The hush that fell upon that Court was supernatural.

" ' Sensation ' 's no use. I want a bigger word.

" Look at the ingredients of this amazing stew. First, Plague's terrific personality. Hang it, the man's only got to ask somebody to pass the salt, to create a sensation. Then the neurotic condition the Court was in—thanks to Plague's conduct of the last case : ready to scream if a cow lowed. Thirdly, the appearance in the dock of an obvious gentleman. Fourthly, Plague's sudden announcement that he proposed to defend a case of whose existence—much less details— until that moment he had manifestly never dreamed. . . . Plague. . . . Plague himself. . . . Sir Andrew Plague. . . .

" So soon as I'd recovered my wits, I just slid back to my old seat and sat down tight. It's as well I was quick about it, for every one else in the building was seized with the same idea. The news must have spread like wildfire. Within one minute I'll swear you couldn't 've got an umbrella inside that room.

" Well, Bench, police and Clerk were obviously swept off their feet. They weren't expecting this, and you can't blame them. The first thing they realized was that they must have time. They told one another so in hoarse, excited whispers—especially the superintendent. If perspiration's anything to go by, I fancy the wretched fellow felt that his hour was come. All the time the solicitor was coolly taking the prisoner's instructions, and Plague was sitting in his seat with his eyes closed.

" Presently the chairman leaned over and, wreathing his face into a winning smile, inquired if Plague wouldn't like an adjournment as he had ' only been so recently instructed.'

" ' No,' says Plague, ' I wouldn't. Proceed with the case.'

" ' Then,' says the chairman, ' we'll hear evidence of arrest.'

" ' You'll hear the case,' says Plague.

" Evidence of arrest was given.

" By the time Plague had done with him, I'll bet that policeman cursed the hour he was born. The way he perspired was frightful.

" Then the superintendent got up, fairly streaming with sweat, and asked for a remand.

" ' Why ? ' says Plague.

" ' To make inquiries.'

" ' What inquiries ? '

" The superintendent boggled and said it was usual.

" Plague fairly let fly.

" ' Usual ? ' he blazed. ' By gad, it's as well I'm here. Usual to clap a gentleman in gaol for seven days while you rake over your dunghills to scratch up some lies against him ? ' He threw up his head and looked the Bench up and down. ' I demand,' he barked, ' to be told if that is the Prosecution's case. If it isn't, let them go on. If they can't, then it's closed.'

" The superintendent tried, stammering, to stick to his rotten guns. The Bench, who had always looked upon him as a sort of Rock of Ages, shivered and writhed. . . .

" ' Enough,' says Plague. ' He presses for a remand. I say it's an iniquitous request. I'll address you on this point now.

" ' Loitering, *per se*, is no offence. We're all of us loitering here, the more fools we. It only becomes an offence when it is proved that he who is loitering is loitering with a definite, wicked object—that of stealing, or murdering, or committing some other felony. The police must satisfy you that the defendant was loitering in the flesh, with felony in his heart. They've not done the one, and they can't do the other. I'm assuming you're reasonable men with reasonable minds. I'm bound to. Now listen to me. . . .

" ' *Loitering in the flesh.* The ball some children are using falls into a yard. They cry. The defendant climbs into the yard and restores them their ball. He goes on his way. Half an hour later he finds he has lost some money. He thinks it fell out of his pocket when he was scaling the wall. He returns to look for it. While he is looking, he's found— by the vigilant police. They ask and are told his business. *He is not believed.* I asked that ornament why. What did he say? *Because the defendant could not produce the money which he said he had lost, for which he was looking.*

" ' There goes one half of the charge. Now for the other.

" ' *With felony in his heart.* No evidence forthcoming: but if you will imprison the defendant for seven days, some might be procured. . . . I've every right to stamp this board-school argument underfoot, but I'm not going to. I'm going to pretend it needs a proper reply, and I'm going to blow it into atoms about as small as the greasy brains that conceived it. . . .

" ' Which looks most like a felon—the accused or the fool who accused him? Or that ass of a superintendent, for the matter of that? Don't be afraid.

I'm not going to go any further. But, if you're hard
up for sense, for Heaven's sake use your eyes. D'you
think those finger-tips there are recorded at Scotland
Yard ? 'But,' whine the police, 'he gives no account
of himself.' Why should he ? He's not even trespassing. I'm half a lawyer—I take it you won't
dispute that. And I say he's not even trespassing.
Why should he give an account ? Yet give an account
he did—which is more than I would have done. He
gave his name and he said he had no address. He
told them where he was going and whence he had
come. He said he was looking for work, and asked
if they could tell him where hands were wanted.
. . . But that pelting Jack-in-office won't be beat.
He's out to find a worm—an evil worm. The
more evil worms he finds, the better for him. He's
looking so hard for worms that he never sees that
the very soil he's sifting is fuller's earth. Probably
he doesn't recognize the fuller's earth of honesty.
But he knows a worm in a minute—an evil worm.
Discretion doesn't count with him. Worms count.
And evil worms count two. But you're not police,
and that's where you come in. . . .

"'If, in the face of these facts, you like to grant
a remand, do so. But, so sure as you do, I'll post
up to London, have a Judge out of his bed and a
Writ of *Habeas Corpus* to-night. Please yourselves.
I was at school with his father, the famous surgeon,
and I'm not going to have my godson . . .'

"He let the sentence go and flung himself down
in his seat.

"I thought those wretched Justices were going
to faint. For a moment there was absolute silence.
Then the earnest, throaty gent gave a gurgle of dismay.

. . . With a superhuman effort, the chairman pulled himself together.

"'Of co-course,' he stammered, with a frightful grin, 'I ne-need hardly say, Sir Andrew, that we had n-no idea——'

"'Not the faintest,' whimpers another Justice.

"Plague waved them away.

"'Dismiss the charge,' he says. 'Dismiss the charge.'

"'Of course,' says the chairman, watching the superintendent being helped out of Court. 'The charge is dismissed, and—er——'

"'Should never have been brought,' howls another Beak.

"'Oh, shameful!' wails Throaty, raising his eyes to heaven.

"'I trust, Sir Andrew,' mouths the chairman, 'I sincerely hope——'

"'Where's my hat?' says Plague, and follows the late defendant out of Court. . . .

"Well, there you are.

"I found out the fellow's name—same as my own, curiously enough. 'Jonathan.' Surname, 'Wood.' And, after a lot of thinking, I remembered who he was like—that fellow Valerie French took such a toss over. But it obviously wasn't him. His name was 'Lyveden,' wasn't it? Besides, they found his body. . . . Yes, I remember."

*   *   *   *   *

The sweet o' the day had come in, and the village of Ruby Green was looking its best.

At noon the place had been superb—a beautiful, clear-cut study in black and brilliant white—a thing

for strangers to photograph. Now that the sun
was sinking, the clear-cut study was gone. The
shadows were there still, but they were grey and
blurred : the brilliancy had faded to a glow : the
white had become rosy. The place was alive with
tones no camera could ever catch. Always the
village was lovely—a perfect sheet out of the folio
of Time : but while at midday it had worn the last-
ing beauty of a rare old print, now at even it was
a piece of exquisite tapestry—delicate, memorable.
There was a peace, too, which had displaced its noon-
tide sleepiness—a mellow, dulcet atmosphere of
labour done. Sounds that had gone unnoticed during the business of the day stole into earshot : the
steady rush of water over a sluice, the lisp of the
wind in elm-tops, the distant drone of a thresher. . . .

Seated upon a bench outside *The Yew Tree*, Jonathan cared for these things with a full heart.

Sir Andrew Plague had given him three commands.
The first was to find the man upon whose hat he
had sat, and to pay him two pounds. The second,
to go to the inn and get a square meal. The third,
to await instructions.

The first two orders had been obeyed, and now
he was waiting at ease till Porthos should have finished
his tea. A dozen paces away, Hamlet, who had
had enough of prison yards, was making horseplay
with a retriever.

If Jonathan felt thankful, he also was greatly moved.
This is not to be wondered at. He was upon the
edge of great matters. The interview, the summons
to which he was awaiting, must be momentous.
Thereat, for better or for worse, he would learn his
identity and his past. His future, too, would in

some sort be settled in that same small room where
Plague—his godfather—was having tea . . . *his godfather*. . . .

Not that he cared about his future. His past was
the thing. ' His father, the famous surgeon. . . .'

Jonathan began to wonder what he had done.

He had an uneasy feeling that he had done wrong.
There was some mystery about him. If Sir Andrew
had known him in Court, he had known him equally
well that day by the side of the road. Yet he had
never declared himself—would not have done so
now, but to save his (Jonathan's) skin. That was
as clear as daylight. Oh, indubitably he had erred
—in some way. So much the nicer of Plague to
have befriended him. But for his intervention . . .

He wondered what Plague would say to his loss
of memory. A thousand to one he'ld call him ' a lying
hound.' Still, he'ld believe what he said.

Here his thoughts flew back—as far as they could.
He remembered that terrible night when he had
walked with Death. He thought of that morning,
a short four days ago, when he had first discovered
the virtue of his misfortune—perceived the excellence
of his lot in all its glory. . . .

With a shock Jonathan realized that that very
freedom from care, which he had found so precious,
was about to be withdrawn. The thought of such
subversive dispossession daunted him. For a second
of time, indeed, he was minded to rise up and go.
His state was blessed. Why, then, should he sur-
render it ? He had no real desire to know the past.
If such knowledge was to cost him his freedom from
care . . .

Jonathan started to his feet.

Then he sat down again and shook his head.

"No," he said, frowning. "No, I can't run away.
I'm sorry it's come so soon, but I can't run away.
Besides . . ."

Here the spruce little chauffeur appeared in the
inn's doorway. . . .

Jonathan called Hamlet and put him under his
arm.

A moment later he was ushered into the presence.

Stretched luxuriously upon two easy-chairs, Sir
Andrew, cigar in hand, regarded the pair.

"Didn't I tell you," he said, "never to help anyone ? "

"You did, sir."

"Then why the devil d'you do it ? "

Jonathan shrugged his shoulders.

"I suppose I forgot, sir."

"Don't lie to me," snapped the other. "You'ld
do it again to-morrow. You know you would. And
next time I shan't be by, to pull you out of the fire.
I wouldn't have done it to-day, if I'd thought twice.
And turn that dog round. I don't like his ugly face."

Obediently Jonathan reversed the Sealyham.

"I should like to——"

"Ugh ! He's still looking at me, the brute. Put
him down, can't you ? "

Placed upon the floor, Hamlet advanced upon
Sir Andrew and, fixing his eyes upon him, sat up
and begged.

The K.C. covered his face.

"I have to thank you, sir," said Jonathan, subdu-
ing a smile, "for a most handsome action. But
for your generous——"

"That'll do. I enjoyed myself. Besides, I've a

weakness for seeing justice done." He plucked a
case from his pocket and pulled out some notes.
" Here's twenty pounds. Don't go and drink it.
If you aren't on your feet again by the time that's
finished, you ought to be flogged."

Jonathan stared at the money with saucer eyes.

" Take it, you fool, take it. I'm not going to hold
it all day."

Jonathan took the notes with trembling fingers.

" You're very kind, sir," he stammered. " Of
course I'll pay you back."

" As you please," jerked the other, and fell a-whist-
ling. " Good-bye."

Jonathan could hardly believe his ears. The
interview, which was to be so memorable, was at an
end. His fortune had not been told. . . . It occurred
to him in a flash that he must be a very black sheep
—a family skeleton, in fact. Recalling Sir Andrew's
charge, he began to wonder if liquor had been his
downfall. . . .

For a moment he hesitated. Then he turned dully
away. . . .

Arrived at the door, he swung round.

" Tell me one thing," he said quietly. " Who
was my father ? "

Sir Andrew stared at him.

" How the devil should I know ? "

Jonathan put a hand to his head.

" But you were at school with him. You must
have known him well to be my godfa——"

The other leapt to his feet, kicking over a chair.

" Is this blackmail ? " he demanded.

" ' Blackmail ' ? " echoed Jonathan. " *Blackmail ?* "

"Because," said Sir Andrew, advancing, "because, if it is . . ."

The cold, deliberate tone was more terrible than any rage. The countenance had lost its grossness and become a grim mask. The keen blue eyes had narrowed to mere points of steel.

Jonathan felt as though he had crossed a king.

Then—

"I may be a waster," he said, "but I've not sunk so low as that." He threw the notes on the floor between the two of them. "I'm deep enough in your debt. I suppose I've given you cause to think this vile thing of me, though why, if I have, you didn't spare your talent this afternoon, I fail to see."

With that, he called the dog and turned again to the door.

"Stop!" Jonathan stood still. "Why on earth did you ask me your father's name?"

"Because you know it, and I do not."

"Why should I know it?"

Jonathan wheeled about.

"Two hours ago you stated in Court——"

Sir Andrew waved his arms.

"Lies, you fool. All lies." The other recoiled. "I had to say something to shake those Justices up. Up to that moment I hadn't a rag of a case."

Jonathan stared and stared. Then he leaned against the wall and began to laugh. . . .

After a long look at him, Sir Andrew returned to his chairs. Sitting down, he proceeded, snorting, to mop his face.

"There's something wrong with you," he burst out suddenly. "What is it?"

"This," said Jonathan weakly. "I've lost my memory."

He told his tale there and then. The eminent lawyer listened with closed eyes. When the recital was over—

"And what," he demanded, " do you propose to do ?"

Jonathan shrugged his shoulders.

"Work," he said simply. "At least, I've one recommendation. I've got a clean sheet."

" You haven't a sheet at all," snapped Sir Andrew. "And that's what'll lay you low. That and your cursed folly of helping fools."

"If I'm believed when I say——"

"Would you believe such a tale ? "

"I would," said Jonathan.

Sir Andrew let out a squeal, as though suddenly stung, and Hamlet, considerably startled, began to bark.

"I knew it," yelled Plague. "I knew it. In spite of all I've said, you'ld help the liar that told it." He turned upon Hamlet with a roar. "Stop it, you venomous swine ! Don't yap at me." He snatched *The Times* from the floor and flung himself back in his seat. "What of your friends ? " he demanded.

"I don't even know if I have any, much less who they are."

"You can make inquiries."

"I think that's for them to do. They've something to go on. I haven't. Besides, I've got to live."

"In fact, you're content as you are ? "

"Perfectly. The past has been taken from me. I don't want it back."

"You may be a millionaire."

Jonathan smiled.

" Felicitate me," he said, " upon my release."

A ghost of a grin stole into the great red face. . . .
Then, as though to obliterate the impression that
he knew how to smile, the giant snorted like a wild
beast and beat and wrung *The Times* into the shape
he desired.

For a moment his eyes were scanning a column of
print. Then—

" There's a fool's advertisement here," he announced,
" for a secretary. I happen to know the fool. If
you like to offer yourself, I'll get you the job."

Jonathan hesitated.

" D'you think I could give satisfaction ? I don't
want to let your friend down. You see, I've no
idea of what I can do."

" Fools go with fools." Sir Andrew dabbed at
the paragraph. " You'll suit him admirably." He
nodded at pen and ink. " Write a reply now, and
I'll take it to Town."

Jonathan did as he was bid.

> *The Yew Tree,*
> *Ruby Green.*
> *August 5th.*

Sir,

 *In reply to your advertisement, appearing in to-day's
issue of* The Times, *I beg to apply for the post you are
seeking to fill.*

 *An interview will better enable you to appraise such
qualifications as I may have, so, if you entertain this
application, will you be good enough to write to me c/o
The Poste Restante, Oxford, giving me an appointment ?* *I am, Sir,*

> *Your obedient servant,*
> JONATHAN WOOD.

He addressed the letter to the Box, and, rising, humbly offered it to Plague for his inspection.

The latter read it carefully.

"You've told me a pretty tale," he said, without raising his eyes. "As I've tried to point out, not one in a million fools would ever believe you. A sudden loss of memory's too convenient."

Jonathan nodded.

"I see that now," he said slowly. "I realize that. I shall always proudly remember that you believed what I said."

"'M not sure that I do," grunted Plague. "An' now take up that money you flung in my face. Those clothes won't win an appointment, and there's your fare to Town. You'll have to get rid of that beastly dog, you know."

Jonathan started. A finger flew to his lip.

"Hamlet!" he breathed. "Hamlet! I quite forgot."

A touch made him look down. It was the terrier's 'Adsum.'

One paw raised, his soft, brown eyes alight with eagerness, the dog was awaiting his bidding with a heart no wages can buy. As their eyes met, his tail began to move to and fro. Surely never squire so hung upon the lips of his lord. . . .

Jonathan stooped and patted the small rough head.

"Perhaps they'ld let me keep him," he said lamely. "We're rather friends."

"You're mad," said Plague shortly. "The advertisement asks for a man, not a menagerie."

Jonathan straightened his back.

"I can't give him up," he said.

Sir Andrew Plague rose and clawed at the air.

" You blithering fool ! " he roared. " It's the dog or the post."

" I choose the dog," said Jonathan quietly enough.

With a fearful effort, the other mastered his voice.

" So," he said hoarsely. " Vagabonds and rogues hang together. Well, I'll keep my word. I'll send your letter along. If you like to cut your own throat, that's your affair."

" I'm afraid you think me ungrateful."

" Never mind what I think," snarled Plague. " But learn of me. Never help anyone." He turned on his heel. " And now go," he added. " I'm tired of fools."

Jonathan went.

*　　　*　　　*　　　*　　　*

On the morning of August the eighth he was given a letter.

He thrust this into his pocket and left the Post Office. Crossing St. Aldate's, he passed into the meadows. . . .

Presently pacing that majestic nave—that peerless robing-room where youth, panting, barelegged and thoughtless, unconsciously puts on the magic mantle of Tradition to his own use for ever, Jonathan drew out the letter and turned it about meditatively.

Blithely Hamlet preceded him, going upon three legs—indisputable evidence of his approval of The Broad Walk. Abstractedly his master watched him. . . . After a little while he shook his head.

" I can't give him up," he said shortly. " It's out of the question."

With that, he ripped open the envelope.

45 *Kensington Palace Gardens,* W.
August 6*th.*

SIR,

We have had our interview.

I am satisfied that you are stubborn, sentimental, and credulous—three most abominable failings.

Upon the understanding that you will correct your behaviour in these respects, you may become my secretary at a salary of five hundred pounds a year.

Yours faithfully,
ANDREW PLAGUE.

Jonathan Wood, Esq.

P.S.—*Acknowledge this letter and be here in three days' time. I have told the steward that your dog will eat sausage-rolls. If this diet is wrong, you had better instruct him direct.*

CHAPTER III

FIGS OF THISTLES

HERE is a letter, sirs, out of a Cardinal's bag. His Eminence will not mind my setting it forth. I am a privileged person, like the King's jester.

> *Villa Narcisse,*
> *Dinard.*
> *August 3rd.*

DEAR UNCLE JOHN,

It seems impossible that it is not yet one year since I wrote to tell you that I was in love with a footman. I remember writing so well. Just as in another year's time I shall remember writing this letter, which is to tell you—not that Anthony is dead, because you know that, or that I still love him, because you know that too, but that I am sane again and that the power of caring has come back. Of course my occupation is gone. I have not the slightest idea what to do. But I must and mean to do something—take some action of some sort, and that is more than I could say a week ago.

It is, in fact, just five days since I fell in with a girl—a complete stranger—who was unhappy, too. Her trouble was that she was in love with my darling. She had no idea, of course. . . . I don't think she knew

66

*he was dead. But she had been very hard hit, and—
the clouds had returned after the rain.*

*I have stated the truth baldly. I do not feel able to
comment. It is too big. Truly Fate is an amazing
thing. Out of the millions of women—surplus women,
Uncle John, of whom your niece is now one—this girl,
a Miss Strongi'th'arm, selects me for her peculiar
confidence. . . . I owe her a debt. When I heard
her mourning Anthony, it set my heart going again,
and I was able to cry.*

*I think that's all my news, but I'ld like your advice.
Tell me about the dead. Can they take part in our
lives, assuming they want to? Or are we too small
fry? I mean, Death's really a promotion, isn't it?
One's given a better brain. New lenses are fitted to
our understanding, aren't they? Immensely more
powerful. ' Now we see through a glass, darkly. . . .'
Well, when those lenses have been fitted, how will this
old life look? Shall we be able to see it at all? Or
will it be out of focus—beneath contempt?*

*You see what I'm driving at. I not only want Anthony
—I need him. His is the only presence that can help
me to stand his loss. I can't realize that he's dead—
yet. But I shall soon. And I want his shoulder to
lean on—the hem of his garment to clutch at when that
realization comes. It's like a wave approaching:
already I can see its crest. If I could feel that he saw,
felt, understood, perhaps even loved me, looking down
from his peak, I think I'ld be able to breast this terrible
wave—I think I'ld feel less famished than I do. I
tell you I'm just starving. And Memory's bitter fare
—very bitter . . .*

*Now that I've written all this, I see I've wasted our
time. You can give me only one answer It would*

*be brutal to give me any other. Besides, you can only
guess. You may be a Cardinal, but you're still alive
and so as blind as all the rest of us. Your fine red
hat was made in a tailor's shop, probably by sweated
labour. The point is, it's a hat, not a halo.*

*No. I may have wasted your time, and I'm sorry
for that: but I haven't wasted my own. I feel better
for having got rid of all this sob-stuff. For that's all
it is.*

*I am so glad you knew him—so awfully glad. He
was so splendid, wasn't he?*

Your loving

VALERIE.

*P.S.—I'll write again when I'm through this phase.
I leave for London to-morrow, without Aunt Harriet.
I won't let her come. I'ld like to go to Bell Hammer,
but I can't stand that . . . yet. I suppose you know
he left me every penny. Which means that, with what
I already had, I must be worth considerably over a
million. Isn't that nice?*

*Yes, I know. But you must admit I've a lot to
make me bitter.*

Valerie French, spinster, was as good as her word.
Ere her letter had reached Rome, she and her maid
had lain one night in London.

The following morning she left for the Cotswold
Hills.

The impulse which drove her to Girdle was natural
enough. It was, indeed, with the idea of visiting
Lyveden's grave that she had left Dinard. She
wanted to see where he rested, desperately. More.
She was most pitifully thankful for an object in life.
Never pilgrim journeyed to Canterbury one half so

undistractedly. The girl had no need of tales to beguile the way. This was all too short. Had her shrine stood in the Antarctic Zone, she would have praised God. Once she found herself wondering what pilgrims do when they have made their pilgrimage. One heard of their going. Whoever heard of their return? Upon that point even Chaucer had broken down. . . . Clearly the return was empty, flat—an appalling anticlimax. For one thing, of course, they were no longer pilgrims. A frightened look came into Valerie's eyes. To-morrow her pilgrimage would end . . . to-morrow. And after that . . . She was only twenty-six. Supposing she lived to be seventy. . . . She brushed the thought away and pictured her shrine anew.

This was much what she had figured—a low, green barrow, seamed across and across, where the late-cut turf had not healed. Valerie was directed to it by a mumbling sexton. She hardly heard what he said and forgot him, so soon as he had spoken, as one forgets a finger-post. The truth is, the girl was overwhelmed. She had hoped so hard that Anthony might lie in a pleasant place: she had never dared to dream that he was buried in a King's Corner.

The Abbey Church of Girdle stands a mile from the village in a most lovely yard. Its day is over, of course The town it was built to serve has disappeared. Each Sunday a handful of worshippers plod resolutely to Matins, stare for an hour uncomfortably about their heritage, and go their way. Occasionally strangers appear, to glory in the flying buttresses, marvel at the fan-tracery above the choir, and sweat the altar-screen an anthem wrung out of stone. For the rest, the great church sleeps, stately and exquisite, amid its whispering elms. As for its ancient retinue, with one superb exception, this is clean gone. Only the footings are left, to turn the shadowy plot into a close. One gentle spokesman of another age remains. There by the southeast corner three lovely arches tell where the cloisters ran. With these the afternoon sun will print three matchless windows upon a little greensward. There is only one grave there yet. And that lies under the silver birch—a low, green barrow, seamed across and across. . . .

After a long half-hour Valérie rose to her feet and sought the sexton. Ten minutes later she rang the Vicarage bell.

Here we are upon the edge of three several interviews, all of which were painful and are relevant. Two, as you shall see, may be swallowed whole; but the third must be chewed. Bear with me, sirs. He who would gather grapes of thorns must at least pick over the brambles.

The first interview—between Miss French and the Vicar of Girdle—took place at a quarter to one. It was distressing, as was the second, because the Reverend Simon Barley was not a lady's man. Moreover, he suffered, poor fellow, from St. Vitus's Dance and was acutely conscious of his infirmity. Both parties were very thankful when it was over.

The second—between Miss Strongi'th'arm and the Vicar of Girdle—took place at two o'clock. This ended abruptly with the slam of a door and left the unfortunate priest a nervous wreck.

The third—between Miss French and Miss Strongi'th'arm—took place at two-fifteen.

Valerie had lunched at Girdle and had returned on foot to the churchyard. Thither her car was to follow at half-past three.

The poor girl was almost cheerful. She had won sanctuary. Sitting on the turf of the cloister, marking the bulwarks of the grey old church, she found an ease of spirit she had not known for months. The old steady look began to steal into her eyes. The atmosphere of the place was ministering to her mind. Viewed from this belvedere, the scenery of Life became less desolate. Far in the distance stood peaks, which the sun was touching. . . .

Valerie took off her hat and, leaning her back against its delicate trunk, stared at the hanging garden which the silver birch made.

A footfall made her look down.

" You ? "

Framed in one of the archways, Miss Strongi'th'arm was regarding her with burning eyes.

" You ? " blazed André again. " What are you doing here ? "

For a moment Valerie gravely returned her gaze. Then she rose and came forward.

" Of course you live near here," she said quietly. " I'd quite forgotten." With that, she put out her hand.

The other stared at this, biting her lip. Then she took it uncertainly.

" I'm sorry," she said jerkily. " You'll—you'll think I'm not safe to be about. The first time we meet I behave like an idiot child : and now, like —like a maniac." She laughed mirthlessly. " I suppose you know where you are . . whose grave that is ? "

" Yes," said Valerie.

André shot her a long and searching glance. Then
she fixed her eyes upon an adjacent headstone.

When she spoke again, her voice was strained
and low.

" It was my earnest desire to put up a memorial.
. . . I went to see the Vicar ten minutes ago. . . .
He tells me he's given permission to somebody else
—some other woman." She paused. " I asked if
she was a relative, and he said she had told him
' No.' "

" That's right," said Valerie quietly. " He gave
it to me."

" So I was right," breathed André. She turned
upon the other with smouldering eyes. " What's
your imagined authority for doing this ? "

" Major Lyveden and I were engaged."

Miss Strongi'th'arm stared.

" When ? "

" At the time of his death."

" But he was mad."

Valerie shook her head.

" We got him all right," she said. " Apparently,
perfectly well. It——"

" ' We ' ? Who's ' we ' ? "

" His friends," said Valerie. " It was only right
at the end that he had a relapse."

" D'you swear this ? " demanded André.

" Of course."

" Why didn't you tell me at Dinard ? "

" Until you opened your mouth, I hadn't the slightest
idea. When you'd opened it, it was too late."

" ' Too late ' to stop me telling my rival the details
of how her lover had turned me down ? " She pointed

to the grave at their feet. " I wonder what he'ld think about it."

" He'ld understand," said Valerie. " So would you, if you'ld only think for a moment. I never dreamed, of course, I should ever see you again."

The other gave a short laugh.

" No," she said dryly. " I don't suppose you did. One doesn't bother, as a rule, about a sucked orange."

Valerie lifted her eyes and stared at the tops of the elms.

" I'm sorry," she said gently, " you take it like this. God knows I meant you no harm."

" Then why did you let me talk—strip myself ? Because you wanted to see my nakedness. You'd landed the wonderful thing I'd lost my heart to, and so my failure was interesting . . . a posthumous titbit . . . the hell of a feather in your cap. That *I* was sticking it there was simply superb. You must have screamed when I'd gone."

" Do I look that kind of woman ? "

" I wish you did," said André bitterly. " Then I'ld 've held my tongue."

" You know I never laughed when you'd gone."

The other shrugged her shoulders.

" A woman who'll do such a rotten, shameless——"

" Why do you talk like this ? " said Valerie. " Why are you so unfair ? I never invited your confidence."

" You abused it."

" I never abused it. Listen. For one thing, you know I was ill—almost out of my mind."

" Rot," said André. " Your nerve was like iron."

" I say," repeated Valerie, " that I was almost mad. Anthony was dead. You find his loss hard enough. What d'you think it was—is, to me ? Well, you offered to tell me your tale, and I offered to listen. Suddenly, without any warning, I found you were giving yourself away. . . . I had to decide what to do—instantly. There was no time to think. I had to decide whether it was better to stop you —make things desperately awkward for both of us, and drive you wild with yourself for having spoken, or to let you go on and away without knowing who I was. I don't think I ever decided. While I was trying to think, you went on talking, until it was clearly too late."

" How could I help in the end finding out who you were ? "

" It didn't seem likely then. I never expected to come to see his grave."

" Till after I'd spoken ? "

Valerie nodded.

" I owe you a debt," she said. " When you spoke so handsomely——"

" Rub it in," said André.

With a gesture of despair, Valerie turned away.

" In fact," said André, " it was only when you found that there was some one who *cared*, living a couple of miles from where he lay . . . some one whose *right to care* was technically smaller than your own . . . some poor rotter who *might* be ' expected to come to see his grave,' that it occurred to you to use your authority and put up a gravestone—' In Loving Memory.' After all, what's the use of a door marked ' Private ' if you've nobody's face to slam it in ? " She stamped her foot upon the ground. " Upon my soul, I wonder you don't order me out of this churchyard."

Valerie stepped to the birch and picked up her hat. Her face was very white, and when she spoke there was the chill of death in her tone.

" Before I go I'll tell you what you've done.

" I came here to-day, laden and desolate, after two solid months of horror, misery and despair. And here, for the very first minute in all these frightful weeks, I felt at peace. The weight that was breaking me was taken : that awful, desolate feeling fell away. Perhaps you can imagine the relief—after two solid months. I could have cried with gratitude. In fact, I did. Then I went to the village and took a room at the inn, so that I might be able to come here every day. . . .

" And now—you've smashed my sanctuary . . . sown it with stinging memories . . . poisoned the peace I found here . . . hunted me back into the night. . . . I tell you, you've robbed the destitute. You say you're poor. You fool. I *am* Poverty. And yet you've found a pocket in my rags—and rifled that."

She turned and passed out of the pleasaunce like a stricken queen. . . .

Her red lips parted, wide-eyed, the other watched her go, and, after she had gone, stared at her point of disappearance.

Presently her brown eyes narrowed, and she began to frown. . . .

*   *   *   *   *

It took a good deal to stagger Miss André Strongi'-th'arm, but the trick had been done. For this, a finer personality, a blow from an unexpected quarter, and an air of frozen dignity were together responsible.

She had been shaken much as a confident boxer may be shaken by the shock of the sudden punch of a better man. She walked home thoughtfully.

That same night, in her chamber, she threw herself, dressed, on her bed and considered her plight. Her windows were wide open, and from where she lay she could command the dark heaven, literally crammed with stars. These afforded, as ever, a majestic spectacle, conducive to meditation. Occasionally one of them would leave its place in the pageant and take its dying leap into eternity. . . . After a little André began to feel that Fate not only was pretty powerful, but possibly knew its job rather better than she.

For more than six dragging months she had been most deeply in love with Anthony Lyveden. Never once in all that time had she viewed this passion impersonally. It was, of course, a question of effort, purely : and the effort had never been made. She had let herself go—let herself love, dream, suffer. Six months ago she had stumbled upon a pool, sunlit, inviting. Without an instant's thought, she had flung herself in. . . . Soon the sunlight had gone and the waters begun to grow chill. She had stayed there desperately. Gradually the waters had become icy : but she would not come out, because they had once been warm and the sun had lighted them. To-night, for the very first time, she saw herself crouched in the pool, wide-eyed, frozen. . . . She was only just in time. A moment later the pool was empty.

A feeling of resignation stole into André's heart, as blood that has been congealed begins to liquefy.

The reason for this is plain.

The girl was a fine lover, handsome and careless. This morning she would have given her life to bring back Anthony, and given it gladly, without a thought. But to-night—no. She would not have crooked a finger. This morning she would have asked no questions, made no conditions, but would have gone to the block with the shining eyes of a zealot. To-night she would have seen eternity end before she brought him back for another woman. André was neither selfish nor unselfish. She was just human.

Continuing to look through her new, impersonal lens, she perceived that Lyveden's death had been predestinate. This discovery relieved her immensely. Till now she had always felt that she might have saved him. The millstone of self-condemnation began to slip from her neck. . . . Still using this comfortable lens, she found it perfectly manifest that Anthony was not for her, because he was for no woman. This finding was more than a relief: it was a positive cordial.

The glow of resignation began to course through André's veins, as blood which has got going begins to circulate.

Staring up at the regalia of Destiny, it struck her that Anthony Lyveden had crossed her path like one of those falling stars, flooding her life with his radiance, dragging her heart with him in his dying leap. Pondering the truth of this simile, André found him ethereal, made of the silver stuff of dreams, a prince passing. The man began to change into a memory —a most important transition.

Out of the highway of Life there runs a sable lane whose name is Mourning. Down this we, that are quick, walk with our blessed dead. Sooner or later, sirs, the lane will bend—sooner or later. And there at the turn, the dead enter in at the gate which is that of Memory, but we, that are quick, pass on, and lo! an instant later, we are back upon the old highway.

When Anthony became a memory, André came out of mourning. The prince had passed.

After all, our emotions are nothing more than a set of hooks on which we hang things. And Lyveden had been transferred from the hook of passionate love to that of affectionate remembrance. Of this the direct result was that the hook of passionate love was now unoccupied. Nature abhors a vacuum. Miss Strongi'th'arm's nature went further. Her hook of passionate love *had* to be filled. Never in all her life had it gone spare. Dolls had hung there. So had horses, often. Dogs, dancing, Donegal, men —one after another, these had been tenants at will —a very uncertain will. But that is beside the point, which is, as I have hinted, that the hook was now empty. . . .

André switched on the light and slid off the bed. Then she crossed to her table and opened a drawer.

Here lay a letter which had arrived that morning.

Sitting upon the edge of the table, she re-read it carefully.

MY DEAR ANDRE,

They tell me you know that I am well, but that, after all you have been through, you do not feel able to see me just yet. I am not surprised. (Remember, I can only take their words literally, without trying to read something which may or may not be written between the lines.) I neither know nor desire to know the circumstances of my loss of reason—I am told that it was caused by overwork at that place which was recently burned, Gramarye—but, however it came about, the shock to you must have been awful.

You see, my dear girl, I know that, when my mind was taken, you and I were engaged.

That my love for you should have survived my illness, is not surprising. I was, in a sense, less affected than anyone else. But I want you to know, André, that it has survived, and that I can think of no one else.

Whether you love me still, is another matter. You may. If you do not, I can most perfectly understand. Possibly you may not know whether you do or not.

In any event, write to me candidly: and what you wish, my lady, that I will do. If you think it better, I will keep away—for a while, or for ever. If you would like to see me, I will come—as a friend. If . . .

André, my darling, I have tried to write dispassionately. In return, don't let me down. Tell me the absolute truth, however harsh it may be. It's far kinder.

Always,

RICHARD WINCHESTER.

Now, André believed firmly in going whither the winds of Fate were minded to carry her. How little she practised this faith she was sublimely unconscious. She was fully persuaded and often averred with conviction that she had done so all her life. As a matter of hard fact, she went where she listed: and the winds of Fate had usually to work themselves into a hurricane before she became aware that any suggestion was being made. In the present case a whole gale had been driving for over twelve hours.

Only two people knew that her engagement with Richard had been broken off. Of these, one—Anthony—was dead, while the other—Richard himself—had forgotten. 'When my mind was taken, you and I were engaged.' Probably they were. That night when she had flung down her ring he was already mad—obviously.

Of her affair with Anthony, of course, he knew nothing at all. As likely as not, he did not remember Lyveden. 'That place which was recently burned.' *That place* . . .

There was no doubt about it. By an amazing accident the clock had been put back, and André was being offered her 'time' over again. The question was, whether to accept it or no.

André flung back her head and stared at the light.

Richard . . . Richard Winchester . . . normal, was a most splendid being. She had been crazy about him—till she had met Lyveden. When he had asked her to marry him, it had been the proudest moment of her life. . . .

Harlequin-like, the scene flashed into her mind, gallant and glittering. The two were riding home after a hunt. It was a mild evening, and the rain, which had been falling, had slackened and died. With no wind to carry it, the smell of the soaking earth rose up sweet and lingering. On either side of them a beechwood gave back the jingle of bits and the hollow slap of hoofs. Far down the silent road an early light was whipping on the dusk. . . . Suddenly Richard had leaned forward and caught her bridle. 'Will you marry me, André?' 'I will.' Without a word he had lifted her out of her

saddle and gathered her in his arms. Then he had
kissed her mouth and set her upon his saddle-bow.
. . .

André closed her eyes and drew in her breath.

Of course he needed a job—a job which would
give him a chance to use his amazing powers. Big-
game hunting, for instance. If she had realized
that twelve months ago, things might have been
different. But she had not. She had resented the
way in which he had courted occupation. All the
time it had been the man's nature. She might as
well have been jealous of his appetite. . . . If the
clock had been put back, not so her experience.
She had been shown most clearly what cards to play.
Big-game hunting. . . . Well, she would love that.
That was a job she could enter into heartily. And
if Richard hadn't much money—why, she was rich.
. . .

André began to appreciate that she was a most
fortunate girl. She had come an unearthly cropper,
and—the record had been expunged. Not a living
soul was aware—yes. One was. Not that she mattered, still . . .

Which brought her to Valerie French.

A faint frown of vexation gathered on André's
brow.

"I am a fool," she said sharply. "A headstrong
fool. I had no case at all. If I'd liked to show her
my cards, it wasn't her fault. All the same . . ."
She gnawed at her underlip. "I am a fool," she
repeated "I suppose she thinks I don't know any
better. There, of all places. . . . I wish to Heaven
I'd pulled myself together before—before she went.
Of course she thinks I'm just rank. *She*, of all people

F

—to think that of me." André flushed red with mortification. "With what I told her at Dinard and then what I did to-day—— Oh, of course she thinks it. She must. So would anyone. It's just like shouting ' I'm rank. I'm the cheapest, rankest bounder you ever saw.' Hell! Why was I such a fool? Such a rotten fool?"

She stepped to a box by her bed and took out a cigarette. When she had lighted this, she flung herself into a chair.

"I shall have to see her," she said. "Somehow. Barley's probably got her address. Yes. That's the only thing to do. I can't leave things as they are—possibly."

It was, of course, a question of self-respect. While Valerie did not respect her, André could not possibly respect herself. This was unbearable. That her own respect should depend on that of somebody else, was humiliating. That it should depend upon that of her idol's darling, made André writhe. In a mad moment she had pawned her dignity. Now, at whatever cost, this must be redeemed.

That she was quite unrepentant must not be charged to her account. Fate had been rough with her. That she should have chosen Valerie to be her confidante was most outrageous fortune. What had resulted, if distressing, was natural enough. At two-fifteen that day Miss Strongi'th'arm had had no reason to believe that she was not upon dry ground. At two-fifteen and a half she had made the unpleasant discovery that the ground was not dry at all, but a particularly odious slough, in which she had for some eight days been standing up to her knees. Few girls would not have floundered. André's mettlesome nature had sent her in up to her neck. Incidentally, it was the same vehement spirit which was now peremptorily demanding to be released from this plight. Mettle is a good subject, but, as an autocrat, apt to cost rather more than he is worth. The cheques he draws upon Humiliation are cruelly fat. It is good to think that in Miss Stroni'th 'arm's case these were invariably honoured.

André tossed her cigarette into the night and began to make ready for sleep. . . .

Before nine o'clock the next morning she sent a telegram.

This was addressed to Winchester, and was most eloquently brief.

Come.

*   *   *   *   *

Valerie s sudden decision to keep a diary was a desperate move. She was prompted by much the same motive as prompted political prisoners who were not sculptors to carve the walls of their cells. She *had* to do something. But, since she was not a diarist and never could be, she kept it only so long as there was nothing—to her mind—worth recording. Indeed, this fragment ends abruptly upon the fifth day. After all, I will wager that such political prisoners as were eventually released alive did not keep up their carving.

August 7th.—Breakfast at nine. Tried to decide whether to return to Dinard or not. Couldn't. Wrote to Aunt Harriet and said I was staying in Town and would wire before I left. Asked her to try and think of some ' Professions for Girls.' I cannot get that sordid business of yesterday out of my head. Is everything to be denied me? I've only to scratch up some wretched, miserable crumbs, for these to be taken away. I feel like the prisoner who managed to tame a rat; and then one day they found him feeding his pet, and killed it. The flat needs decoration. Made up my mind to send for —— to-morrow. But I shall not. What is the good? We may not ever come here again. Even if we do. . . . Walked in the Park before luncheon. Something impelled me to ring up Daphne Pleydell. Happily, she was out of Town. Of course, everyone is. Luncheon—a solitary meal. Pity the idle rich. Then I had the car round and drove into Hertfordshire—to The Dogs' Home. The superintendent seemed pleased to see me again. I was a fool to go. I was a bigger fool to have tea at *The Leather Bottel*. Even they remembered me. They also remembered Joe . . . and Patch . . . and him. I never asked. They just rambled on and dragged them all into the fairy tale. I came home and dined in melancholy state. Afterwards I tried to read, but I could only think. Why did I leave Dinard? I am getting frightened. This loneliness makes me afraid. Yet I cannot go back. I can't face the villa again. That girl was there, for one thing. Besides . . .

August 8th.—I think waking is the worst time of all. For a fraction of a second, after I'm awake, everything's rosy and golden. Then, with a paralysing shock, I remember. . . . What a cruel thing Life is! Every morning now, for nearly a month, I have been informed most bluntly that my darling is dead. And every morning I am stunned with the awful news. I suppose I must be thankful that

I sleep as well as I do. This morning I rang up
Forsyth. He begged me to come and see him. I
promised to go to-morrow. I dread it terribly.
Sole legatee, sole executrix. The misery it means.
I shall tread the steps he trod—that awful day:
sit in the chair he sat in: use the same pen. The
clerks will stare at me. Forsyth will temper the
wind to the shorn lamb. He'll think he's doing
it beautifully—he's done it so often. . . . And
I shall sit and watch him, just as one watches a
photographer moving his screens about. A letter
from Betty Alison came by the second post. A very
sweet note. I feel I should like to see her, but of
course she can't get away. And I daren't go to
Hampshire. *Dear old Val*, she says, *we think of
you all day long. Lift up your beautiful head. Don't
say there's nothing to lift it up for. Lift it up and
wait.* I must try. After luncheon I put on a coat
and skirt and drove to Richmond Park. I tramped
all over it for hours. I should like to be able to say
it did me good. It didn't. Coming home, I saw a
dog run over—rather like Patch. The owner—a
little girl—was like a mad thing. I took her home
in the car with the dead dog clasped in her arms.
. . . It is obvious that I am to be spared nothing.
Soon I shall be afraid to go out. I spent a bad
evening and was thankful to go to bed.

August 9th.—I went to Lincoln's Inn Fields. Forsyth was very kind—not at all what I had expected.
If he moved any screens about, I didn't see it going
on. He said I must try to regard him as an old
family butler—four-fifths servant and one-fifth friend.
He showed me the Will—a very short document.
Another longer one had been prepared, to be signed

after our marriage. I saw this, too. There was really no difference, except that there was a memorandum attached to this, suggesting that, if I liked, I should give George and Betty and Anne ten thousand apiece and Slumper two hundred a year until his death. Of course I shall do this delightedly, as soon as ever I can. I came home to luncheon, not so much comforted as relieved. I am very fortunate in Forsyth. What a misleading thing anticipation is! The wind you dread turns out a zephyr. The wind you hail cuts like a knife. After luncheon I wrote to Aunt Harriet and said I was coming back—probably to-morrow. I cannot stand it here. All the same, I dread Dinard. Perhaps, because I dread it, it won't be so bad. If only she wasn't so comfortable there, I would suggest Paris. For some inexplicable reason I don't want to go far afield. Then I went to the Wallace Collection —rather desperately. I felt that awful depression coming on. I stayed there till I was turned out. Fragonard's *Villa d'Este* and Rembrandt's *Landscape* did me a lot of good. I kept going back to them. I came in to find a letter from Uncle John—very short, very wise, very honest. *My dear, I am not going to risk my position, as your adviser, by giving you valueless advice. For one thing, you are no fool, and, for another, I love you too well. I can only say this. Do not lose heart. Refuse to let yourself go. There is, I know, a breaking-point. Nine girls out of ten would have been broken by now. But you, if you please, need not be broken at all. I tell you, I cannot think of any calamity which could subdue your high spirit, if only you opposed its assault There lies the danger—that you will let yourself go. You*

*are tired of holding on. Of course. Remember, there
is always one more ounce of resistance left in us than
we believe. It seems a pity not to use it. Why?
Because, if you use it, you will come through . . .
and out . . . into the light.* 'Into the light.' Then
there is light ahead. I'm thankful I didn't ask him,
because I should have suspected his reply. But
he would never volunteer a lie. I am going to bed
more hopefully than I have for weeks and weeks.
'Into the light.'

August 10th.—This morning arrived a letter from
André Strongi'th'arm. The moment I saw the
writing I knew it was hers. And I felt cold. *Ashamed
of my barbarous behaviour . . . cannot rest till I have
seen you. . . . I am very much changed . . . my
eyes have been opened. . . . I know I'm asking a
lot, but will you see me? If you are in London, I'm
coming up on Thursday for two or three days. Will
you send me a line to the Berkeley?* I'm glad in a
way she wrote, but I don't want to see her at all.
Why can't she leave it at that? It isn't as if we
were friends. There's nothing to be made up. Now
that she's written, the incident ought to be closed.
Yet she's keeping it open—setting her foot in the
door. Why? I suppose she wants to show me
she can behave. As if I cared. The obvious thing
to do is to leave for France. I had meant to to-day.
But I don't want to go, and, after Uncle John's letter
I felt I could stay. . . .

I went to the Wallace Collection again this morning. I might as well have stayed in the flat. That
wretched letter kept cropping up all the time. I
don't want to see her, and yet I suppose I must. After
luncheon I took the two-seater and drove down the

Portsmouth Road. I shan't do it again. I found
the traffic a strain, and London's too big. By the
time you're out of it you're tired. At least, I am.
This is the first sign of age I've seen in myself. I
welcome it. Dinner—a ghastly meal, because I
knew after dinner I must decide. I've tried to argue
it out—for and against. I couldn't get far. The
only thing against seeing her is that I don't want
to. On the other side, I don't want to seem to be
keeping it up. (Keeping what up? I can't recognize
any hostility. I've never drawn my sword.) Besides,
if I see her, I can snuff the whole thing out. After
a lot of hesitation, I wrote and asked her to come
on Friday at twelve. After all, when the morning
comes, I can send her a wire. But I shan't. I
know I shall see her. What does it matter? I
think everybody would say that in this I was at
perfect liberty to please myself. Even Uncle John.
Yet I'm not going to, and I am right. I feel instinctively that I am right. I suppose it's another phase
—a draught's only got to be nasty to be worth drink-
ing. Late as it was, I took the letter to the post
—to make certain. I suppose I am right.

August 11th.—I have had a bad day. Anthony
is dead. Years—centuries ago I made a terrible
mistake. I paid most heavily. Then I paid again
—most heavily. Each time I thought the debt was
settled. Each time I was wrong. I was paying
the pence . . . the shillings. The pounds were to
come. And now I have paid the pounds. I hold
the receipt. It came before breakfast this morning. *The Executors of the late Major Lyveden, Bell
Hammer. Dr. to Benjamin Punch, Saddler, 7 Castle
Street, Brooch. June 9th. To Dog's Collar, 4s. 8d.*

Anthony is dead. Yet everything is just the same.
Boys have been whistling in the street, cars have
swept on their way, and once a band passed. I
know. I have not been out. Of course I do not
expect the world to stand still, but *there is no difference*. This frightful tragedy does not count. Is
it nothing to them? Nothing. They don't know.
If they knew, they wouldn't care. Betty says, 'We
think of you all day long.' Yes, but they eat just
as well. They're just as put out, if they run out
of jam. No jam—and Anthony is dead. Can such
a hideous catastrophe be so confined? Is it possible?
Yes. Outside the room I sit in, it doesn't count.
I think I must have some straw put down outside
in the street. Then when people go by they'll toss
a thought to the dying person inside. There will
be no dying person. That doesn't matter. The
straw will make them think. I must make people
realize that there's something wrong. This present
frightful indifference is unendurable.

I had breakfast. I had luncheon. I had dinner.
The thought of that interview to-morrow has driven
me nearly mad. Yet I must go through with it.
'Lift up your head.' 'Refuse to let yourself go.'
'One more ounce.' I suppose to-morrow will bring
the breaking-point. But I shan't break. Why?
Because I *can't* break. I'm not naturally made.
There's some terrible stuff in my composition which
can stand any strain. The hell I go through doesn't
matter. My mind may be twisted and wrenched,
but it will not give way. It's like those rag-books
—untearable.

A letter from Aunt Harriet arrived this evening
—a kind, rational letter, full of good things. But

they are wasted on me. I am too wretched. It shows that my absence has done her a lot of good. Which is hardly surprising. I'm glad I didn't go back. Poor woman, by now she has my letter, saying I'm coming. I must send her a wire to-morrow, that she may breathe again. I must be terrible company. I have read the letter again. I can see that its wit is brilliant, but I cannot smile. The salt has lost its savour. Anthony is dead.

Ten o'clock is striking. Only another hour, and, with any luck, I shall be asleep—until to-morrow. That's the awful part—' until to-morrow.' I'm never out of it. My bed has been brought into the torture-chamber. I have slept there for weeks. And I shall. I do not see that I shall ever come out any more. How can I? Anthony is dead.

* * * *

As André turned into Hill Street, a neighbouring clock began to announce midday. Three minutes later she was seated in a cool morning-room, looking composedly about her.

She had come, as we know, to regain Valerie's respect. This was not her hope, but her intention. It had never occurred to her that she might fail of her quest. Delicate mission as this was, she had thought out nothing to say. The time would provide the sentences. . . .

Sitting on the arm of a chair, she surveyed the tip of a little patent-leather shoe with infinite satisfaction. There was no doubt about it, —— made the best shoes in London. . . .

Then the door was opened, and Valerie came in.

I think it was the quiet, grave smile which hung

in those tired blue eyes that knocked Miss Strongi'-
th'arm out.

Be that as it may, it is quite certain that she was
greeted, shaken hands with, and quietly thanked
for her letter, before she could try to speak, and it
is equally indisputable that, when her hostess had
finished and was standing silent, André stood in
front of her, nervously wringing her gloves and trying without success to use her tongue.

"Let's sit down," said Valerie. André did as
she was bid. "And now please tell me your news.
I'm sure from your letter it's good, and I'ld like to
hear it."

"You—you've made it seem very small," said
André, slowly. "It seemed important when I wrote,
but now I'm ashamed to tell it." She hesitated.
"After all, what am I to you? What if I did care
about your—the man who was engaged to you?"

"Did care?"

"Did. I see my mistake. I shall always remember him with a grateful heart—as your affianced
husband. I'm very lucky. Richard loves me,
you know, and I'm going to marry him. He's quite
himself again—speaks of Gramarye as 'that place.'
He hasn't mentioned . . Major Lyveden. I don't
think he remembers him."

"Please call him 'Anthony,'" said Valerie. "And
why should you think that the fact that you cared
about him would mean nothing to me?"

"Oh, I don't know," said André, looking away.
"I expect a good many girls cared about him, if
the truth were known. But that's their pigeon,"
she added, with a half-hearted laugh. "The general
doesn't know every soldier."

"You'ld like me to like Richard."

"I wouldn't like it if you rammed the fact down my throat and, when he was dead, came and heckled me at the graveside."

There was a moment's silence.

Then—

"That's very handsome of you," said Valerie, quietly. "And I'm awfully glad you're going to marry Colonel Winchester. I didn't know he was well."

"You know that Gramarye's burned?"

"I heard so at Girdle."

"The day it was burned out, his mind came back."

Valerie stiffened suddenly and went dead white.

After a long minute, she drew in her breath sharply and bowed her head. . . .

A thoroughly frightened André fell on her knees.

"What have I said?" she cried. "What have I said?"

For a moment Valerie made no answer at all.

Then—

"Oh, nothing," she said quietly. "Only . . . only it seems a pity that it wasn't burned a little earlier . . . before—Anthony—died."

"My God!" said André. And then again, "My God!" She buried her face in her hands. "I never meant it," she breathed. "I swear I didn't. It never occurred to me. Oh, what a fool I am! What a poisonous, blundering fool! I came to try and repair what I did last week. I've made it a million times worse. I've . . ."

Her voice broke and she began to weep passionately.

'One more ounce . . . one more ounce. . . .'

The words danced before her, searing Valerie's

brain. It occurred to her that they were a satire upon her misery—a sham, a cheat, a trick of the torture-chamber. They were the carrot hung in front of the donkey's nose—the grapes of Tantalus —the national anthem of the damned. ' One more ounce.' Then the words stopped dancing and fell into step with the tick of the Vulliamy clock beside the fireplace. *' One* more—*one* more—*al*ways—*one* more . . .*'* André's sobs got in the way of the rhythm, and Valerie wished she would stop. She began to beat time with her foot, to try to preserve the sober, measured tread. . . . Suddenly the words stopped marching and came to rest. The fine, firm handwriting of Cardinal Forest appeared, with the phrase set in its context at the top of the sheet. *Remember, there is always one more ounce of resistance left in us than we believe.* And there, a little lower down, *into the light.* . . .

With a tremendous effort, Valerie lifted up her head.

" It's not your fault," she said gently. " I was bound to know one day. Besides, it's nothing new. The whole affair is studded with the words ' If only.' Every tragedy is. That's what makes a tragedy."

Still sobbing, André shook her head.

" You'ld never 've known," she wailed, " if I hadn't told you. If I hadn't come to-day, you'ld 've been spared that." She dropped her hands and looked up at Valerie's face. " You do know I didn't mean it ? " she added desperately.

" Of course I do," said Valerie. " I don't bear you the slightest grudge for—for anything."

" You do, you do. You must. You wouldn't be human if——"

" I don't," said Valerie. " As I live, I don't. Because there's a curse on me, that isn't your fault." She laughed bitterly. " Tell me of Colonel Winchester. I know a little about him, but not very much."

André started and glanced at the watch on her wrist.

" I think I've lost my balance," she said, wiping her eyes. " I did a senseless thing. He had to go into the City, and I told him to call for me here at half-past twelve. I'm afraid I felt I'ld like you to see him. I actually thought it might interest you."

" So it will," said Valerie.

André got upon her feet.

" How can it possibly ? " she said. " You can't say anything else. I'm afraid I'm very self-centred," she added miserably, " as well as an awful fool. And now I'm going. I'm frightfully, terribly sorry for all I've done, and I'll never forgive myself for——"

Here the door was opened, and a servant came in.

" Colonel Winchester."

A man like a Viking was ushered into the room. Confusedly, André introduced him.

Valerie and he shook hands.

" I'm afraid I'm late," he said in a steady, deep voice. " You said ' a quarter past twelve.' "

" Half past," corrected André.

"Did you ? That's a relief." He turned to Valerie. " I hate being late, Miss French. But while I was driving up Fleet Street I saw a man I knew going into the Temple. By the time I was out of the cab he was out of sight, and I wasted a quarter of an hour trying to find him. I shouldn't have bothered, but I've not many friends, and he was a very good chap." He turned again to André. " I don't think you ever met him. Lyveden, his name was. He was with me at——"

The sentence stopped in its stride, and Winchester stared at his audience with a dropped jaw.

Valerie was standing, shaking, with a hand to her brow. André had shrunk against her and was clutching her arm. The eyes of both were starting out of their heads.

" B-but he's *dead !* " shrieked André. " He's dead ! He's buried at Girdle."

" *Dead ?* " shouted Winchester. " Nonsense ! I'ld know him anywhere. Besides, he had his dog with him—a Sealyham, with a big black patch on his back. And he heard me call his master, though Lyveden didn't. He turned and looked about him, the moment he heard my voice."

CHAPTER IV

BLIND ALLEY

A GIRL with auburn hair stared out of a window. It was a blazing afternoon.

Immediately below her the traffic of Piccadilly advanced in an everlasting series of short rushes, like infantry going into action. The laboured breathing of the 'buses in the intervals between their spurts at once lent colour to the illusion and made up a stertorous foundation of uproar, above which little but coughs and hoots of warning, the sudden storm of an engine or the crash of a taxi's gears managed to rise. Beyond, raked by the afternoon sun, a somewhat stale Green Park belied its name. The pitiless drought waxing, London's precious fields had come to look second-hand.

But the girl with auburn hair was spared tumult and shabbiness alike. She neither heard the one nor perceived the other. In a word, André Strongi'th'arm was preoccupied.

Hers was not the case of the widow who, after she has re-married, encounters her first husband, but it was pretty closely allied to that most awkward condition. Her plight was that of the dog—unaccountably omitted by Æsop—who, after considerable hesitation, has preferred substance to shadow, only to find that the shadow was, after all, no shadow, but stuff just as good as it looked.

She had officially renounced the late Anthony Lyveden. She had resigned all claim to the deceased in favour of Valerie French. Also she had resumed her engagement with Richard Winchester. Renunciation, resignation and resumption had all worked together very well. They were, of course, jointly and severally founded upon Anthony Lyveden's death. And now, without any warning, the rock had crumbled away. Anthony Lyveden was alive and in London. He had been seen that morning.

These were the hard facts. Now for the little ironies.

It was Richard Winchester who had seen Lyveden : it was she who had arranged for Richard and Valerie to meet : it was at this meeting that Richard, in all ignorance, had announced his amazing news. More. What I am sure would have pleased Sophocles was that Richard was at this moment most capably assisting Valerie to find his rival. . . .

Pell-mell the three had repaired to the Temple, where Anthony had been seen. There Richard had posted each of the girls at a point commanding two exits. Himself he had sworn delightedly to answer for the rest, while a transfigured Valerie had thanked him with a smile out of heaven itself. . . . So soon as he was out of sight, André had made her escape and had returned to her hotel. The limit had been reached—passed. Labouring under a delusion, she had conveyed her freehold : she could not bring herself to subscribe to the livery of seisin. To be pressed enthusiastically into such monstrous service was more than André's flesh and blood could endure. . . . She

G

could not know that two minutes after she had deserted her post Anthony Lyveden had followed her out of the Temple.

André stared at the sunshine decking the havoc it had wrought.

What should she do? Was she to lie in the bed which she had made? Or should she declare her position, demolish her existing couch, and set herself forthwith to make another? The idea of setting to work without telling Richard and Valerie never occurred to her. André was honest to a fault. She would not have deceived a dog. She could strike, and that without pity, but she could never feint. Craft of any sort she abhorred utterly. It was as much this very abhorrence as anything else which, though she did not know it, had compelled her to leave the Temple two hours before. . . .

Supposing she made a new bed, what would it be like?

First, Richard must be sent packing. The stage had to be cleared. Then Valerie must be told that she—André—was out for Anthony Lyveden. Finally, for the bed to be anything other than the planks of misery, Lyveden, when found, had to be made to love her.

There is nothing like looking the future full in the face . . . André observed that, viewed from this standpoint, its features left much to be desired.

For one thing, if Richard were dismissed, he would never re-enter her service. That was as clear as daylight. It was hardly likely that the clock would be put back a second time. André disliked the proverb which sets the poulterer's shelf above the butts. She found it unsporting. All the same, the saw edged its way into her mind and sat there, looking very wise and unpleasantly worthy.

What was less certain, but very possible, was that Anthony Lyveden would not come up to the scratch. Once before he had failed signally. Besides, he was Valerie French's affianced husband. . . . Thackeray's tremendous dictum bundled into her mind. 'A woman with fair opportunities, and without an absolute hump, may marry WHOM SHE LIKES.' Yes, but Thackeray left himself a tremendous loophole. 'Fair opportunities.' Noun and adjective alike were extremely flexible. And her opportunities were not fair. In fact, she had none. Like the prospective bed, they had to be made.

Indeed, the one and only thing to be said for such an attempt was that the bed, successfully contrived, would knock her existing couch into a cocked hat. The deal, if compassed, would make the audacious speculator unearthly rich . . . if compassed. . . .

Always the flame of speculation was flickering in André's heart. She was so built. Her daring in the hunting-field was a byword. Only her love of horses restrained her at all. But for that, she would have been killed years ago.

And so, madness as it may seem, before the radiance of the prize André almost went down. Inspired by some false god, almost she determined 'to put it to the touch to gain or lose it all.' Blinded by the glory of a phantom success, she could not see failure. So it was not the certainty of failure which stopped her dead. Neither—to her discredit—was it the thought of Richard, that splendid, honourable giant, which brought her up all standing. It was a pair of violet eyes, very beautiful and very, very tired, but smiling gently and easily for all their weariness. . . .

Success meant that Valerie French, her rival, would be broken, body and soul, upon the wheel.

As I have hinted, André was not of the kind that waste their pity. If others went to the wall on her account, that was their own look-out. They should have shoved harder. But here was a difference. Twice she had done Valerie most grievous wrong. She knew it. The fact could not be blinked. That the injuries were now repaired was beside the point. She had not repaired them. She owed the girl something. She had kicked her when she was down. Now she was on her feet, it was out of the question that she should administer the *coup de grâce*. Anthony or no, it could not possibly be done. . . .

Of course, if Anthony saw her—preferred her to Valerie—made the running himself, that would be different. As it was, she could not move in the matter . . . could not, possibly. . . .

Noblesse oblige.

Where reason, decency, common sense—even the instinct of self-preservation had gone for nothing, magnanimity of all emotions had done the trick. And this was no daw in peacock's feathers, but the real thing. André honestly considered that she was standing aside, letting Valerie French go in and win.

That same evening André visited Valerie and told her in very plain terms why she had deserted her post. She added that, if Valerie would allow it, she would henceforth do her utmost to help her find Anthony Lyveden.

Valerie laughed gaily.

"I should think you ride pretty straight," she

said simply. " And now it's my turn. I very nearly
kissed your Richard this afternoon. I had to drag
him away, or he'ld 've been there still. Not that
I wanted to go, but Rome wasn't built in an eight-
hour day. I know that Anthony's alive and here
—in London. The rest will follow. I'm sure of
it. Colonel Winchester was kindness itself—and
efficiency. He went home swearing that Anthony
should be found and that he'ld find him. I asked
him why he was so good. He simply stared. ' But
you're a friend of André's,' he said. ' Aren't you ? ' "

" I hope you said ' Yes,' " said André Strongi'th'arm.
Valerie nodded.

*   *   *   *   *

When Colonel Richard Winchester affirmed that
he had seen Anthony Lyveden alive and walking,
exactly twenty-eight days after the remains of Anthony Lyveden had been reverently interred at
Girdle, it will be seen that he was making a statement which might easily have been questioned. That
it was accepted wholly by his hearers was due in
some measure to the fact that, while both of them
had seen the grave, neither of them had seen its
contents, but, mainly, to Winchester himself. The
man's personality simply compelled belief. . . .

And so, though the days went by, and Lyveden
was neither seen again nor heard of, Valerie found
no fault in her portion. Indeed, she held herself
blessed. True, she was not yet in Paradise, but she
had escaped out of that Pit which hath no exit. Her
dead had been raised. The ' great gulf fixed ' no
longer mattered : Anthony and she were both upon
the same side. Paradise could wait. . . .

Not that she and her councillors wasted their time. The most exhaustive inquiries were set on foot : advertisements appeared : Winchester himself conducted a house-to-house investigation of the Temple. Indeed, short of setting a price upon Anthony Lyveden's head, everything possible was done to locate the gentleman. With it all, the latter obstinately defied detection.

And there, of course, was the rub—the riddle which no one could read.

If Lyveden was alive and up and doing, why did he make himself scarce ?

I have not discussed it because it was not discussed : Valerie never referred to it, nor did the others : it did not depress her, because an eccentric lion is so much better than a dead one. But . . .

Speculation, wrote Lady Touchstone, *is idle— nothing worth. Anthony holds the answer in his fine, grey eyes. When we find him we shall know—instantly. Personally, I am convinced that there is nothing seriously amiss. He is not mad. That ghost was laid when Gramarye was burned. Probably he thinks he is not wanted. Once before he thought so, and with good reason. And now his mind has thrown back. . . . Meanwhile we wait—triumphantly. We know that it is only a matter of time. Such confidence would be ridiculous, if it were not sublime. (I am trying to write coherently, but there is a distracting buzzing noise which I cannot locate.) Talking of eyes, if ever veiled pity looked out of anyone's orbs, it looks out of the lawyers'. Need I say that they are wholly sceptical of our discovery ? They do not believe a word of it. Not that they say so. Oh, no. They listen attentively to what we say, fall in with our plans, respectfully*

*endorse our enthusiasm. They 'hope very much
that we shall find Major Lyveden very soon.' But
they know that we shan't. They simply cannot get
over the death certificate. That Somerset House should
be harbouring an impostor is to them incomprehensible
—a heathenish suggestion. Anthony is legally dead.
I had it out with Forsyth the other day. "Why,"
I said, "are you so hide-bound?" "Ma'am," says
he, "there is a faith which can remove mountains.
I have always coveted it." "So have I," said I. "But
I don't covet common sense, because I've got some."
Forsyth spread out his hands. "Pity the weaker
vessel," he said. "Pity the legal mind," said I, "that
places black and white before flesh and blood. I'll
dance at their wedding yet—but not with a lawyer."
"No, don't," says he. "They'll trip you up every
time." I could afford to laugh. (I wish this mysterious
noise would stop. I cannot think what it is. It sounds
so indignant.) If you could see Valerie, John, your
heart would leap. Her radiance, her eagerness, her
joie de vivre make me feel that I must paw the ground.
I actually do so sometimes, under the table. Her beauty
takes away my breath. Her eyes alone. . . . I tell
you, people stop still in the street and stare after her.
And I see them and try not to burst into tears. The very
gods must be amazed at the effects of their gift. Her
confidence would frighten me to death, if I did not share
it. But, as I have said, it is sublime, not of this world.
We have no doubt—this time. Anthony will be found,
if not to-day, to-morrow. It is inevitable. We are a
singular quartette—Valerie, André Strongi'th'arm,
Colonel Winchester and I, and should, I think, go very
well in a revue. Valerie contributes the life, Winchester
the drive, André the dash, and I the low comedy, as a*

sort of confidential groom-of-the-chambers, fat, forgetful, superfluous and spending half my life asking people to 'spell it' over the telephone. Which reminds me, I've left the receiver off. . . .

* * * * *

Sir Andrew Plague was in Chambers.

That the Temple was empty and the Law Courts closed did not matter to him. The man was above custom. He went as he pleased.

A desultory fire of snorts and grunts of indignation, audible in the clerks' room and greatly relished by the two 'juniors,' suggested that their master was perusing Case Law, while the occasional crash of a volume declared the K.C.'s contempt for a dictum which should not have been printed and might have been left unsaid.

After a while the objections suddenly ceased, and from the succeeding silence a listener might have assumed that Sir Andrew was asleep. The clerks knew better, and fell to whispering or, if they had occasion to move, did so a-tiptoe. Sir Andrew was not asleep : he was using his brain.

By dint of supreme concentration he was at once shaping, ordering, compressing and expressing his conclusions regarding a question of law, and doing it about thirty times as swiftly and twice as skilfully as could anyone else alive.

There was nothing traditional about his pose. His huge arms folded upon the table, his massive head bowed, his great red face buried in his sleeve, the man might have been dead. From a tray by his side a cigar sent up a slender, swaying column of smoke. Before him an old chronometer measured the moments with the deliberate dignity of a forgotten age. . . .

Presently the thinker lifted up his head. For a moment he stared at the chronometer. Then he sat back in his chair and blew through his nose. His work was done.

Sir Andrew stretched out his hand and smote with great violence the hand-bell upon his table. The instrument, which had survived outrageous treatment for nearly two months, followed the example of its predecessors and broke. With an oath, Sir Andrew flung it into a corner.

" 'Streuf," said one of the ' juniors ' in the adjoining room. " If 'e ain't done in that bell. An' the place where I got it, they said I could stan' on it."

" Yes, but they didn't say 'e could," snapped his superior, hurrying out of the office.

A moment later he stood before his master.

" Destroy that bell," said Sir Andrew, jerking his head at the corner. " And sack the fool who bought it. Oh, and return that brief, and tell 'em that Lincoln's Inn 's the other side of the street."

Mr. Junket swallowed.

" I did remark, sir," he said, " that it was a point of Chancery law, but they said they knew that, and they'ld rather 'ave your opinion than any in Lincoln's Inn."

" Lying hounds," replied Sir Andrew. " What they mean is, every one else is away."

" I don't think it's that, sir," cautiously ventured the clerk. " There's plenty the other side would give an opinion. But Mr. Firmer 's attendin' to this 'imself, an' you know what 'e thinks of you, sir," he added proudly.

" I don't ! " shouted Sir Andrew. " I haven't

the faintest idea. Send me the shorthand clerk. If they like to waste their money, that's their look-out."

"Very good, sir."

Mr. Junket retired precipitately, and a moment later the shorthand writer appeared. As he closed the door, Sir Andrew began to dictate. . . .

"*My opinion is valueless. I know little of Chancery doctrines, and, happily, nothing of those appointed to administer them. It is a principle of law that* . . . (here followed a masterly 'opinion,' dealing root and branch with the matter and setting intricacy by the ears) . . . *In these circumstances, provided that the Court before which the case would ordinarily come has discretion sufficient to enable it to distinguish right from wrong, your client will not be permitted to proceed with the development of his property, so long as the lord of the manor, however base his motive, requests that such permission may be denied.* That's all. Send Junket."

The senior clerk reappeared.

"I told you to destroy that bell," said Sir Andrew. "Why the devil don't you do it?" Junket made a rush for the corner. "I'm leaving in five minutes. Produce it to me destroyed before I go."

"Very good, sir." Arrived at the door, the clerk hesitated. "There's—there's rather an urgent case, sir," he said uneasily, peering at a pile of papers upon his master's table. "A case to advise—from Mincing's. They've been pressing me now, sir, for over a week. An' another from——"

"D'you want to kill me?" demanded Sir Andrew. "This is the Long Vacation. If they don't want to wait, they can take their matters elsewhere. I won't do another stroke until to-morrow. Destroy that bell."

"Very good, sir."

The next moment Junket was in the clerks' room.

"'Ere, George," he said, handing the bell to his subordinate. "Take that out an' break it. Look sharp."

"'Break it'?" said George, staring at the battered instrument. "But it's broke already."

"Never mind about that," cried Junket, thrusting the bell into his hand. "'E wants it 'destroyed.' 'E's got to see it 'destroyed' before 'e goes. An' 'e's goin' in four minutes. For gauze sake, be quick. You know what 'e is." He turned to the shorthand writer, who was transcribing the 'opinion.' "Do the las' paragraph, Jim, 's quick as you can. So 's I can get 'im to sign it before 'e goes."

"But look 'ere," protested George, "I ain't a blecksmith. 'Ow can I——"

"Look 'ere," rejoined his senior, taking out his watch. "D'you want the bird? 'Cause, if 'e asks for that bell before it's ruined, you can 'ave it in one. Take the blighter out," he added fiercely, "an' keep on chuckin' it down on the flegstones till——"

A sudden bellow from Sir Andrew's room threw the three clerks into a panic.

George rushed out of the Chambers: Jim drove his pen like a madman; while the unfortunate Junket wiped his brow and, nervously adjusting his collar, prepared to answer the summons.

Beyond, however, that Sir Andrew observed darkly that the bell was due to be demolished in three minutes' time, Mr. Junket was merely ordered to send four ' cases to advise ' to his master's private house.

The clerk withdrew relievedly.

George, meanwhile, was working feverishly.

After four violent collisions with the flags, the condition of the bell seemed rather improved than anything else, and, what was worse, upon being tested, it rang smartly.

George broke into a sweat.

Indeed, but for the sight of a dray standing in Middle Temple Lane, he would, I think, have retired at once from the Temple and the unequal contest. . .

Necessity knows no law.

A moment later the bell was in position beneath the off hind wheel, and George was backing the horses like an Artillery driver under fire. . . .

Sir Andrew surveyed the fragments with grim satisfaction. Then he signed his ' opinion ' and called for his hat. . . .

As he stepped on to the Embankment, a ragged fellow passed him, with misery in his eyes.

The K.C. called him back. He came uncertainly.

" What's the matter with you ? "

The wretched eyes avoided Sir Andrew's look.

" I'm—I'm 'ungry," faltered their owner, and turned away.

Sir Andrew counted ten shillings and put them into his hand.

" That's for food," he said shortly. " Not drink."

He turned to wave his stick at a passing cab. . . .

A moment later he was being carried westward at an unlawful pace.

Here let me say that Lady Touchstone's courage was of a high order. Danger, for instance, merely

sharpened her wits. I do not think that she knew
any physical fear. Yet, as she frankly admitted,
each visit she paid her dentist undoubtedly shortened
her life. To point the paradox, her anticipation of
the ordeal was always far worse than the encounter.
Compared with that of the waiting-room, the atmosphere of the condemned hold seemed to her almost
jovial. Indeed, she so much abhorred the former
that she was always most careful to arrive late, with
the result that her detention in the ante-chamber
of horrors was seldom more than a matter of sixty
seconds. How, in the teeth of such provision, upon
this particular morning she came to make such a
mistake is incomprehensible, but it is a hard fact that
she alighted in Brook Street precisely at four minutes
past eleven, in painless ignorance that her vivisection
had been fixed for a quarter to twelve.

For a while she fully believed that she was being
kept waiting, but when twenty minutes had passed
and she was still unsummoned, she rang the bell
and inquired if Mr. Sleeseman was aware of her
presence. . . .

Upon learning the awful truth, the unfortunate
lady's first impulse was to withdraw ; but, realizing
that, if in her present nervous condition she emerged
into the smiling streets, she would never have the
fortitude to re-enter the house that morning, she sank
into a chair and began to pluck at the pages of a
periodical upon which the blessed gift of immortality
had been apparently conferred.

Ten frightful minutes had slunk by, and Lady
Touchstone, who had the room to herself, was half-
way to nervous prostration—starting at every footfall, finding cause for nameless suspicion in every

unfamiliar sound—when a bell was pealed with
great violence and a blow upon the front door shook
the house to its foundations.

After one tremendous bound the poor lady's heart
stood still. . . .

A moment later came a rush of steps, the front
door was opened, and an uproar of furious quarrelling
was launched into the hall.

"Summon me, then," roared Sir Andrew, "you
slanderous thief! You know who I am. Go into
Court and swear that I've broken your springs. A-a-ah,
you blackmailing villain! . "

The door was slammed with the shock of an explosion,
tremendous footsteps pounded along the passage, and
an instant later Sir Andrew was ushered into the
room.

More dead than alive, Lady Touchstone, who had
risen to her feet and stumbled towards the window,
regarded his entrance with a palpitating indignation
which knew no law.

The giant flounced into a chair and closed his
eyes. . . .

"You brute," said Lady Touchstone, deliberately.

At the third attempt Sir Andrew recovered his
voice.

"Were you addressing me?"

"I was," said Lady Touchstone.

Sir Andrew rose to his feet.

"Madam," he said, "how dare you?"

"If you don't like it," said Lady Touchstone,
who was feeling much better, "you can leave the
room. You're a brute."

"A brute?" said Sir Andrew, taking a step forward.

"A brute," said Lady Touchstone. "And don't

talk about 'daring' to me. You ought to be on your knees, suing for pardon. This isn't a bull-ring. It's—it's a confessional."

"It's a public——"

"No, it isn't," was the disconcerting reply. "I've no doubt you'ld feel more at home if it were. It's a place of mental affliction for patients who have a sense of their duty towards their neighbours. I suppose you're here with the object of receiving attention : apparently the idea exhilarates you. That alone is indecent. But when you flaunt such monstrous emotion under the noses of more reasonably-minded beings, it's—it's worse than brawling."

Sir Andrew Plague gasped. His eyes began to protrude.

"Brawling ? " he repeated, as though unable to believe his ears. "Brawling, madam ? What do you mean—' brawling ' ? "

"Brawling," said Lady Touchstone, "is the offence of quarrelling in a noisy and indecent manner upon holy ground. They used to do it at that very high church near the Cromwell Road. I say advisedly that your behaviour is still more abominable. At least, they had the excuse of religious fervour."

"Madam," said Sir Andrew, in a shaking voice, "you presume upon the privilege of your sex. I am not in the habit of having my conduct criticized, still less of hearing it condemned."

"The more's the pity," flashed Lady Touchstone, bristling. "If those unfortunate enough to be associated with you occasionally corrected your failings, you would be less of a menace to society."

"Goats and monkeys ! " yelled Plague.

Lady Touchstone stifled a scream.

" How dare you shout at me ? " she demanded.
" How dare you ? "

With a frightful effort the lawyer mastered his
voice.

" Madam," he said thickly, " you have spoken
of bull-rings and brawling. Twice you have used
the word ' indecent ' in a context and with a meaning
which admitted no possibility of misconstruction.
Finally you have thought proper to style me ' a menace
to society.' Madam, this may not be slander, but it
is vulgar abuse, and while the Law will take no——"

" You will please," said Lady Touchstone, " withdraw that expression. I believe it to be a purely
legal term, but it offends me."

For a long minute the two eyed one another across
the mahogany table.

Then—

" I beg your pardon," said Plague uncertainly.

Lady Touchstone inclined her head.

" I regret," she said, " that I cannot return the
compliment. Your conduct has been outrageous.
Regardless of the feelings of others who, cast in a
less—er—vigorous mould than yourself, may be
awaiting in agony the attention to which you apparently look forward——"

" I don't. I loathe it. And my conduct's not
been outrageous. You've no right to——"

" I have every right. You might have shattered
my nerves. Because you have been annoyed, why
should I suffer ? Why should you vent your vile
wrath——"

" Madam," cried Plague, trembling, " you go too
far. If you have been inconvenienced by over-
hearing such protest as I thought fit to lodge against

a scandalous attempt at blackmail, that is regrettable. It confers upon you no authority to insult a complete stranger, whose rights to the quiet enjoyment of this chamber are co-equal with yours, and——"

"When you speak," said Lady Touchstone, " of 'the quiet enjoyment of this chamber,' you make me feel faint. So please don't do it again. I say you've behaved disgracefully. What did you knock for ? "

Sir Andrew swallowed.

"To gain admittance," he said.

"Then why did you ring ? "

"I refuse——"

"Why did you ring ? "

"For the same purpose."

"Did you really think that your usage of the bell could be misconstrued ? "

"I was particularly anxious," blurted Sir Andrew Plague, " not to be kept waiting."

"Rot," said Lady Touchstone. " You were particularly anxious to vent your wrath—vile wrath. Why did you shout at the potman ? "

"It wasn't a potman. It was——"

"Cabdriver, then. Was he deaf ? "

"He was da—extremely insolent."

"Was he deaf ? "

"Not that I know of."

"Of course he wasn't," said Lady Touchstone. "Why did you slam the door ? "

"Damn it, madam, I——"

"Don't swear at me. Why did you irrupt into this room ? "

"I didn't," cried Plague, writhing.

"Don't be absurd," said his tormentor. " Your entrance was barbarous. You knocked, you slammed

H

the door, you raved at the potman and irrupted into this room—all by way of indulging your horrible wrath. It's as plain as a pikestaff."

" It isn't at all. And it wasn't a——"

" Don't contradict me," snapped Lady Touchstone, " because I won't have it." Sir Andrew choked. " Besides, you've been rude enough. You haven't a leg to stand on. And if I've done anything to show you the error of your ways, this encounter, however distasteful, will not have been endured in vain."

With that, she picked up a paper, shook it into position, and took her seat upon a settle as if it had been a throne.

" It *wasn't* a potman," said Sir Andrew doggedly. " It was a cabdriver."

My lady replied with a look of unutterable contempt. . . .

Then the door was opened and the servant appeared.

Head in air, Lady Touchstone swept from the room. . . .

For a minute the giant stood as she had left him. Then he picked up his hat and stole out of the house.

*   *   *   *   *

That Sir Andrew Plague swore by his new secretary was common knowledge. A good many others, who had to do with the knight, also swore by his secretary —the tall, good-looking fellow with the fine grey eyes, who stood them in so good stead. Indeed, though it was not yet one month since Jonathan Wood, Gentleman, had entered the K.C.'s service, between him and his testy patron there was existing an understanding which was almost too good to be true. Sir Andrew Plague, who despised most men and regarded none, actually respected Jonathan. The latter was, of course, a squire in a million—faithful, patient, swift-brained, ridiculously honest. . . . What turned the squire into the compeer—an office no man had ever hitherto filled—was his strength of character. He would stake his job—which is to say, his livelihood—upon a point of principle. He did so stake it a dozen times in the day. The giant in his wrath gave him an unjust order : respectfully enough, Jonathan quietly declined to carry it out. . . . After a little the storms had become less frightful, and twice in the last week Sir Andrew had laughed. (This the steward, who had been told by the butler, flatly refused to credit. But then he was a sceptical fellow, and had served Sir Andrew Plague for twenty years.) There was no doubt about it. Beneath his secretary's influence the leopard was changing his spots. He was, moreover, lying down, not with a kid, but with a blood-horse. Between the two of them a little white dog with a black patch made himself thoroughly at home. . . .

From the very first day Hamlet had taken for granted Sir Andrew's goodwill and had proceeded to bask in it. That there was no goodwill to bask in did not occur to him. He basked contentedly—and presently had his reward. The goodwill was induced.

On the morning after his arrival he had visited the K.C. in his bedroom and had removed one of his slippers at the moment at which the knight, who was at his worst before breakfast, was proposing to insert his foot. Sir Andrew, whom the intrusion had rendered speechless, watched the asportation as a man in a dream. Then he let out a squeal of fury and launched his remaining slipper at Hamlet with the might of a maniac. The terrier sprang upon it in ecstasy and, after shaking it as if it were a rat, placed one paw upon it and sought to detach the tongue with his teeth. . . . For movement and uproar, the pursuit of a native by a rogue-elephant upon enclosed premises must pale beside the racket of the next five minutes. The household, unable to conceive what was happening, and terrified to go and see, huddled together downstairs : Jonathan, splashing in a distant bathroom, heard nothing at all : and Hamlet, as full of beans as an egg is of meat, decided that as an exponent of horseplay Sir Andrew more nearly approached perfection than anyone he had ever seen. Indeed, after leaving the ravening knight jammed between his bedstead and the floor, and conveying one of the slippers to the library, there to dismember it undisturbed, he determined to repeat so highly successful a visit the following day. Since Sir Andrew slept with his door open, he was able to do this—and did it, with the acme of ease. . .

At the end of a week the horseplay had been suspended and a compromise reached. Thereafter between seven and eight every morning the Sealyham slept luxuriously upon Sir Andrew's bed. By the time a fortnight had passed, the knight reviled Hamlet if the latter was late. . . .

Of such was life in Kensington Palace Gardens. From being a nightmare, it had become a cheerful masque. The old situations cropped up—frequently, but they were always saved.

It was upon the evening of the day upon which he had broken his bell that Sir Andrew laid down the paper and stared into the dusk.

Dinner was over, and the knight was reclining, as was his wont, upon a mighty sofa eminently adapted and, in fact, specially constructed to accommodate his tremendous frame. From behind him a table lamp threw a convenient light directly into his lap. On the floor by his side reposed a silver ash-tray and a cup of cold tea. Opposite, writing at a great table, sat Jonathan Wood. A second table lamp illumined at once his labours and the bowl of his pipe and, when he bent lower than usual, threw his clean-cut profile into sharp relief. For the rest, the room was in darkness. Without an open French window a small white sentinel sat peering down into the garden, motionless, vigilant. Hamlet loved the terrace. It added cubits to his stature. . . .

Suddenly the secretary looked up.

" I quite forgot to ask, sir, how you got on at the dentist's."

Sir Andrew's stare slid into a scowl.

" I didn't," he said.

" But didn't you——"

" I never saw the brute," said Sir Andrew savagely. " He—he was engaged."

Jonathan frowned.

" I was afraid he might be," he said. " You must let me ring up next time and make an appointment."

For a moment the other said nothing.

Then—

" Telephone to-morrow morning," he said shortly, regarding the end of his cigar.

" I will," said Jonathan. " When would you like to go ? "

" It's not a question of going," replied Sir Andrew.

" I want a name and address. A woman preceded me—probably took my turn, the graceless shrew Find out who she is."

Jonathan thought very fast.

" I hope . . ." he said tentatively.

" Then don't," snapped Sir Andrew. " Do as you're told instead."

" Very good, sir."

There was nothing else to be said, but Jonathan was far from easy. He scented trouble. That the lady had crossed Sir Andrew was perfectly clear. Probably there had been a scene. What worried him was that the knight's curiosity was never idle. He had some reason for wanting to know her name. Jonathan hoped very much that he was not contemplating a renewal of hostilities. . . .

The terrace growing chill beneath him, Hamlet rose to his feet and entered the room. For a moment he stood as if uncertain : then, with an apologetic look at his governors, he selected the deepest chair, leaped into its arms, and lay as still as death. The strained look in his eyes betrayed his concern lest he should be commanded to seek less luxurious quarters, and when he perceived that Sir Andrew was frowning in his direction, he gave himself up for lost and, laying back velvety ears, started to wag his tail in the hope of charming aside the dreaded sentence.

His fears were groundless.

" Has it ever occurred to you," said Sir Andrew Plague, " that if that dog could speak he could tell you who you are ? "

Jonathan sat back in his chair and laid down his pen.

" No, sir," he said. " It hasn't. Why should
he ? I only found him by chance."

" You found him beside you when—when you
recovered consciousness."

" I know. But he had no connection——"

" He was your dog."

Jonathan started.

" I never thought of that," he said slowly.

" That," said Sir Andrew explosively, " is because
you don't use your brain. Because you deliberately
reduce yourself to the level of the congenital idiot.
Ugh. . . . You were in evil case, and so was he.
You were dying of hunger, and so was he. You were
foul and beastly, so was he. He was your dog."

Jonathan crossed to the chair, picked up Hamlet,
sat down and set the terrier upon his knee.

" I wonder," he said, " that never occurred to
me." Sir Andrew snorted. " Of course you're right
. . . of course. There's not a shadow of doubt."
He looked into the bright brown eyes. " You know
—everything." The Sealyham licked his nose. " You
know what happened to me . . . how I came to be
starving . . . how——" He broke off and turned
to Sir Andrew. " Think of the way he stuck to
me," he said suddenly. " I had to carry him that
night. He couldn't walk. He must have——"

" Of course he did," said the knight. " You'd
fed him before : he expected you to feed him again—
the gluttonous brute. And don't go and get maudlin
about it, or you can leave the room."

Jonathan laughed.

" You hear ? " he said, pulling the terrier's ears.
" You're not faithful at all. You're just a gluttonous
brute."

" And a damned ugly one," added Sir Andrew.

" In fact," said Jonathan, smiling, " I can't imagine why we let you sleep on our beds."

Sir Andrew turned a rich plum colour. Then he picked up his cup and drank deep and violently. . . .

As he replaced the vessel—

" How long," he demanded, " are you going on like this ? "

" Like what, sir ? " said Jonathan.

" Masquerading."

Jonathan raised his eyebrows.

" I'm very happy," he said.

" That," rejoined Sir Andrew, " is beside the point. You can't go through life in a domino."

" I see no reason——"

" Well, I do," snapped the other. " You're guilty of *suggestio falsi*, and I'm abetting you. Not that I care about that," he added fiercely. " My back's broad enough—and to spare. But it's—it's out of order."

" So long as you don't mind, sir, I'ld rather stay as I am."

" Under an assumed name ? "

Jonathan shrugged his shoulders.

" If I knew who I was," he said, " and deliberately concealed my identity, that would be one thing. But I'm doing nothing of the kind. I'm hiding nothing. I've nothing to hide. I don't know who I am, and I don't care."

" Others may," said his patron. " Supposing you're married ? "

" I've thought of that," said his secretary, " and, frankly, the idea frightens me to death."

" I dare say it does," said Sir Andrew. " But what of that ? "

" Well, sir, you see . . ."

Jonathan hesitated.

" Proceed," said Sir Andrew mercilessly.

Jonathan set down the Sealyham and crossed his legs.

" I don't think I *can* be married," he said desperately.

" Why ? "

" I know so little of women."

" That's no argument."

Jonathan laughed.

" Well," he said, " if I am, surely it's better that I should stick to my domino until my memory returns."

" Why ? "

" Well, sir, supposing a girl was suddenly produced to you, and you were bluntly informed that she was your wife. . . ."

" I should take appropriate action."

" So, I hope, should I.   But it'ld be fearfully awkward—for both of us."

" Why ? "

Jonathan decided to plunge.

" Well, I shouldn't—shouldn't love her, you know."

Sir Andrew let out a squeal of agony.

" Ugh ! " he raged.   " Ugh, you maundering fool ! "
He covered his eyes and waved the other away.
" Didn't you undertake to mend your ways ?   Didn't you swear you'ld eschew all sickly sentiment ?   Ugh, you make my gorge rise !   Love ?   A poet's licence !
A libertine's excuse !   Besides, you might.   You're fool enough, Heaven knows."

" Have a care, sir," cried Jonathan, laughing.
" Don't drive the gods too far."

Sir Andrew sat up and looked at him.

" D'you want the sack ? " he demanded.

" I do not," said Jonathan.

" Then hold your tongue," roared the other. " And don't squirt venom at me."

" I only said——"

" You made a most vulgar suggestion. You implied that my mind was diseased—that that disgusting emotion to which you just now referred could infect my reason."

" I'm perfectly sure," said his secretary, " that the woman you delighted to honour would have to——"

" She'ld have to change her sex," was the grim reply. " Only to-day I was subjected to the grossest insult at a woman's hands." Jonathan repressed a start. " A most respectable-looking female proved to be a harridan of the very worst type. For no reason whatever she reviled me."

" Reviled you ? "

" Reviled me," said Sir Andrew, rising. " Most foully. Omitting no circumstance of indignity. I tell you, I was amazed. She actually accused me of brawling."

Jonathan swallowed.

" She can't have known——"

" Oh, yes, she did ! She defined it most accurately. She even referred to a leading case on the subject."

" But what had you done, sir ? "

" ' Done,' you fool ? Nothing. She heard me correct a cabman. The swine demanded compensation, alleging that I'd broken his springs. I rebuked the man—naturally. Then I passed into that swab of a dentist's waiting-room, to be pounced upon by this—this scold." The lawyer began to stride up and down the room. His secretary, who had a pretty good idea of Sir Andrew's methods of reproof of cabmen and entrance into rooms, began to see daylight. "At first," continued the latter, warming, as he went on, "I could hardly believe my ears. Then, so soon as I could speak, I demurred. . . . My protests were interrupted, infamously perverted and ignored. When I sought to point out that my rights to the user of the room were co-equal with hers she made ready to swoon. Of common decency I let the point go, to be told I was 'a menace to society.'"

"'A menace . . .'"

"The vixen's words," said Sir Andrew. "You could have knocked me down. I tell you, Wood, it was a perfectly hellish business. Indeed, I can only think that, presumably mad with pain, the creature resented my intrusion and lost her balance. Mercifully, I kept my head and, at the expense of my dignity, calmed her before—before I left. She actually wandered towards the end. Poor woman, it was most distressing. She seemed to think I had emerged from a public-house."

With a fearful effort Jonathan subdued an impulse to yell with laughter. Wholly absorbed in his outrageous retrospection, the K.C. proceeded, frowning.

"Yes. The more I think of it, the more satisfied I am that she was temporarily deranged. Indeed, she referred to the house as 'a place of mental affliction.' Therefore I blame myself. . . . Not that I replied to her abuse. That course, as I have indicated, was denied me. But I should have humoured her, Wood. . . . She spoke of bull-rings and confessionals —in the same breath. Of course I was taken by surprise. And instinctively I strove to defend myself against what I fairly considered to be an unprovoked and provocative assault. Did I tell you she styled me a brute ? "

" No, sir "—incredulously.

" She did," said Sir Andrew, wiping the sweat from his brow. " Twice. I tell you the woman was possessed—like the Gadarene swine."

" And, to judge," said Jonathan, eager to encourage this lenient view of the affair, " to judge from her behaviour, by the same tenants. Only, last time it was a place they ran violently down."

Sir Andrew laughed. Then he knitted his brows.

" Be that as it may," he said, " her frenzy took the form of vituperation. And I feel that, as she was unattended and, so far as I know, I am the only being who witnessed her—her humiliation, it would be becoming if—er—if I inquired after her health."

" Coals of fire," said Jonathan, stroking his chin.

" Er—perhaps. You see, I have no wish to be thought unsympathetic. I should like it to be understood that I bear her no illwill. I should like her to realize that if my manner was somewhat—er—stilted, that was due to my failure to appreciate her plight. . . . I—er—I feel—er. . . ."

To interrupt Sir Andrew was, speaking generally, to invite, if not personal violence, at any rate execration of a very unpleasant sort. Here, however, it would have been plainly brutal to do anything else. He who was never at a loss for an expression was searching desperately for words.

" I'll find out her name to-morrow," said Jonathan Wood.

He retired that night, blessing the anonymous lady and all her works. Whatever her shortcomings, she had proved herself a red herring of conspicuous merit. . . .

*   *   *   *   *

When, two days later, Sir Andrew, who was standing in a cool drawing-room, awaiting his hostess's appearance, perspiring with great freedom and savagely asking himself why the devil he had come, perceived a large photograph of his secretary handsomely framed and sharing a Louis XV table with a blotter and a Lowestoft bowl full of roses, he stood as though rooted to the floor. Then he went backward, caught his foot against an ebony stool, lost his balance and, with a rattling oath, fell into the miniature palmarium which had till then been 'camouflaging' the hearth.

It was at this juncture that Lady Touchstone, wondering who 'Sir Andrew Plague' might be and what he wanted, opened the door. . . .

For a moment she thought the room was empty. Then—

"Ten thousand devils," said a familiar voice. "Ugly ones."

Lady Touchstone started violently and caught at a chair.

"Where are you?" she said faintly.

"Behind the sofa," said Sir Andrew, making frantic endeavours to rise. "Who's that man on the table?"

"Wh-what man?" stammered his hostess, staring about her.

"Sitting with Hamlet in his lap," cried Sir Andrew, prising himself out of the foliage.

"'Hamlet'!" shrieked Lady Touchstone. "'Hamlet'! Oh, he's mad," she continued, thinking aloud and trembling violently.

" No, he isn't," roared Plague. " He's lost his memory."

By a superhuman effort Lady Touchstone retained a hold upon her wits. . . . Valerie was out : the servants were not within call. It was a case for strategy.

" Has he ? " she said, smiling. " How very awkward."

" He doesn't find it so," said Plague, staring. " As a matter of fact, he rather likes it. At the present moment he's my secretary. What's his name ? "

Lady Touchstone side-stepped, as if by accident, towards the door.

" Oh, I shouldn't bother about his name," she said gaily. " What's—er—what's in a name ? "

Sir Andrew choked.

" But—but you know him ! " he cried, jerking his head at the table. " You must. Don't you want to hear news of him ?   I tell you he's in my service."

" Of course he is," said Lady Touchstone. " Oh, and devoted to you," she added ecstatically.

" Madam," said Plague, trembling, " this pleasantry is ill-timed. If that man means nothing to you——"

" But he does," cried Lady Touchstone earnestly, regarding the Louis XV table with starting eyes. " He does indeed."

" Then don't you want," raved Sir Andrew, " to know where he is ? "

" I'ld—I'ld give anything," wailed Lady Touchstone frenziedly trying to preserve her mental poise.

" Well, I can tell you," roared Plague. " I've just left him. He's in Kensington Palace Gardens."

Lady Touchstone's brain reeled.

Then—

"I know," she said brightly. "A charming spot. So open. I always think the air there——"

The look upon Sir Andrew's face cut short the sentence.

Twice the giant strove to speak—ineffectually

At length—

"There," he said thickly, "the air is at least sincere. If we care for nobody, at least we do not advertise a regard which we do not feel." He passed to the door. "Madam, I take my leave. Why I came is of no consequence. I regret extremely that I should have disarranged your ferns, and still more that I should have revived an acquaintance which I shall strive to forget."

As he passed into the hall—

"Stop!" cried Lady Touchstone. "What on earth do you mean?"

Sir Andrew swung on his heel.

"Mean?"

"Mean. I thought you were mad." Sir Andrew recoiled. "You said there was a man on the table and—and other things. But never mind. Why am I insincere?"

"I said there was a man on the table?"

"You did indeed," said Lady Touchstone. "With Macbeth in his arms."

Plague started against the wall.

"I—said—that?"

"You did."

Sir Andrew looked wildly about him. Then he clapped his hands to his head.

"Then it's time I was gone," he said shakily.

He seized his hat and stick. "I *must* be mad—raving. My fall. . . ."

He lurched to the flat's door, opened it, blundered almost into the arms of Valerie French, muttered an apology and stumbled uncertainly downstairs. . . .

Valerie stood in the doorway, watching him go, wide-eyed.

Presently she turned to her aunt.

"What on earth . . ."

"That," said Lady Touchstone faintly, "is the man. The one I met at the dentist's."

"But what——"

"Don't ask me," wailed her aunt, putting a hand to her head, "because I can't tell you. One of us is insane." She passed into the drawing-room and sank into a chair. "I came into this room to find him behind the sofa—enumerating ill-favoured devils."

"*What?*"

"It's a fact," said Lady Touchstone. "Then he began to see things. He declared there was a man on the table, and kept on demanding his name."

"What table?" said Valerie, staring.

"That one," said Lady Touchstone, pointing to the Louis XV. "He said he was in his service, and didn't I want to hear of him. All the time, as I tell you, he kept on demanding his name. As if I—— Whatever's the matter?"

Vouchsafing no answer, Valerie flashed from the room. A moment later she was flying downstairs. . . .

Hill Street appeared to be empty.

With a beating heart she rushed to the nearest corner. . . .

Upon being interrogated the policeman had seen no one at all corresponding to her description of

Sir Andrew Plague. Desperately she turned and ran in the opposite direction. . . .

After a fruitless ten minutes she burst into the flat.

Weakly her aunt regarded her.

" What was his name ? " panted Valerie. " What was his name ? "

The revival of this terrible query confirmed Lady Touchstone's worst fears. Insanity was in the air.

With an unearthly shriek she clapped her hands over her ears and subsided upon the floor.

As a servant came running—

" What," said Valerie, " was that gentleman's name ? "

For a moment the man hesitated.

Then—

" Sir Andrew Plague, miss."

A second later Valerie was at the telephone. . . .

After an interminable delay—

" Is that Sir Andrew Plague's ? " cried Valerie French.

" It is," said Anthony Lyveden.

CHAPTER V

" **A** NTHONY ! Anthony ! "

Anthony Lyveden swallowed.

Then—

" This is Sir Andrew Plague's," he said, speaking distinctly.

" Anthony ! Don't you know me ? " cried the voice.

The man frowned into the mouthpiece.

" I think you're making a mistake," he said quietly. " This is Sir An——"

" I know ! I know ! "

Anthony raised his eyebrows.

" Who is that speaking ? " he said.

" It's me, Anthony. *Me*—Valerie ! "

With an air of amused vexation, the man held off the receiver. After a moment he replaced it against his ear.

" I'm awfully sorry," he said, " but I assure you you're making a mistake. This is Sir Andrew Plague's, and I'm his secretary. Can I——"

" It's *Valerie*, Anthony. VALERIE — Valerie French."

The man took a deep breath.

" Could you—would you mind telling me what

130

want ? " he said desperately. " Sir Andrew himself is out, but——"

" Isn't that Anthony Lyveden ? "

" *No*," cried the man, " no."

" Then who is it ? "

" It's . . ."

The sentence died there and then.

For a second of time the man stared at the telephone with a dropped jaw . . .

Then he clapped his palm to the mouthpiece and set the receiver down.

" *It's come !* " he whispered. " It's come ! My God, it's come ! "

He began to tremble.

For a moment he sat, shaking. Then he rose to his feet and stepped to the bell. . . .

A servant appeared.

" Answer the telephone," said the man. " Say I've been called away, and ask for the lady's telephone number and—and name."

The fellow took the receiver and picked up a pencil.

" Hullo ? "

" Who's that ? " flashed Valerie.

" May I have your number, m'm ? The gentleman you were speakin' to has bin called away, m'm."

There was a long silence.

" Hullo ? " said the servant, straining his ears. " Hullo, hullo ? "

" Mayfair nine double nine," said Valerie, slowly.

" Mayfair nine double nine," repeated the servant, writing. " An', if you please, m'm, your name."

" Miss Valerie French."

The servant repeated her words. Then—

" Thank you, m'm. Good-bye, m'm."

Apologetically, he rang off.

Then he made his report to Anthony Lyveden and left the room.

For a while the latter stood motionless, staring out of a window and across the shadowy lawn. Presently he threw back his head and began to laugh. . . .

Here his Sealyham appeared, leisurely patrolling the terrace and keeping a mistrustful eye upon a gardener whose attitude and demeanour were irregular —the one because he was clipping the edge of the grass, and the other because he found life weary and was grunting and sweating aggressively to advertise his misfortune.

" Hamlet," cried his master, " come here ! " The dog obeyed gaily. " Young fellow me lad, we're off. The interval's over, and the curtain's up. _I— have—been—found._ . . . A lady's found me—a lady with a very nice voice. She seems to know me quite well, and she sounds as pleased as Punch. It's most embarrassing, Hamlet. Very exciting, you know, but frightfully awkward. Something's required of me. I ought to respond—make some sort of return. I must, of course. But . . . I've got an attack of stage-fright, Hamlet. I've made my entrance, and now I've nothing to say. I haven't learned any lines —or, if I have, they're forgotton. I can't pick up any cues." Hamlet yawned luxuriously and then stretched himself nonchalantly. " Yes, that's all very well ; but, then, you're not shy. I'll bet you've never seen your own father. But if you were to meet him to-morrow and you didn't like the way he wore his tail, you'ld——"

The slam of the front door cut short the prophecy.

An instant later Sir Andrew Plague floundered into the room.

"Never again!" he roared. "Never again!"
He shook his fist at Lyveden and flung himself into a
chair. "I seek to read your riddle and get bogged for
my pains. Bogged and badgered and fooled, till I
lose my wits! Ugh! It serves me right," he added.
"I was a fool to go."

His secretary stared at him, open-mouthed.

"B-but what's happened?" he stammered.

"Happened?" yelled his patron. "I've placed
you, you long-limbed fool. Seen your photograph."

"Where?"

"Where I've been, you idiot. At that wretched
woman's abode. The place is crammed full of stools.
You can't move without falling over them. I fell
over one into a gimcrack fernery and hurt my head.
I meant to ask your name, but I talked rubbish—trash
. . . frightened Lady Touchstone to death. . . .
But you're there all right." He waved his hand at
the telephone. "Ring her up, you fool. Don't
stand there gibbering. Ring her up and find out
your name."

"I know it. A girl's just told me. She rang up
ten minutes ago and knew my voice."

So soon as Sir Andrew could speak—

"Who?"

His secretary stepped to the table.

"Miss Valerie French," he read. "She rang up
and asked if this was your house. When I said it was,
she called me 'Anthony.' I thought she'd made a
mistake, but she wouldn't have it. She said I was
'Anthony Lyveden.'"

"I've no doubt you are," said Plague. "But
you've got some damned funny friends. What did
you say?"

"Nothing. I was too rattled. I sent for William and told him to take her number."

"You never replied?"

Anthony shook his head.

"I couldn't," he said. "I was too much taken aback. But——"

The sudden stammer of the telephone-bell erased the sentence.

For a moment the two men looked at each other. . . .

Then Sir Andrew rose and grabbed the receiver.

"Yes?" he said fiercely. "Who's that?"

At the other end of the line Lady Touchstone repressed a scream.

"It's—it's me," she said faintly. Sir Andrew started violently. "Harriet Touchstone. . . . There's—there's been a terrible mistake. . . . I believe you were trying to tell me that a friend of ours was with you."

"That," said Sir Andrew heavily, "was my ambition. But you——"

"I know. It was dreadfully stupid. But when you spoke of Hamlet, I——"

"*Hamlet?*" screeched Plague. "You said '*Macbeth*'!"

"I mean Macbeth."

"No, you don't!" yelled Sir Andrew. "Hamlet's his dog."

"Macbeth's?"

"No, *no*, NO! What's-his-name's. Er—er—Augustus."

Lady Touchstone laid down her receiver and looked at her niece.

"Valerie," she said weakly. "I cannot continue this conversation. Perhaps, if I knew my Shakespeare better, I should be in a position to compete. As it is . . ."

Valerie picked up the instrument.

" Is that Sir Andrew Plague ? "

" Get off the line ! " raved Sir Andrew. " Get off the line ! I'm engaged. Lady Touchstone ! Where's Lady Touchstone ? "

" I'm speaking for her," shrieked Valerie. " I'm her niece. Please will you come back at once ? "

" *Back ?* "

" Yes. To Hill Street. And bring your secretary ? "

" Was it you who rang up just now ? "

" Yes."

" Ah," said Sir Andrew relievedly. " What's the matter with your aunt ? "

" Nothing," said Valerie, laughing. " What's the matter with your secretary ? "

Sir Andrew smothered a grin.

" You must excuse him," he said. " He's lost his memory."

*　　*　　*　　*　　*

Anthony Lyveden proceeded to Hill Street alone. Alone Valerie French awaited his coming. Their respective supporters had failed—for the same reason. Neither felt equal to facing the other again. Later, perhaps, when the monstrous tide of confusion had had time to subside. . . . So Lady Touchstone girt up her loins and fled to the hairdresser, in ignorance that Sir Andrew had sent his secretary packing and then withdrawn to his chamber and pulled down the blind.

It follows that Jack and Jill had a couple of hours together—very momentous hours. . . .

As in a play, the servant shall take up the curtain.

" Mr. Lyveden."

Valerie's heart leaped.

Anthony passed into the room.

" How d'you do ? " he said, smiling.

The girl tried to speak, vainly. As in a dream, she shook hands. . . .

It was he . . . Anthony . . . her darling. It was his blessed voice . . . his eyes . . . his hair. . . . She wanted to hang on to his hand—kiss it—hold it against her breast. She wanted herself to sit down and him to kneel, so that she could draw his head down into her lap. . . . Her wonderful, dazzling lover had been restored to her. She wanted to hold and be held by him. . . . It was her right.

Almost she swayed towards him. The desire to put her arms about his neck was almost irresistible . . . almost . . .

' Very pleasant hast thou been unto me.'

As for Anthony, he was profoundly moved. It was, of course, a tremendous moment for him. He had stepped over the threshold into another life, through which—at first, at any rate—this glorious, shining creature was to be his shepherdess. . . .

Little wonder that they stood for a minute like two beautiful children—shy, tongue-tied, colouring.

Then—

" You must forgive me," said Lyveden.

" What for ? " whispered Valerie.

" For this embarrassment. It's of my making, of course. I gather we used to know one another well—you used my Christian name. . . . But, as I heard Plague tell you, my memory's gone. Why,

I don't know." He spread out his hands. " I know nothing."

" You're well ? "

" Perfectly."

" Well . . . let's sit down," said Valerie. " One moment." She picked up a frame. " Look."

Curiously Lyveden inspected his own photograph. It was an enlargement of a snapshot—a very good picture. He saw himself seated upon a sunlit lawn, with Hamlet at ease in his lap.

" Where was this taken ? " he asked.

" You were staying with us in Hampshire, three months ago."

" Only three months ? "

" That's all," said Valerie.

Anthony set down the frame with a laugh.

" Three centuries or hours," he said. " What does it matter ? When you've dropped your brain into a bottomless gorge, the breadth of the gorge doesn't count." The girl sat down, and he took his seat by her side. " Do I make you feel dazed ? "

Valerie smiled.

" You do a little," she admitted. " It's awfully hard to grasp. You see, you're just the same— exactly. And it's almost impossible to realize that you—well, that, for instance, you can't remember that photograph, there, being taken."

" You do, obviously."

" I took it."

Anthony laughed.

" You're clearly an artist," he said. " It's the image of Hamlet."

" Hamlet ? "

" The dog."

Valerie cried out with joy.

" Patch ? Have you got him still ? Oh, I'm so awfully glad. To—to tell you the truth, I thought it was hopeless to ask."

" He's as fit as a fiddle," said Anthony. " And a very great friend of Plague's. They're together now. He wouldn't come, you know. He said he'd wrought enough havoc for one afternoon. . . . Which brings me to my affairs. Shall I tell you my story—at least, as much as I know ? "

" Do," breathed Valerie.

The six weeks' tale was told quietly, without emotion. The girl listened spell-bound. . . .

" And there you are," concluded Anthony. " It's been a wonderful experience—intensely interesting, amazingly happy. It's been an Arabian Night. And now—the dawn's come."

" Are you sorry ? " said Valerie.

Anthony turned and looked at her.

" May I speak frankly ? " he said. " Remember, I'm not a man. I'm a shade—feeling its position acutely and very anxious to do the right thing."

" I'm sure you'll do that," said Valerie, smiling. " So please don't be anxious. Still, if it'll make you easier, we won't count to-day. Say what you like, please."

" Well, then, I think you're just the most wonderful thing I ever saw." The girl gasped. " Until I entered this room I was wretched—growing more gloomy and scared every step that I took. You see, I loved my interlude—my backwater. I'd been so happy in my Arabian Night. And the cab that brought me here was rushing me out of my happiness into —I knew not what. I only knew that it couldn't ever be so jolly as what I was leaving behind. Then I saw you. . . . Don't think I'm being impertinent, or making love. I'm not. I'm stating facts. I'm a shade. I say—I saw you. . . . On the day I die, I shall see you, standing as you stood when I came into this room, and the sight will comfort me. . . . The cold, grey dawn I was so afraid of, you made golden and rosy. You cast out my fear. When I touched your hand, I felt glad to be alive. . . . And all at once, looking back, my interlude seemed very cold, very dull, very empty." With a sudden movement, he rose and picked up her hand. " I should be a graceless fellow if I didn't praise God that I had such a very sweet friend." He stooped and kissed the slight fingers. " You see," he added, letting fall her hand, " I've taken you at your word and spoken out. If I wasn't a shade, this would be a declaration of love. As a matter of fact, it's just pure gratitude. You've lifted up my heart."

Her eyes like stars, Valerie rose to her feet.

" I told you you needn't be anxious," she said tremulously. Abruptly she turned to a bookcase, disordered two or three volumes and then pushed them back into place. " The duster is mightier than the pen," she explained, over her shoulder. " I—I have to do this every day." She whipped a tear from her cheek and turned to her guest with a smile. " Let's go to the morning-room, and I'll give you some tea."

Anthony followed her thoughtfully out of the room. . . .

He would not eat, but was glad of a cigarette.

" I'm so excited," he said ingenuously. " You would be if you were me."

" I am," said Valerie.

" That's very nice of you."

" It isn't," cried Valerie. " It isn't. I can't help it. You see, you—we knew you so well. You were staying with us when it happened, and——"

" What ? "

Valerie put a hand to her head.

Straining her mind's eye, she was hunting for some indication of the course she must shape. Two things stood out of the water—the race down which she was sweeping, was being swept. One was a wreck —the rotting tackle of an old nightmare, which might be no longer dangerous, but must be avoided. *This was the fact that Lyveden had been insane.* The other was a bank of yellow, inviting sand stretching beside her channel for as far as ever she could see. *This was the fact that Anthony and she had been betrothed.* Of the two, Valerie would sooner have driven upon the wreck. . . .

Come what might, never, save of his own memory, must Anthony Lyveden learn what their relations had been . . . never. . . .

" You disappeared," said Valerie. " Quite suddenly —for no apparent reason. We traced you to the Cotswolds, and there a body was found. They said it was yours. . . . A month ago you were seen going into the Temple. We've been searching for you ever since."

Anthony stared upon the floor.

" I think your construction of the laws of hospitality is very handsome. Have I no—no people ? "

Valerie shook her head.

" No one ? "

" No one," said Valerie.

" What am I ? "

" A man of considerable means, of no occupation, a Major and a D.S.O."

" Un-unattached ? "

" Yes."

" Thank Heaven for that," said Lyveden fervently. " I had a terrible fear that I might have a wife. That was one of the things which made me cling so fast to my Arabian Night. It would have been very awkward, wouldn't it ? "

" It might," said Valerie, laughing.

" It would," said Anthony positively. " You know it would. Talk about a one-sided affair . . . "

" You'ld 've forgotten all her shortcomings," said Valerie.

" And her virtues."

" Oh, she'ld tell you all those."

" But what about me ? Love's very sensitive. Force Love's hand, and however sweet the fruit you take from him, it's bound to be a bit sticky."

" How do you know ? "—mischievously.

" Instinct," said Lyveden promptly. " Besides, I've a dog called Hamlet. And now you're evading the question. What about me ? "

" I hope," said Valerie, " you'ld remember a certain appropriate proverb—about ignorance and bliss, and thank the good St. Luke for the nice, warm summer he was providing."

" I hope so, too," said Anthony. " But, after this afternoon, I fear the good St. Luke would go empty away. You see, I'm sure my wife wouldn't have stars in her eyes." Valerie laughed joyously. " We agreed that to-day shouldn't count, and it shan't. I promise you that. But I'ld like you to know that you'll always stand alone. Your niche——"

" I'm human enough," said Valerie. " Don't make a statue of me. As to-day doesn't count, I can tell you it's meant—a good deal to me."

" You 're awfully sweet," said Lyveden.

" No, I'm not. I mean what I say. When you walked into that room—I nearly cried."

" That's because of your very sweet nature. I felt embarrassed, overwrought. Out of your gentle pity, you felt the same."

" But I don't pity you. Why shouldn't I be glad ? "

" Glad—yes. If you please. But it wasn't the sort of gladness I was expecting. You weren't boisterous. I'd often pictured my recognition. I always assumed I should be found one day. I saw myself being stopped—perhaps in the street. I saw people wringing my hand, slapping me on the back, stamping. . . . And I dreaded it all. I knew that I couldn't respond, and I dreaded it terribly. But you did none of these things. You seemed to feel my trouble— to understand. You were so quiet, but you seemed so very pleased."

" I was. I am," cried Valerie. " It's the biggest . . . surprise I ever had," she concluded tamely.

Anthony fell upon the substantive.

" I know. But you never showed it. That's my point. You might have been waiting and watching, with your precious eyes riveted upon the door through which you knew I should pass. And when I came stumbling out, there was your little, firm hand to hold me up." He threw back his head and put his hands over his eyes. " You must forgive me. I —I can't get you out of my head. I ought to be asking all manner of questions, I know. I ought to be wild to hear all about myself. But I'm not. I don't

care. I don't want to know." He let fall his hands
and leaned forward with burning eyes. "I want to
make the most of to-day. The rest can wait. I've
all my life to listen to the mistakes I've made. But
to-day . . . I feel I'm standing with you, looking
down on the world. To-day our position is sublime,
because I'm a shade. I can exult in your company . .
stare at my exquisite guide . . . open my heart,
because—to-day doesn't count. To-morrow you'll
be Miss French and I shall be Mr. Lyveden. To-day
I'm a child, and you're—just Valerie. You've seen
a child run to its betters, cling to their knees, look up
into their faces. If you asked it why, it couldn't tell.
Neither can I. But I think it's because it—knows—
they—understand."

Valerie crossed to the hearth and stood by his side.

"I'm not your better," she said, "but I—understand. Take hold of me, if you will. To-day the
clocks have stopped. There is no time."

Very gently he took her in his arms.

"You wonderful creature," he breathed. "You
glorious, wonderful thing. How can you understand?
Why am I not afraid to take you like this? Why do
I dare to lay my cheek against yours? Why do you
suffer me? Convention's not dead. But you. . . .
to-day . . . We're out of the world; we must be.
I hardly know your name; yet we speak the same
tongue. I've called and you've answered—and nobody else would have heard. We're alone on the
edge of some cliff overhanging the earth. . . . I was
alone . . . and now you've come to my side." He
turned his head sharply and peered into her eyes.
"Am I mad?" he demanded. "Do I speak as a
fool?"

"No," said Valerie quietly. "You've spoken the absolute truth. I let you hold me like this because it's my will that you should—because I have need of your arms. I hoped that you'd put them about me, and then you did."

"Why? Why did you hope it? What's this astounding language that only you and I speak? It isn't love. It can't be. I haven't been here half an hour. . . . I throw an invisible ball—you catch it and throw it back. I lose my head, to find I've not lost it at all. I flounder, to find I'm on rock. What does it mean? . . . Never mind. I don't want to know. I'm a king—for an afternoon."

"Listen," said Valerie. "What made you want to—to set your cheek against mine?"

"I don't know. I don't care. I——"

"Try to think."

She felt his temples contract.

"It sounds absurd," he said, "but it seemed—it seemed so natural. The moment I saw you, you filled the whole of my brain. The questions I've asked, I've asked with difficulty. Up to just now I was acting, Valerie. Now I'm myself. I feel at—at ease, somehow. Why don't you mind?"

"I feel at ease, too."

"I know, I know. Why? You don't know. You can't say. It's natural and yet unnatural. It's out of order, yet right. It's like a fairy tale, where the poor boy kisses the beauty he's never set eyes on before. And nobody minds, and even Convention approves." He held her off firmly. "But this is Life—where there aren't any fairy tales and where this sort of thing isn't done."

Her eyes upon his, the girl was thinking furiously.

Should she tell him the truth . . . explain that *his heart had thrown back* . . . shatter the brilliant bubble which he had blown? The time seemed ripe. Surely no harm could result. And the bubble would not be shattered, but rather turned to crystal. Yet . . . ' Love's very sensitive. Force Love's hand, and . . .' The jest rang in her ears. Her imagination turned it into the bell of a buoy, swinging to mark that yellow, inviting sandbank she had determined to shun.

" I know," she said gravely: " I know that as well as you. Yet I'm not cheap in your sight."

" *Cheap?* You're the finest gold that ever gladdened man's eyes."

" Then why do you frown so, Anthony? To-day I can read your fairy tale and share your dream."

He drew her head down on to his chest.

" I love your hair," he said simply. " It smells so sweet. You can't be a princess, or it'ld be all golden. And so you must be a queen."

" For an afternoon," she whispered.

He put a hand under her chin and raised her head.

" For ever," he said, smiling. " We're in the land of Oxymoron. To-day doesn't count, yet it will last out Time. It's not in the almanac, yet it's gold-letter. I've lost my memory, yet I can never forget. And heresy's orthodox, and fairy tales are fact. . . . D'you think, if I kissed your mouth, it'ld turn into a flower? It's awfully like one."

" I—I don't think it would."

He kissed her tenderly. . . .

Presently she put up a hand and touched his hair.

*   *   *   *   *

Anthony walked back across the Park with his head in the air.

The man was exalted. The dog had just had his day. And, while all days are as grass, the splendour of this afternoon would never die. That he had been born again was nothing at all. His heart had leaped and had been caught and held at the very top of its bent—so held that it would never come down—sink any more. Of this he was quite certain. No disaster could alter his state. Not even the sudden production of a duly accredited harem could shatter this illusion. He had been given the original—the model after which illusions are made. Like fire, it had been filched out of Heaven.

That he did not perceive what any fool could have told him, is not surprising. His memory was gone. It lay like a silent pool, walled up with rock. Upon this pool, for more than forty days his eyes had been riveted. And nothing—no sight, or sound, or scent had stirred its waters. Then had come Valerie. . . . The moment he saw her he knew that if ever the pool was to be troubled, now was the appointed time. Peering at its surface, he found it motionless as death. She whom no man, having seen, could ever forget, with whom he had once been familiar, had failed to wake the faintest ripple upon those silent waters. Therefore Anthony *knew* that the strange exhilaration he had felt was not out of Memory. And if it was not out of Memory, neither was it by Love. That was obvious. Love was a slippery fellow, but he was not so swift as all that. Besides, it was to be hoped that he (Anthony) had not lost all control. As for the lady. . . Oh, indubitably it was not love. . . :

His mental arithmetic was, I think, sound. Anthony

had done his sum right and had got the wrong answer.
Any fool could have got the right answer without doing
the sum at all. But that is because lookers-on see
the best of the game. And if anyone but a fool had
done the sum, he would have seen instantly that the
error lay in the premises. Whereupon he would have
worked backwards, with the result that in about two
seconds he would have located the mistake. This
was that, while the surface of the pool of Remembrance
was motionless as death, its depths were considerably
troubled. Still waters run deep.

It was as he was approaching Kensington Palace
Gardens that Anthony Lyveden realized with a shock
how very slight was the report which he was prepared to render. Sir Andrew would naturally expect
to be regaled with a wealth of crisp information regarding the former existence of his *protégé*. . . .
Anthony began to wonder what on earth he should say.
He could not explain that he had been in Paradise.
For only one thing, not to put it too high, the knight
would hardly appreciate such a translation. . . .

With his key in the lock, Anthony fingered his chin.
Then he made a grimace and tiptoed into the hall.

The drone of a voice in the library fell upon his
ears. He stepped to the door.

" And so, you see, young fellow, we've got to part.
I'm a creature of habit—bad habit. Don't think I
don't know that. It's not my fault. My temper's
spoiled. Men are such maddening fools. . . . And
when you're a creature of habit, your habits—good and
bad—count higher than anything else. Well, you're
a habit of mine—a bad one, of course. Whoever
heard of a dog getting up on a bed ? Bringing his fleas
and dirt into your blankets ? The moment you're

out of the house, I'll have 'em cleaned. . . . The point is, I'm used to you. D'you hear? Used. And there's the rub. In a sense, you've been—my dog . . . my little dog. . . . I know I've been rough, but I think you've understood. You've never been afraid. You've—— Damn it, you ugly swine, you've seemed to like me. And I'm—I'm a man of few friends. . . . Habit, habit, habit—that's all it is. Why does one feel the breaking of habits so much? You and your man Wood—Lyveden, are in my pocket. I shall feel lost when you're gone. I contracted for service: he's given me infinitely more. Why? Heaven knows. But he has. Something that's not for sale. And I've got used to it, you brute, as I've got used to you. . . . Well, it's my own fault. The whole affair's been fantastic, and fantasy's not in my line. I knew it, of course. I'm guilty. I stole by finding. And now I've got to pay. . . . Come here. . . . D'you remember, a week ago, I threw a book at you? And it—it hurt you, and—you—cried out? . . . . I'm sorry for that —very. Ah, you're a forgiving swine. . . . But I— I'ld give a hundred pounds to call that moment back . . my fellow . . . my little dog. . . ."

Anthony stole upstairs like a thief in the night.

By the time he had bathed and changed, his plans were made, and when Sir Andrew descended at eight o'clock, his secretary was seated at the great table, writing assiduously.

"Hullo," said the knight, "I didn't know you were in."

"I expect you were dressing," lied Anthony. "I hurried rather, because I'm a little behind." He picked up a sheet of paper. "There's a letter here, sir, from——"

" I dare say there is," said Sir Andrew, crossing to a great French window and opening it wide. " Tell me your news."

Lyveden laid down the paper and rose to his feet.

" First and foremost," he said, " by the grace of God, I'm unattached. I've no dependents and no responsibilities. Beyond that, I don't know a great deal. I shall hear more to-morrow, and if you can spare me——"

" Yes."

" —for one or two hours——"

" Your time's your own," rapped Sir Andrew over his shoulder. " You needn't bother about notice. If you want to go to-morrow, go."

" I don't want to do that."

" If it's any convenience to you to stay in this house until——"

" If you will keep me," said Lyveden, " I'ld like to stay on." Sir Andrew swung round. " I don't want to leave your service."

" Don't think I can't spare you, you know."

" I know you can," laughed Anthony. " But it seems that, when I went down, I was out of a job. I hope you're not going to sack me because I've changed my name."

For a moment the giant stared at him. Then he turned on his heel and walked out of the room . . .

When, five minutes later, his secretary came to tell him that dinner had been announced, the knight was pacing the garden with Patch at his heels. And when, still later, the two men were sitting at meat, the sober candle-light revealed three short white hairs adhering to Sir Andrew's sleeve.

Master and man observed them simultaneously.

For a moment the giant regarded them. Then he grew slowly red.

"Off one o' the chairs," he muttered, slapping his cuff. "The brute must be moulting." Here the butler approached, whiskey in hand. "No, you fool, no. Take it away. Bring two bottles of Clicquot. I—we want a change."

* * * * *

At half-past five the next morning Sleep took his leave of Lyveden and, being gone, flatly refused to return, although importuned to do so for thirty restless minutes. I fancy the whimsical god was getting his own back. The night before he had met with a cold reception—had had, in fact, to cool his heels for a long hour while Anthony paced his chamber, thinking high thoughts. And possibly the repulse rankled. Be that as it may, at six o'clock Anthony yawned, sighed, sat up and then switched on the light.

From the foot of his bed a bright, brown eye, set in a white ball, regarded him.

Anthony stared back.

"I'm sorry, old chap," he said, "but it can't be done. Dogs have the knack, I know; but we poor men haven't got Sleep on a lead." A piece of the ball detached itself and moved up and down. "The question is, my fellow, what shall we do. The tea won't be here for an hour, and I'm not even drowsy." He slid out of bed and stepped to a window. Pulling the curtains aside, he saw the dawn coming up over distant Mayfair. "I know," he said, turning to meet the eye, which was watching him fixedly. "I know." He lowered his voice to a whisper. "*Walks.*"

As a charm pronounced, the word left ' Sesame '
standing. The latter merely opened a door. The
former turned a one-eyed ball into a well-bred Sealyham, panting with excitement and leaping like a young
ram. . . .

A quarter of an hour later the two entered Kensington Gardens and raced for the Round Pond.

It was a perfect morning. Trees, grass and earth
were drenched with a heavy dew ; the air, washed
as a garment, smelled like fair linen ; London was
at her toilet and her best. Then the sun got up, to
overlay the lawns with transient silver, mark out pale
effigies of walks and avenues, and aid a flickering
breeze to send the jolly pond into long ripples of Ægean
laughter.

Anthony and Patch found their adventure sterling
—too good to curtail. Indeed, they were deep in
Hyde Park, when seven o'clock was unbelievably announced. Reluctantly enough, they turned homeward
and, presently skirting the Serpentine, fell in beside
the Row.

Till now the Park had been theirs, but here a sprink-
ling of riders was sharing the brave sunshine. Anthony
watched their going with envious eyes. He must,
he felt sure, have ridden a lot in the shadowy past ;
the saddle attracted him so strongly, and the sight
of a good-looking horse so gladdened his eyes.

There was a beauty coming—a great, rich brown,
walking towards him. Look at that fine, deep chest,
that small clean-cut head, those steady great eyes,
those delicate ears, the elegant line of that neck,
those clean big-kneed legs—above all, that free, true
action. . . . What a horse for a man to ride ! Ah,
it was a girl in the saddle . . . a girl with auburn—

Good God, he knew her ! Her name was . . . was . .
André.

It was at this moment that André Strongi'th'arm
saw Anthony Lyveden for the first time. She started
so violently that the good-looking brown leaped almost
out of his skin, and it took quite a lot of cajolery to
reassure him. When she had him in hand, Lyveden
stepped under the rails and took off his hat.

" How d'you do ? " he said nervously.

André tried to reply, but she could not speak.

The girl was rattled. The sight of Anthony Lyveden
—no shade, but the man himself—had thrown her
into a panic. For a moment she thought she must
faint. More. André knew in a flash what this panic,
this faintness meant, and the knowledge tied up her
tongue and set her heart pounding against her ribs.
She knew that the love she had choked was no more
dead than she was.

André began to tremble.

" I'm—I'm afraid I've given you a shock," said
Anthony, with an embarrassed smile. " You—you
didn't expect to see me."

André's lips were moving, but no words came.
She continued to stare fixedly.

Anthony laughed uneasily.

" I might have risen from the dead," he said.

His brain was thrashing, hammering, wrenching
at a shut-fast door—the door of Memory. He had
remembered—did remember the girl. The door had
been opened, then. . . . He remembered faintly that
he had met her alone—more than once. Where ?
When ? Why ? He could not remember. The door
had been slammed before he could . . . And *she*——
Good God ! Why did she look so strange ? Why

didn't she speak? What was the matter? Who
was she? *André*. Yes, but André *Who?* And
what was she to him? What . . . They had talked
—intimately. Yes. That was right. Intimately.
. . More. Infinitely more. *Looking upon those lips,
he could remember the feel of them—perfectly. They
were soft, warm lips . . . very soft . . . very——* How
did he know? How on earth did he know? If
he remembered this, why couldn't he remember——
Because the door was shut. Because . . . *Was* this
Memory? Or had he dreamed some terrible——
Oh, of course, it was Memory. Undoubtedly. Well,
then . . .

It was, indeed. For an instant a corner of the
veil had been lifted. Then the corner had slipped,
and the veil had fallen . . . back . . . into its place.
For the second time the waters of the pool of Remembrance had been considerably troubled. But this
time the surface had swayed.

The girl was speaking, haltingly.

"You might . . . In fact, we—I did think you
were dead. You—you disappeared. And—and last
time we met . . ."

She stopped dead.

"Yes?"—eagerly.

Her eyes held his for an instant, striving to read
his mind. Then they fell to her knees.

"We won't talk about that," she said in a low voice.

"But I want to," cried Anthony. "Please. You
see——"

"What?"

"Well, I—I don't know what you can have thought
of my clearing out as I did." André started. "You
must have thought it very strange."

There was a moment's silence. Then—

" I didn't expect anything else," faltered the girl.

Anthony stared at her boot—a tiny, patent-leather affair, too small for the shining iron.

" I don't know why you say that," he said slowly.

" D'you mean to say you're glad to see me again ? "

" Of course," cried Anthony, thankful to be on apparently firmer ground. " Aren't you glad to see me ? "

" Glad ? " She leaned far out of the saddle, with burning eyes. " *Glad ?* What d'you think . . Anthony ? "

There was no mistaking her meaning. If ever love flamed in a phrase, it went flaming in that.

" I—I don't know what to think," he stammered, flushing to the roots of his hair.

This was the bare truth. For the matter of that, he did not know what to say, either. He had seen the blow coming : then he had lost sight of it : and now it had fallen, and he had been knocked out. All the time his brain was pounding upon that cursed door—clapping its eye to the keyhole—trying to picture the ghost which lay behind. And this was pure folly, of course. The only thing to do was to study the facts he had and learn of them, to endeavour to piece together this terribly vital document—at least, such fragments thereof as had been vouchsafed him. With a supreme effort, he managed to focus his mind. *This girl—André—loved him. And he . . . Reference to his fragments argued that he had given her cause.* . . . As for his state, it seemed absurd to say that he had lost his memory. Of course she would think it a lie, and with good reason. If he had lost his memory, how did he remember her ?

Oh, why had he come out this sunshiny morning?
Why. . . . No. That was a rotten thought. His
way was clear, if steep. . . .

He lifted his head.

"I haven't been myself for a long time," he said
slowly. "But now, when I looked up and saw you
coming . . ." He stopped and passed a hand across
his forehead. "Tell me what you've been doing,"
he added desperately.

André raised her eyes and stared down the shadowy
Row.

"Oh, floating round," she said carelessly. "Riding . . . thinking . . . trying—trying to forget."

"You sound as if you'd been unhappy," said
Anthony. André shrugged her shoulders. The man
braced himself. "Was that because of me?"

The girl stiffened.

"What right have you to ask?"

"I think, perhaps," he said slowly, "I had a right
once. If I remember . . ." He broke off help-
lessly. "Won't you help me?" he said. "It's
very difficult."

"It was because of you."

There was a long silence. The murder was out.

At length—

"I'm very sorry," said Anthony. "I think,
perhaps, when I tell you everything, you'll understand. I will—very soon. Not now. It's hard to
explain. Don't think too hardly of me," he added
piteously.

André stifled a cry.

"Don't, Anthony, don't. How can you talk
like that?" She set her hand on his shoulder.
"You've said you're glad to see me. What more

do I need? I thought you must never want to
see me again. I thought it was finished . . . dead.
It nearly broke my heart, but I made sure you didn't
—*care*."

Anthony caught his breath. Blow after blow
now. What did it matter? Besides . . . It wasn't
his fault, of course, but—he owed her something.
She'd suffered a lot, plainly. She'd said as much.
And—it—was—all—through—him.

"Poor lady," he said gently. "You won't be
unhappy any more?"

The touch on his shoulder became a grip, tense and
quivering.

Lips parted, eyes blazing, her beautiful, careless
face aglow with ecstasy, for a moment André let
the world slip. . . .

Then the hand slid away, and she took a deep
breath.

"Where are you now?" she said suddenly.

He told her and she turned her horse round.

"I'll ride back with you," she said. "No." She
checked the great brown. "We'll go our ways.
To-morrow we'll ride together. You shall ride
Joshua." She patted the brown's shoulder. "And
now—good-bye."

She pulled off a glove and stretched out a little,
white hand.

Anthony took it in his.

After a moment's hesitation he put it to his lips.

CHAPTER VI

POOR PLAYERS

IT irks me, sirs, that I cannot go two ways at once. But then no man can do that—not even the puppeteer. I have my cap of darkness: my boots are many-leagued: at a nod from me, the sun will stand still in his heaven. I should, I suppose, be satisfied. Yet am I not content, because I have sent one puppet East and another West, and I would follow them both. . . . Since I cannot do that, I must choose. And I choose the lady. And when I have done with her, by your leave, we will have Time back and follow her startled squire about his business.

André rode down the Row as a girl in a trance.

What did it mean? She had always been apprehensive about her next meeting with Lyveden. The last had been so painful that the next must of necessity be most embarrassing. When a girl has told a man that she loves him and the man has thereupon promptly shown her the door, and when, because he will not kiss her, she has taken the law into her own small hands and kissed him wildly upon the mouth, it is hardly to be expected that their next encounter will be convivial. It is still less probable that the man will have executed a complete *volte face* and, apparently regretting his rejection of her advances, will instantly reopen the matter, apologize for his behaviour and, figuratively speaking, take the girl's two arms and put them about his neck. Yet that is precisely what had happened. And Valerie French, to whom he had been engaged, who was simply living to see her lover again, was never referred to. . . . 'When I tell you everything, you'll understand . . . It's hard to explain.' What did it mean? What did it all mean?

André realized suddenly that she was afraid. The meaning was plain—written in shining letters upon the wall. And she was afraid to read it. It was too—too big. . . .

Slowly she raised her eyes.

WHEN ANTHONY LYVEDEN WAS SICK, IT WAS VALERIE FRENCH WHO WON HIM BACK TO HEALTH. OUT OF GRATITUDE HE ASKED HER TO MARRY HIM. ALL THE TIME HE LOVED ANDRÉ STRONGI'TH'ARM. AT LENGTH HE COULD BEAR HIS POSITION NO LONGER, AND SO HE JUST DISAPPEARED.

The thing was plain. There was no other explanation. It was unfortunate—very, but it had happened before. . . . 'The marriage which had been arranged, will not take place.'

Arrived at Hyde Park Corner, André dismounted and gave her horse to a groom. Then she crossed Piccadilly and entered the Green Park.

Ordinarily she drove: but to-day she wanted to think. She must not be rushed. Her hotel stood in the danger zone: there she could be visited, addressed. . . . And she was not ready: she must have time.

She made her way eastward slowly, biting her lips.

Was ever a girl so placed?

She was engaged and pledged up to the hilt, and now Anthony had come and turned engagements and pledges into a bundle of vanities.

Her engagement to Winchester was nothing. As she had given, so she could take away. She was sorry—for Richard's sake. It would shake him up badly. Still, he would understand. It was a nasty business—rather like shooting a horse. But it was just as easy. What was presenting a truly formidable front was her allegiance to Valerie French.

So far as Valerie was concerned, everything seemed to have combined to make her triumph more ghastly than any defeat. If only Valerie had been less mad about Anthony Lyveden—if only she and Valerie had not become such friends—if only their friendship had not been founded upon their love for the same man—above all, if only she had not at first disputed Valerie's right, and then renounced her claim in Valerie's favour. . . . The omission of any one of those protases would have made all the difference. As it was, Valerie stood in her path, radiant and unsuspecting, and she was going deliberately to ride the girl down. And it was not her fault. Fate had her bridle-rein. . . . Fate. . . . And when the murder was over, Fate was going to libel her—publish an infamous slander of what she had done . . . and she would have no redress. She was going to be called treacherous . . . shameless . . . accursed . . . Fate was going to indicate excitedly a hundred other paths she might have chosen, show that she had gone out of her way to ride down Valerie, raise his false eyes to heaven and lament her sin.

Was there ever such a coil—such a monstrous, tragical coil?

André thrust it aside and gave herself up to a contemplation of her amazing fortune. Anthony loved her . . . Anthony . . . all the time—and she had not known it. He had fought not to, and he had been borne down. Once he had turned her away: now he had come, stepping out of the sweet of the morning, straight to her side . . . himself . . . Anthony . . . What if she had to pay for such a prize? What if she was to be slandered—vilified? God in heaven, it was worth while! It was worth *anything*. The price was not even high. No price could be. Such profit was above price . . . She remembered the evening when she had seen him first—how they had passed together up Gallowstree Hill, and he had talked of his work, and she had challenged his zeal. . . . Then she had gone to his cottage—because she loved him, and he, *because he loved her*, had sent her away. . . .

André entered the Berkeley and passed upstairs. . . . A letter addressed by Valerie's hand lay on her table. The girl ripped it open with shaking fingers.

I've been trying frantically to get you all the evening. Anthony's FOUND. *Isn't it wonderful? And he's as right as rain, André, as right as rain. Only —he's lost his memory. He can't even remember Gramarye or anything. He didn't even know his own name. Which, of course, explains why he didn't answer the advertisements. One word, just in case I don't see you before we all meet. He has no idea, of course, that he and I were engaged.* ON NO ACCOUNT TELL HIM, OR GIVE HIM THE SLIGHTEST HINT. *I rely upon you. You can understand why. And dine with us to-morrow at Claridge's—you and Richard—without fail. Say eight o'clock. . . .*

For a long time André stared at the document.
Then she lifted her eyes. . . .

AND WHEN HE WAS PRESENTLY DISCOVERED, IN
DESPERATION HE PRETENDED TO VALERIE THAT HE
HAD LOST HIS MEMORY. THEN HE MET ANDRÉ
STRONGI'TH'ARM. . . .

Now that the meaning was confirmed, what was
to be done?

If André had been at once less confident and less
infatuate, she would not have gathered so naïvely
the chaff into her garner and trampled the wheat
of truth under her feet. Still, since she had had
no say in her construction, and nobody else had had
any in her development, I do not think she can be
blamed for her egregious mistake. This was made
in good faith. And in good faith she decided that
Valerie must be told the terrible truth. She was
faintly surprised that Anthony had shrunk from this
duty. Then the beam in her eye again interfered
with her vision, and she recalled the convenient fact
that it was not yet six months since he had cast off
brain-fever. Still, Valerie must be told, and he
must tell her. . . .

She sent a wire to Lyveden that afternoon.

*Joshua will be by the Albert Memorial to-morrow
at seven o'clock.*

When Winchester returned from the country at
half-past five, his fiancée sent down word that she was
in bed. Winchester raised his eyebrows and pulled
his moustache. Then he went out and bought her
the finest roses that he could procure. And presently,
knowing nothing of his invitation to dinner, he dined
at his club.

* * * *

L

Lyveden was late for breakfast that sunshiny morning. Had he hastened he might have been in time : but, instead, he tramped slowly, as a man who is tired.

His brain was no longer labouring and losing its labour. That burst of frenzy was done. The storm had blown itself out. He was thinking quite quietly and rather dully. His glorious, great adventure had come to a sudden end. All at once he had rambled out of Arcadia into the common thoroughfare of Life . . . real, earnest Life . . . unpleasantly real, mercilessly earnest. His shepherdess, of course, was belonging to Arcadia. She could not step over the frontier into the thoroughfare of Life. It was not allowed. He had passed out of her province . . . out of her care . . . into that of another, who —had—no—stars—in—her—eyes. Their idyll was finished. Something else, not at all Arcadian, *more like a satire*, was being spouted. The pipe had been replaced by the barrel-organ. He had come down to earth.

Anthony felt very cold suddenly. Paradise was lost.

He began to wonder miserably what Valerie French would say. She would be sorry, of course : very sorry, because she was very kind. She would be surprised, too, because she had no knowledge of this clandestine engagement. She would be disappointed —for his sake. She would know what it meant. She—she would understand . . . And then she would wave 'Good-bye' from the edge of Arcadia, and he would see her no more.

He would see her no more.

Anthony stopped and put a hand to his head. Why was he assuming that he would see her no

more? What rot! They had been—great friends.
Now—just because he was engaged—was he to lose
her friendship? And that at the very moment when
his need of it was so sore? What awful rot! And
who said she couldn't leave Arcadia? Just because.
. . .

Then the spurt of revolt died down, and Anthony
found himself looking the truth in the eyes.

He could see her no more, because he loved her.

For an instant the heavens were opened, and he
saw what might have been. Then the sovereign
vision faded—faded into the picture of a handsome,
careless face, with large, brown eyes and a mass of
auburn hair. . . .

Some one laughed—horribly. And Patch ran to his
master and tried, leaping frantically, to lick his face.

I think it was largely because he had been so apprehensive that Anthony had jumped to the conclusion
that the worst was at hand. He had, of course, a
good deal to go on. *André alone had waked his memory.*
Why? Because, presumably, she had meant more to
him than anyone else. *He had met her alone and kissed
her.* So much he actually remembered. *She loved
him.* That he had seen—and confirmed. *She had
read in his disappearance a sign that he loved her no
more.* This showed plainly that he had loved her
once. . . .

To erect a clandestine engagement upon this foundation of fact was very simple. Anyone less scrupulous
would have perceived that the foundations would
have supported equally well an ordinary, not very
creditable, love affair. But that did not occur to
Anthony. It was his memory he had lost, not his
outlook.

Had he been told there and then that he had remembered the wrong girl, he would still have been most uneasy. He was persuaded, of course, that he had given her cause. . . .

As he made his way home that sunshiny morning, had they but known the truth, the very stones must have pitied him. The prince had become pauper. The pauper was being shown the prince's heritage —treasures of love and laughter, broad, smiling roods of happiness, castles of delight . . . gone, all gone, lost, forfeited by some madman's folly—some sudden, fleeting fancy for a Bacchante's face. The prince had sold his birthright for the brush of a girl's lips. The prince had plighted his troth. To keep it meant desolation. To break it, defilement. " What shall it profit a man if he shall gain the whole world and lose his own soul ? "

Later that morning, as Sir Andrew was leaving for the Temple, Lyveden desired his permission to keep two appointments he had made.

" One's at twelve, and the other at half-past one. That means that I shall be out, sir, from eleven to three."

" Do as you please," was the answer. " Do as you please. By the way, d'you think they really want me to come to this dinner to-night ? Or is it some fool's idea of being polite ? "

" I'm sure they do," said Anthony gravely.

Sir Andrew blew through his nose.

" Once for all," he said shortly. " I'll bet they don't ask me again."

He clapped his hat on his head and left the house.

Anthony's first appointment was with Forsyth and Co., Solicitors, Lincoln's Inn Fields. He kept it punctually, to learn quite a lot about himself. Amongst other things, he learned that he was extremely wealthy and possessed a mansion in Town and an estate in the West Country. But, since his fiancée had visited Forsyth at ten, he did not learn that he had been engaged to be married to Valerie French. Once he had asked for his Will: and Forsyth, with bulging eyes and the Will in a drawer, had sworn that he had not made one. The attorney writhed, but the man was resolute. He had given his word.

Lyveden's second appointment was luncheon with Valerie French.

As they had taken tea the day before, so they lunched—by themselves. Lady Touchstone, like Plague, was to appear at dinner.

Valerie was, I suppose, in the fifth or sixth heaven. Anthony was very quiet: very tender, but awfully quiet.

Throughout the meal they discussed his visit to Forsyth and what he had learned. Of their meeting the day before, nothing was said. It had been agreed, of course, that that day shouldn't count. . . .

At last coffee was served, and they were left alone.

Instantly Anthony rose and crossed to her side.

"Valerie, I've something to tell you. Yesterday afternoon I asked you a question—a very vital question. I asked if, when I—went down, I was unattached." He paused.

"Yes?" whispered Valerie, dry-mouthed.

Had Forsyth talked? Surely Forsyth hadn't shown him his Will? Surely he couldn't have been so faithless. Yet . . .

"And you said yes—I was free."

Valerie nodded. She dared not trust her voice.

" Well, I have reason to think that, when I disappeared, I—was—engaged."

'Reason to think' . . . . Then it *was* Forsyth. Something he had said—some slip—some paper—some draft. . . .

Valerie began to tremble.

" You see," he went on slowly, " I've—I've remembered something."

Valerie's heart gave one tremendous bound.

" Yes ? " she breathed. " Yes ? "

Anthony looked at her sharply. He had expected that she would be astounded : instead, she seemed nervous, almost *apprehensive* . . . Why on earth——

A sudden, terrible explanation burst into his brain.

" Valerie ! Yesterday—when I asked if I was engaged—why did you tell me a lie ? "

For an instant the girl hesitated. Then she rose to her feet and put her hands on his shoulders.

" Because," she said simply, " I wanted you to think you were free."

Love is notoriously blind.

Even when she saw the grief in his fine, grey eyes she mistook it for glory. . . .

So they stood for a moment.

Then very gently he took her two hands from his shoulders and let them fall to her sides.

" ' We won't count to-day,' " he quoted. " Of course, I see now. D'you know, I'm not quite certain, but I think you've broken my heart."

He turned and passed out of the room.

Valerie stood paralysed. . . .

She heard him take his hat, and a moment later the door of the flat was shut.

*   *   *   *   *

Lady Touchstone had a grand air. For all that, the moment she opened her mouth, you felt at ease. Not that the grandeur departed. She never stepped down. Instead, she made you step up and sit down by her side. She could have hobnobbed with a swineherd—in fact, she had. And the swineherd had enjoyed her fellowship rather more than that of any crony he had ever known. She made him laugh till he cried, but he never felt an impulse to slap her upon the back. They actually had a drink together before they parted. And ever after the incident the swineherd regarded the bank upon which he had found her with much the same veneration as is due to the Stone of Scone. Indeed, if he passed it alone, he always pulled his forelock.

It was, indeed, the lady's remarkable personality which lifted her out of the ditch into which, this September evening, she had been bundled without any warning and with no ceremony at all.

She had spent the day in the country and had returned rather late—at a quarter past seven, to wit, just five hours after Anthony had taken his leave. And dinner, as we know, was at eight . . . at Claridge's. . . .

She hurried into her room and rang for her maid. Then a note on her table attracted her eye.

DEAR AUNT HARRIET,

Will you depulize for me to-night? I am not myself, and by the time you have this I shall have left for Bell Hammer. Your loving

VALERIE.

So much for the ditch itself. Now for the brambles within.

The object of the dinner was to celebrate Anthony
Lyveden's return to the fold. Of the four guests,
one was coming because he loved Valerie, two to
congratulate Valerie, and the fourth because he was
a friend of Anthony Lyveden. And Valerie had left
for Hampshire, and—it was twenty past seven.

So much for the briers in the ditch. Now for the
convenient culvert by which poor Lady Touchstone
decided to crawl out of her plight.

Upon resorting frantically to the telephone, with
the purpose of stopping the guests, she found that
that useful contrivance was out of order. And Valerie
had left for Hampshire, and—it was seven twenty-
five. . . .

It now became obvious to Lady Touchstone that,
unless the situation was to become a total wreck,
the sooner she made her toilet, the better for her.

Mercifully, her maid had deft fingers. . . .

Half an hour later her ladyship entered a taxi,
admirably clothed, and hoping very hard that she
was in her right mind.

Verily, Valerie's action was enough to unhinge
anyone. Why she had seen fit to take it, Lady
Touchstone did not attempt to consider. She had
had enough of trying to comprehend the incomprehensible. Besides, she was desperately anxious to
spare her wits. If this dinner-party was not to
prove a far-reaching fiasco, she would have to rise
to the occasion, as no understudy had ever risen
before. Valerie was no ordinary star. *Hamlet* was
going to be rendered without the Prince of Denmark
and the play had got to be a roaring success. . . .

Lady Touchstone set her white teeth.

The reflection that Richard and André were to

make two of the guests comforted her. Richard
Winchester was a tower of strength, and André—
—André, at least, was another woman. Besides,
she knew them well. They would understand. She
was a little afraid of meeting Anthony Lyveden.
Scylla and Charybdis were hanging about that encounter. She must not forget that he had lost his memory.
She must not remember that he had once lost his
mind. Above all things, she must forget that he had
lost his heart. Of the fourth guest, Sir Andrew Plague,
K.C., she was actually frightened. Besides, he was
a comparative stranger. She trusted that Anthony
Lyveden would keep him in order. . . .

She entered Claridge's hall at two minutes to
eight.

As she was scanning the lounge, Sir Andrew rose
from a chair and advanced upon her.

Lady Touchstone offered up a short prayer.

" Madam," said the knight shortly, " I am here
under false pretences."

" Good," said Lady Touchstone agreeably. " So'm
I."

Sir Andrew stared.

" I have come without Major Lyveden. While
I was dressing for dinner and wondering where he
might be, I received a telephone message, begging
me to make his excuses and say that he could not
come. I need hardly say that I am extremely angry.
He has forced my hand and he has made fools of
us both."

" And my niece," said Lady Touchstone, " has
done precisely the same. I can only assume that the
mantles of insanity with which you and I clothed
each other yesterday afternoon have fallen upon their

respective shoulders." She turned to look round the lounge. "There ought to be two other fools waiting to catch our eye. But they're probably on the way. Shall we sit down and exchange abuse of our betrayers until they appear? I know some splendid epithets."

"Madam," said Plague, with a grin, "I can confirm that statement."

Lady Touchstone laughed.

"The finger of Fate," she observed, sinking into a chair, "is undoubtedly double-jointed. As you have justly recalled, three days ago I sat upon the opposite side of this street and called you to order." Sir Andrew choked. "Let me take this occasion," added Lady Touchstone quickly, "of apologizing for assuming a rôle to which I had no shadow of right, which I did not adorn."

Sir Andrew threw up a deprecating hand.

"You have chastised me with whips," he said gently, "and my chastisement was deserved. I beg that you will not now chastise me with scorpions. May I add that the object of my visit yesterday afternoon was to offer a profound apology for my misconduct? Then I had the misfortune to fall over one of your hassocks——"

"You must admit," said Lady Touchstone, "that I behaved like a prize idiot. Go on. Without prejudice."

Sir Andrew tried not to grin.

"I have had," he replied, "no opportunity of observing the manners and customs of the happily exceptional class of individuals to which you refer, but, if I may say so, Lady Touchstone, my observation of your intellect suggests that you had reason for what you did. I was foolishly excited and, no doubt, spoke as a fool. If I was misunderstood, I have no just cause of complaint."

"That's very handsome," said Lady Touchstone, "and I should like to keep it. But I must hand it back. You never spoke as a fool. Of my own idiocy I dug myself into the mire, and then picked it up and threw it at you. I think it was very nice of you not to throw it back. And, talking of fools, it looks very much as if these two we're awaiting are wiser than we. If not, then they're knaves as well. It's ten minutes past eight."

"Knaves, if you please," said the knight. "I can't call them wise if they knew they were dining with you."

"Us," said Lady Touchstone. "I quite agree. I think we're excellent company and by no means such fools as we thought."

Sir Andrew rose to his feet.

"Madam," he said, "since our hostess has failed, I have the honour to ask you to be my guest."

Lady Touchstone inclined her head.

"I warn you," she said, "I'm very hungry."

Then she rose and preceded Sir Andrew Plague into the restaurant. . . .

The late opponents made a striking pair.

Lady Touchstone was much more than hand-some, and, if her figure was not what it had been, it must be remembered that it had been the talk of London. An admirable complexion had literally saved her face, and the spirit of youth, which had always inhabited her eyes, was apparently a tenant for life. She behaved as became her years : her soft, grey hair declared that she was over the crest of life, yet all the

time her most attractive countenance was delivering
an astounding rebutter. As for her beautiful eyebrows, they gave demeanour and greyness the lie direct.
Moreover, she knew how to dress, and used the knowledge.

Sir Andrew Plague, in repose, distinguished any
company: in eruption, he overwhelmed. The man's
tremendous personality was royally and, so, suit-
ably lodged. His height saved him from being out-
rageously fat. A man of six feet five who is propor-
tionately broad can wear a big apron. Moreover,
Sir Andrew Plague had no need of a bearing-rein.
His head was always high and his shoulders square.
Between his height and his carriage his stomach fell
flat. As for his looks, the knight was much less
than handsome. Shorn of its strength, his mighty
face would have made the fortune of a thirteenth-
century jester. But nobody ever laughed, because
the strength was no beard. It was, indeed, part and
parcel of the great countenance. The set of the
jaw, the proud curve of the lips, the supremacy of
the keen, blue eyes were all trumpeting a puissance
of another age. Wherever he went, every one heard
the fanfare, and such as were in his path gave him
the wall. And every one who did not know who he
was inquired immediately and in some excitement.
What is still more to the point is that the inquiries
were always respectfully couched. If Sir Andrew
had gone to a ball as the Widow Twankey, I believe
that the other revellers would have laughed more
out of politeness than anything else. After all,
Richard Crookback excited but little derision.

" You know," said Lady Touchstone, when she
was comfortably installed, " I'm really almost relieved

not to be sitting next to Anthony Lyveden. Don't
think I don't like him, because I do. I'm positively
silly about him, and always was. But his present
defect bewilders me. I know exactly how I'm going
to feel when we come face to face. I've had the
sensation before—two or three times. Have you
ever been suddenly presented with the wrong end
of an ear-trumpet ? "

" Not," said Sir Andrew, " that I can remember. Charity is indiscriminate, I know, but not so
indiscriminate as all that."

Lady Touchstone laughed delightedly.

" I see," she said, " that you respect the dictum
of Solon. Yet he was on the Bench."

Sir Andrew heaved with merriment.

" I have," he said, " a fellow-feeling. If you
remember, he was once thought to be mad."

Lady Touchstone choked. At length—

" As I was saying," she continued, " I shall feel
at a loss—tongue-tied. I shall flounder. I shall
fall back upon that vulgar tramp of a topic—that
well-worn copper which is in every dummy's purse—the
weather."

" No, you won't," said Sir Andrew. " He'll see
to that. His charm of manner is quite remarkable.
The servants, who ought to hate him because of his
office, worship the ground he treads. Of course,
I know what you mean. He's your familiar friend,
and the foundation of that familiarity has been cut
away. He was your gossip, and reminiscence is the
breath by which gossips live. How did your niece
get on ? "

" She's said very little," said Lady Touchstone,
guardedly. " But she seemed very happy about

him. He was the dearest fellow, and I gather he's exactly the same."

Sir Andrew frowned.

"Sentimentality," he said shortly, "is certainly among his failings."

"I should," said Lady Touchstone hurriedly, "have said 'lovable.'"

"Madam," said Sir Andrew severely, "I cannot appreciate that adjective. Only the other night Major Lyveden confessed to a dread that he might be a husband. And when, while admitting the horror of such a contingency, I remarked that what had been suffered in the past could probably be endured again, he replied that what was concerning him was that he would not love the woman." Lady Touchstone became extremely interested. "I reproved him, of course," continued Sir Andrew Plague, "but, you will agree that it is distressing to find such a fly in such ointment. Otherwise, his outlook upon life is sane and discerning. And, if he is somewhat stubborn, his charm of manner does much to redeem that fault."

"You say," said Lady Touchstone, "that he was dreading the idea that he might be a married man?"

"Naturally. The first thing he told me last night was that he was unattached. It was plainly a great relief."

Lady Touchstone sipped her champagne. Then—

"Have you the slightest idea," she inquired, "why he has failed to-night? I know he gave you no reason, but do you suspect any cause? Did he let fall any hint?"

Sir Andrew reflected.

At length—

" I have no idea," he said. " But I can tell you this. Last night he was in the very best of spirits. This morning he was late for breakfast—he had been abroad, I believe—and he seemed unusually quiet. He desired my permission to keep two appointments he had made. I gave it, of course. But his subdued manner was noticeable."

" One of those appointments," said Lady Touchstone, " was with my niece. If he is not here to-night, because he is depressed, it looks as if she may be suffering from the same malady."

" Which he communicated to her ? "

" Exactly. You say he went out before breakfast ? "

" So I believe. But what——"

" Cherchez la femme," flashed Lady Touchstone. Sir Andrew started. " I'm sure of it. While he was out, he met some one."

" But what has this," said Sir Andrew, " to do with your niece ? Assume that he met some woman. I think it highly improbable, but let that pass Assume that the encounter depressed him. Why should this depression affect your niece ? "

Lady Touchstone looked her host full in the face.

" I am about," she said, " to commit a breach of trust. I have sworn to Valerie not to disclose a certain fact, and I am going to break my word. I am going to make a confidential communication. I believe that it will go no further."

Sir Andrew smiled.

" Secrets," he said, " never do. Their next step is always the last."

"Don't wither me," said his guest. "That would be inhospitable."

Sir Andrew inclined his head.

"Where forty winters," he said, "have so signally failed, I cannot hope to succeed."

"Fifty-three," said Lady Touchstone, blushing. "You know that as well as I do."

The knight lifted his glass.

"I never flatter," he said. "It is a contemptible practice. You and I, madam, were born in the same year. I have often counted it an ill-starred period : henceforth I shall remember it as a year of grace."

Lady Touchstone drank with a bewitching smile. Then—

"I demand," she said, "to be shown the woman whom you have paid two compliments in the same minute. We are getting on well, aren't we ? " she added naïvely. "At this rate, by the end of the evening we shall have changed hats."

Sir Andrew began to shake with laughter.

"Is that your secret ? " he gurgled. "I can hardly believe that your niece was so optimistic."

"As a matter of fact," said my lady, "it's the champagne. I don't often revel, and I've never attained that dizzy height of communion which is too exuberant for words and can only be expressed by the exchange of headgear. But the idea has always appealed to me. No, the secret is this. When your secretary disappeared, he was about to be married."

"He was engaged ? "

Lady Touchstone nodded.

"And deeply attached—to my niece."

" No ! "

" Yes, indeed. And she, most properly, won't hear of him being told."

" Why not ? " cried the K.C. " The contract stands. And, as a man of honour, Lyveden has only to learn his liability——"

" Which," said Lady Touchstone, " is precisely why Valerie won't have him told. If he was told, he'd want to carry out his contract. And she would never know whether he was following his heart's desire or keeping his honour bright."

" Does she want to marry him ? "

" Only if he wants to marry her."

" He wanted to once," said Plague.

" Very much."

" Then it may be fairly presumed——"

" If you were in her position," said Lady Touch-stone, " you'ld want to *know*. You wouldn't want to take any chances, however slight."

" Madam," said Plague deliberately, " you are talking nonsense. Marriage is notoriously the most reckless gamble in life. You stake your birthright, and once in a million throws you get your money back. What does it matter what subordinate chances you take ? A gambler stakes a fortune, and backs him-self to win for half-a-crown."

His guest put a hand to her head.

" I'm not going to argue," she said, " because, if I do, I shall lose. I can see that. There must be some obvious flaw in your contention, and I shall probably perceive it just as I'm going to get into bed. Valerie's perfectly right, and so am I. Remem-ber, I'm greatly handicapped by your inability to appreciate a common enough emotion, and I consider

M

that I have shown the greatest restraint by not referring to it before.　However, we've wandered terribly. The point is that, whereas last night their relations were happy, this afternoon my niece and Anthony Lyveden are no longer at one.　If they were, they'ld be here. More.　If only one was unhappy, the other would have turned up.　Therefore they are both in distress. *Cherchez la femme.*"

"Is that a command?" said the knight.　"Or only a quotation?"

"I should like it to be a command."

Sir Andrew fingered his chin.　"There were," he said tentatively, "two other guests . . ."

My lady, who was about to drink, hesitated and then set down her glass.

"There were," she said.

"Why have they failed?"

For a moment Lady Touchstone sat motionless, staring at the keen, blue eyes three feet away.　Then she smiled very sweetly.

"You're very obedient," she said, "and very, very clever."

Sir Andrew frowned.

"I have yet to learn," he said, "that the man who slew Ahab was accounted a marksman."

*　　　*　　　*　　　*

When, an hour and a half later, Sir Andrew Plague re-entered his hall to see a telegram lying upon the table, he took and opened the envelope as of right

Joshua will be by the Albert Memorial to-morrow at seven o'clock.

Sir Andrew stared at the writing.

Joshua? Who the devil was——

Then he saw that the communication had not been addressed to him. Also, because he was no fool and had come fresh from the council, he perceived that the flimsy sheet which he held in his hand was the ace of trumps itself.

It was characteristic of the man that he did not hesitate.

He put the ace of trumps into his pocket, entered the library, and rang the bell.

When a servant appeared——

"Is Major Lyveden abed?"

"No, sir. He's not come in."

"When he comes in, say nothing about that telegram."

"Very good, sir."

"And, however contrary his orders, call him at eight o'clock."

"Very good, sir."

"Call me at six."

"Very good, sir."

Sir Andrew's intuition was sound.

Before the knight was in bed, his secretary returned, footsore and dejectedly inquisitive. Happily, the servant he summoned knew how to obey. . . .

"No message at all?"

"No, sir."

"Ah! Well, call me at half-past six, please."

"Very good, sir."

"And be sure you wake me. I'm tired."

"Er—yes, sir."

"Good night."

The servant retired, and Lyveden sank into a chair and stared before him.

" Feet of clay," he muttered, " feet of clay. Those little, shining insteps—vile clay. And yet . . . My God," he burst out suddenly, " what's the good of pretending ? I'ld rather kiss those insteps than André's mouth. Clay or platinum—what does it matter ? They're *hers* . . . *her* feet . . . *her* little, precious feet. . . ." He looked upon his terrier and laughed. " And that's the naked truth, my fellow. Anybody want to buy a soul ? "

Patch, who hoped he was being asked whether he was hungry, sat up and begged.

*   *   *   *   *

There, the long day is over, and all but one of my puppets are gone to their rest. The strutting André, the fretting Lyveden, conspirators Plague and Touch-stone, honest, unwitting Winchester—all are up on their shelf until to-morrow. For the last of all, sirs, we will not wait, because she will lie awake the whole night long, hearing the owls cry and the merci-less stable clock telling the sluggard hours. She might be dead—this puppet with the thick dark hair—so very still she lies, so cold are those glorious temples, that delicate throat, those beautiful, slender arms. But for her eyes, she might be some fairy queen, sleeping in dull, cold marble to mark her majesty's tomb . . . but for her dark-blue eyes. These are restless. Their field is limited, because she lies so still, and so is their vision, because the night is dark, but so much as they can compass they know by heart—the dim silhouette of the table against the black of the wall, the faint, familiar outline of the great pier-glass, the panelled foot of the bed and, beyond, the square, black mouth of the open window, breathing the cool night air and, now and again, a sigh of the wandering wind. See, she is moving at last. She is sitting up, while her thick dark hair falls like a cloak about her breast and shoulders. She is drawing up her knees, setting her chin upon them, clasping her hands about her insteps. She can peer into the park now, and very soon her eyes will pick up the line of the woods against the sky. Yet, but for those restless eyes, she is still the fairy queen and still sculpture. And, as I have said, we will not wait for this puppet, that neither struts nor frets nor sleeps, because the stable clock is merciless and the hours sluggard.

CHAPTER VII

THE SIEVE OF VANITY

SIR ANDREW PLAGUE approached the Albert Memorial with the sober steps of one who has no objective, but is merely taking the air. This, by the way, was worth breathing, for it was fresh from Night's cellar and had not lain long enough in Day's parlour to lose its cool bouquet. Sir Andrew marked this and snuffed luxuriously.

He might have been deep in meditation. As a matter of fact, he was looking for a gentleman of Jewish extraction, who, he had reason to think, would, upon being accosted, prove suspicious and obstructive.

Joshua will be by the Albert Memorial to-morrow at seven o'clock.

Sir Andrew lifted his head and looked about him.
The shrine, however, seemed to be alone in its glory.
The knight perambulated it, frowning.

Its precincts were deserted. More. Except for a distant horseman and two park-keepers, there was no human being in sight.

Sir Andrew glanced at his watch and began to pace up and down. . . .

As he turned for the second time, a clock struck seven.
A moment later, the horseman, who was now abreast

of the Memorial, stopped, dismounted and began to make much of his horse. Then he ran his eye over his charge, flicked a speck of dust from the great quarters and looked about him.

Sir Andrew blew through his nose. He was not in the mood for company, least of all for that of a groom, who was doing the same as himself. He was there to watch, not to be watched. Damn it, how the fellow was staring! Why couldn't he mind his own business? Why didn't his master come and send him packing? Why——

Here the servant approached and touched his hat.

"Major Lyveden, sir?" he ventured.

"That's right," said Sir Andrew faintly, trying to recognize his own voice.

Without a word, the groom turned Joshua round. Then he stepped to the saddle, whipped his head under a flap and proceeded to tighten the girths. This seemed to annoy Joshua, for the moment he felt the pressure he laid back his delicate ears, raised an itching hind-leg with a meaning which was not to be mistaken, and, flinging round his head, snapped viciously in the direction of his aggressor. Beyond, however, conjuring the horse to 'get up,' the servant ignored his vexation and, after a glance at Sir Andrew, lengthened the stirrup-leathers to their full extent.

The knight, who had not ridden for thirty years, watched the preparations as a man in a trance.

He was to ride this—this brute. Almost immediately. He was to put his foot into that stirrup and haul himself up into—into hell. It was ordained—necessary. He had put his hand to the plough. He had to be brought to the woman—*la femme* of the proverb. And this brute would bring him. There

was no other way. *No other way?* Goats and monkeys!
Had one to hark back to the Iliad to do a neighbour
a service? He wasn't a bushranger—a highwayman.
This was the twentieth century—not *Jack and the
Beanstalk* or any other damned pantomime. A-a-ah,
the vicious swine! The——

Here the groom looked over the withers and touched
his hat.

With a shock, Sir Andrew realized that his hour was
come.

For one frantic instant he considered whether he
could with decency lead Joshua to meet his mistress.
Then that fantastic hope was still-born, and with a
frightful grunt the giant heaved himself into the
saddle. . . .

As he gathered the reins—

"Miss André'll be i' the Row, sir. Comin' this
way."

Sir Andrew swallowed.

"Right," he said thickly. Then: "Make the
brute walk."

Obediently, the groom took the bridle and started
Joshua off. . . .

As horse and rider passed down the broad road, he
watched their going gloomily, fingering his chin.
Presently he sighed profoundly.

"An' a major, too," he muttered. "Must 'ave bin
i' the Camuel Detachmen'."

Now, Joshua was a very sound judge—not of men,
as a whole, but of such as got upon his back. Sir
Andrew's seat and hands told him that the knight was
no horseman. His instinct told him, first, that the
latter was not in the least afraid, and, secondly, that
he was a man who meant to have his own way.

Accordingly, Joshua respected him, hoped very much that he would be content to be a ' passenger,' and decided that, if his directions were given with a heavy hand, they must be accepted in good part.

He walked along slowly, as one who has a charge to fulfil.

As for Sir Andrew, he was concerned entirely for his dignity and his convenience. For the desperate venture upon which he had set out to be successful, he would need every grain of wit and every ounce of assurance at his disposal. And here, right at the commencement of his enterprise, he had been placed at an appalling disadvantage. He not only felt a fool; he was leaning upon the shoulder of Discomfiture itself. The brute between his knees had only to toss its head to distract his attention : while, if it elected to shy . . .

He rode out of Kensington Gardens, cursing bitterly, to cross a taxi's bows with the air of an Earl Marshal. . . .

As he passed down the Row, the feeling of liability began to wear off. The brute he was riding seemed to be able to behave . . . seemed . . .

Very gently, by way of proving his ox, the lawyer drew the reins towards his chin.

Instantly Joshua eased his pace to a standstill.

Sir Andrew was greatly relieved.

When, however, upon his lowering and, presently, shaking the reins, the big brown stood like a rock, the knight became less easy.

" Go on ! " he cried, clacking vigorously with his tongue. " Go on, you swine ! I don't want to stand here all day."

Utterly failing to appreciate that he was being

addressed, Joshua looked cheerfully about him and, perceiving no horse within sight, whinnied to proclaim his isolation.

The sympathy which Sir Andrew had always felt for Balaam ripened into an *entente cordiale*.

"Shut up, you fool!" he roared. "And go *on*, can't you?" He shook the reins frantically. "Proceed. WALK, you blithering ass!"

That Joshua immediately advanced was due partly to the fact that Sir Andrew's delivery was that of the parade-ground, but mainly to the fortunate circumstance that the brown had once put in a month of squadron drill.

The two made their way eastward agreeably enough. . . .

When André Strongi'th'arm perceived them, she at first imagined that she had made a mistake. And when, upon a closer inspection, she observed that the approaching centaur was indeed composed largely of her best hunter, she could hardly believe her eyes. As a matter of fact, it was her obvious, blank astonishment which enabled Sir Andrew to identify a girl he had never seen.

As he came up, frowning, he raised his hat.

"Miss Strongi'th'arm, I think." An almost imperceptible nod confirmed his statement. "Major Lyveden was prevented from coming, and I am here in his stead."

André favoured Sir Andrew with a suspicious stare. Her sword was out.

"Who are you?" she said shortly.

So far as she was concerned, she could not have said a worse thing. The abrupt demand, the haughtiness of her tone, were like a stoup of wine to her opponent.

Sir Andrew forgot himself and Joshua. The peppery knight became the King's Counsel—patient, bland, merciless.

Slowly he drew his rapier.

" My name is Andrew Plague."

" Why isn't Major Lyveden here ? "

" Because he's in bed," said Sir Andrew.

" Is he ill ? "

" Not yet."

A dangerous light slid into the big brown eyes. Then, because she was André, their owner rushed in.

" What do you mean—' not yet ' ? "

" This. Since he met you yesterday, Major Lyveden has been a desperate man—dull, spiritless, shunning the fellowship of friends."

" What friends ? "

" His friends," said Sir Andrew, " of whom I have the honour to be one."

André laughed.

" You're very lucky," she said, " to know two such charming people."

Up went the heavy eyebrows.

" Two ? "

" Major Lyveden and Valerie French."

" I have never set eyes upon the lady."

André shot the speaker a long and searching look. Sir Andrew blinked back lazily.

" Then why are you here ? " she said coldly.

" Because," was the deliberate reply, " a man who has lost his memory is not fair game."

André gasped. Then she went very white.

" D'you mind getting off that horse ? " she said. " It—it happens to belong to me."

" I will dismount " said Sir Andrew coolly, " at the

close of this interview. I may add that upon this interview your relations with Major Lyveden entirely depend. I have put no pressure upon him, and, if you will deal with me frankly, I shall put none. Otherwise, he will leave the country to-morrow—for the good of his health."

The threat went home. Sir Andrew saw it go. . . .

For a moment the girl hesitated. Then she lifted her head and stared at the gay, blue sky. After all, she could afford to laugh.

" In your opinion," she said, " Major Lyveden must be protected ? "

" Should occasion arise. A man who has lost his memory——"

" —can be told anything? I see. I suppose, if you'd lost your memory and somebody told you you owed them five thousand pounds, you'ld hand it over ? "

" I should not," said Sir Andrew quietly. " Neither, I think, would you. But Lyveden would."

André frowned. Then—

" Perhaps you're right," she said gaily. " He's got a very sweet nature. I suppose," she added, flicking her boot with her whip, " the object of this interview is to get from me a confession of the lies I told him yesterday morning ? "

The K.C. studied his finger-nails.

" I've told you," he said, " the position. If you want to see him again, you must first of all satisfy me that that's to his advantage."

" D'you know," said André silkily, " that I've a very good mind to whip you across the face ? "

" Isn't that Colonel Winchester's job ? "

" As a matter of fact," said André, " it's Anthony Lyveden's."

" I don't think he'll do it," said Plague, grimly.
" But let that pass. Why isn't it Colonel Winchester's ? "

" Because he is not concerned."

The master of cross-examination applied the lash.

" Have you released him ? "

André winced. Then she flushed red as fire.

" If he knew of this," she flashed, " I believe he'ld
break your neck."

" Then," said Sir Andrew agreeably, " pray for my
soul. I'm to see him at ten o'clock."

" What for ? "

Sir Andrew gazed abstractedly into the middle
distance. At length—

" To ask him," he said dreamily, " to ask him to tell
Major Lyveden who is your *fiancé*."

With the knob of her switch Miss Strongi'th'arm
tapped her white teeth, reflectively.

" I see," she said quietly. " Well, if he gives the
wrong answer, refer him to me."

It was impossible not to admire such consummate
nerve. Indeed, Sir Andrew afterwards confessed
that at this juncture he was within an ace of throwing
up the sponge.

Instead—

" I hope," said the K.C. gently, " I still hope that
it will be unnecessary for Major Lyveden to leave
England."

" So," said André, " do I. What makes you think,"
she added, " that I'm so bad for him ? "

" I have told you."

" You've quite decided that his depression was
not apprehensive ? "

Sir Andrew's eyelids flickered.

" What do you mean ? "

" You're sure that it was due to what happened here yesterday morning ? Certain that it was not the shadow of some coming event ? "

Sir Andrew wrinkled his brow.

" When I know," he said, " what happened here yesterday morning, I shall be in a position to judge."

" But you have judged."

" No. I'm here for that purpose."

" And supposing the information is denied you ? "

" I shall still be in a position to judge."

" You mean . . . ? "

" That those who decline to speak," said Sir Andrew Plague, " must take the consequences."

" What shadow of right have you to——"

" None."

" Why don't you ask Major Lyveden ? "

" If you can't help me, I shall. But a man who's lost——"

" Because you know he'ld tell you to go to hell."

" I don't think he would," said Plague, " before a stranger."

" What stranger ? "

" Colonel Winchester. I know they were friends once, but . . . "

There was a pause.

His face like a mask, the knight sat motionless, staring with half-closed eyes across the park. André eyed him intently, savagely biting her lip, striving desperately to read his thoughts. She could have sworn he was bluffing. He must be. Yet . . . How much did he really know ? And who—who had told him ? And was he honest ? Or was he out, if he could, to tear her garland ? If he was . . .

A mounted policeman passed, self-conscious and jingling, and shot the unwitting pair a curious glance. A squall of sparrows' bickering convulsed the slumber of an adjacent tree. Already from between the high walls of Knightsbridge the confluence of hubbub was beginning to swell into a steady background of uproar, against which the sudden crisp note of a trumpet stood out in bold relief.

As the call faded—

" If I told you the truth," said André, " you wouldn't believe me."

" Be sure that I shall."

" We shall see. You think Major Lyveden has lost his memory ? "

" I know it."

" Yet he accosted me yesterday morning—here, in the Row . . . came up and wished me well . . begged me to forgive his behaviour . . . used my Christian name . . . at parting kissed my hand . . ."

There was a long silence. At length—

" What was the behaviour," said Sir Andrew, " which he asked you to forgive ? "

André hesitated. Then—

" Some people," she said, " might call it—desertion."

" No doubt," was the dry reply. " What was it ? "

André's eyes narrowed till they became two gleaming slits.

" You said that you would dismount at the close of this interview. Well . . . this interview is closed. You came to protect Major Lyveden. You were gallant enough to say ·so. If you believe what I've told you, it may occur to your intelligence that he is perfectly capable of taking care of himself."

" In fact," said Sir Andrew imperturbably, " **you**
think that his loss of memory is assumed ? "

" Naturally."

Sir Andrew rubbed his nose.

" I don't know that I blame you," he said. " Still
. . . Why should he make belief ? "

André took a deep breath.

" I have said that this interview——"

" I know, I know. If you like, I'll beg your pardon.
I believed you a knave. I'm going to save you **now**
from being a fool."

" Will you get off that horse ? "—passionately.

" No," said Sir Andrew, " I won't. Now, listen **to**
me. Lyveden's lost his memory. You may take that
from me. From what you tell me, it seems it's begun
to return. He's remembered you—and your works.
To-morrow—perhaps to-day—he'll remember——"

" What ? " said Anthony Lyveden, quietly enough.

André jumped violently, but Plague never moved.
The man was unshakable. He continued to address
his opponent.

" *The ring you wear*," he said steadily, " *upon your
engagement finger.*"

There was an electric silence.

André began to tremble suddenly. Instantly
Lyveden set a hand upon her knee. The man was
out of breath and fairly streaming with sweat. He
controlled his voice somehow.

" Try me," he said, smiling. " Don't be afraid of
him."

Gently he took her left hand and drew off its
glove. . . .

The emerald which Winchester had set there winked
in the young sunlight.

For a moment Lyveden peered at the gem.   Then—
" That's right," he said quietly.   " We chose it
together.   It had to be made smaller to fit your
finger."   He put her hand to his lips and let it go.
Then he turned to his dumbfounded employer.   " You
will please," he said coldly, " apologize to this lady
for a presumption which no patronage can warrant
and no friendship survive."

Twice Sir Andrew opened and shut his mouth.   Then
he slid off Joshua, uncovered, attempted ineffectually
to speak, turned and walked uncertainly away. . . .

" Oh . . . Anthony ! . . ."

The sorrow with which that cry was laden wrung
Lyveden's heart.

" What ? "

André began to weep silently.

" What ? " cried Anthony.   " What ?   What have
I said ? "

" God forgive me," wailed André.   " I'm very
wicked."

" What d'you mean, André ? "

" I thought," sobbed the girl, " you were pretending
you'd lost your memory "—Anthony started—" pretending, because—because you loved me best."

" *Best ?* "

" And now—you pretend—you haven't lost it,
to—to save—my—rotten—face . . ."   She sat up
suddenly and shook the tears out of her eyes.   " Get
up," she said, pointing to Joshua.   " Get up, you
splendid gentleman, and come with me."

For a moment Anthony hesitated.   Then he swung
himself into the saddle. . . .

André was cantering up the Row.   He followed
her amazedly.

N

They overtook Sir Andrew, bareheaded, sweating, shaking his fists at heaven and audibly condemning all women to an inferno of which—to judge from his report—Dante can never have heard, to which Rabelais alone could have done justice.

"Mr. Plague!" cried André. "Mr. Plague!"

The knight let an adjective go and stopped still where he stood.

"*Begone!*" he bellowed. "*Begone!*"

André flung herself out of the saddle and ran to the rails.

"I've something to say to you," she panted, "which I want Major Lyveden to hear." Sir Andrew waved her away, and Anthony approached dazedly. "I want to beg your pardon." At the word the knight started. Then he let fall his hand and turned to the speaker. "This ring is *not* Major Lyveden's. He said what he did just now out of loyalty—loyalty to me . . . misplaced loyalty. He threw your friendship to the winds to save my face. He doesn't care a damn about me. But, because I'm weak as water and he's strong, he took my part against you, no matter what it cost. And I can't let you go like this. You're *right*. D'you hear? *Right*. Right all along the line. God knows how you saw the bog I've jumped in when I couldn't see it myself. But you did. And you've opened my eyes. I'm in up to the neck—and now I'm going to get out." She swung round upon Lyveden. "Ever since yesterday morning you've thought you were tied to me. I gave you that idea. I never meant to. I didn't know you'd lost your memory. You recognized me, and you knew there'd been something between us. But that was all. *So there had*—but not of your making. I don't

know how much you remember, but you can take it
from me—your hands are clean . . . spotless, as
mine are foul. You're brave and gallant and faithful.
I'm not fit to lick your boots. But—I forgot all
that . . . yesterday morning." Her voice broke,
and she stamped, as if impatient of this evidence of
emotion. "And now give me Joshua and go. I'm
going to the man I'm engaged to, to tell him the truth.
If he's fool enough to stick to me after that, that's
his funeral. And you go to Valerie French, and say
I sent you. Tell her she doesn't deserve you, because
no woman does that. And tell her I never meant
to do her down, black as it looks. Mr. Plague'll
tell you I'm not a knave. Only a fool . . . a crazy,
vain-glorious fool . . . with her heart on her
sleeve."

She whipped about, vaulted—habit and all—on to
Joshua's back, twitched the bridle over the other
horse's head, and flung down the Row with irons
flying.

The two men stared in her wake.

After a little they turned and looked at one another.

"How the devil," said Plague, blinking, "did she
make that horse move?"

*   *   *   *   *

The next two hours were crowded.

Anthony's one idea was to see Valerie : Sir Andrew's
was to communicate with Lady Touchstone. The
one, of course, was depending upon the other. Only
her aunt knew where Valerie was. Food and raiment,
however, had to be considered. Anthony had neither
shaved nor bathed. Sir Andrew had done both,
and felt as though he had done neither. A second

bath was, of course, essential. Then, breakfast had to be swallowed. . . .

The most pregnant moment of all was that at which Sir Andrew excitedly informed the cook-general of a Bloomsbury boarding-house that 'the misunderstanding had been cleared up, and his secretary was ready and willing to fulfil his contract of marriage with her niece.' It was not the knight's fault that he had been given the wrong number, and, having regard to the war conditions invariably prevailing at Tomb Street during the ' rush ' half-hour, Miss Ada Margetts may be forgiven for admitting that she was Lady Touchstone. The result, however, was exhausting. Twice did Miss Margetts desire Sir Andrew to repeat his amazing news, and twice, literally squinting with suppressed emotion, did the knight, to his eternal credit, comply with her request. Then he was asked to ' 'old the line.' . . . After a hideous two minutes, during which Miss Margetts helped a cabman to transport an American trunk from the third floor to the street, communication was re-established.

" 'Oo d'you want ter speak to ? " inquired Miss Margetts.

" Goats and monkeys ! " shrieked Plague.

" Nothin' doin'," said Ada, replacing the receiver and picking up a pair of boots.

She did not even smile. She had no time. It was the ' rush ' half-hour.

Sir Andrew did not replace his receiver. Instead, he detached it with great violence and hurled it into the garden. There it was presently found by Patch, the Sealyham, who played with it for an hour, and then buried it providently under the rhododendrons.

The disruption of the telephone rendered indispensable a visit to Hill Street. . . .

More electricity was induced later, when Lady Touchstone, whose hold on topography was always treacherous, found herself unable to give the direction of Bell Hammer and could only tearfully insist that ' you always passed through Ealing.' Even when it was established that the estate lay in Hampshire, the poor lady continued to confound, by declaring that the passage of Ealing was a condition precedent to anyone's successful arrival at Bell Hammer, and an attempt at joint map-reading, in the proportion of one small-scale map to three shaking forefingers, resulted in Sir Andrew's being assisted into the morning-room and set in a draught. Indeed, had she not finally chanced to refer to the notoriety which Ealing had earned as a haunt of highwaymen——

" *Ealing ?* " shrieked Anthony. " You mean Hounslow ! Hounslow Heath ! "

Lady Touchstone stared. Then she clapped a hand to her mouth.

" That's right," she whispered. " I meant Hounslow. Not that I like Ealing, but that doesn't matter. It's Hounslow you go through. Did ever you know such an idiot ? I'm dreadfully sorry, Anthony. Most dreadfully sorry. And simply frightened to death. I'll go and get under a bed while you break it to *him.*"

* * * * *

The limousine flung through Basingstoke at an unlawful pace, and presently happening upon a ten-mile stretch of metalling, which clearly owed its being to the Roman ruler, swallowed it whole in thirteen minutes dead.

Five minutes later my lady sailed into Brooch, slid past the castle, dropped down the busy main street and then, coming to a carfax, crept to a policeman's elbow humbly enough.

"Bell 'Ammer?" said the peace officer. "Bell 'Ammer lays on your right." He pointed to a slit in an old half-timbered row. "Keep along there till you see the Close on your lef'. Then bear right-'anded on to the Bloodstock road. Bell 'Ammer's the secon' lodge after you pass the village o' Napery Green."

The direction was sound and the road good. The car made up for the check handsomely. . .

Indeed, she finished her business at a quarter to one by coming to rest at the steps of a broad mansion, upon which its spreading mantle of wistaria was blooming for the second time.

Anthony Lyveden alighted and rang the bell.

A moment later he was standing before Valerie French.

The girl looked tired, as one who has slept but ill the night before, and, when she spoke, her tone was that of the soldier who has retired from the fight—not because he is beaten, or afraid, or weary, but because he has perceived that he is not destined to prevail.

"Why have you come?"

"Because I love you, Valerie."

Valerie turned her head and stared out of a window.

"Do you?" she said listlessly. "Why?"

"I think it's very natural," said Anthony Lyveden. "I loved you the moment I saw you—that afternoon. I didn't know it then. But I do now."

"Who's told you?" said Valerie. "My aunt?"

Anthony shook his head.

"I realized it myself—yesterday morning."

A faint frown gathered on Valerie's brow.

" Yesterday morning ? " she said, as one who is troubled with a problem he has no desire to solve.

" Yesterday morning," repeated Anthony, " before I saw you, or Forsyth. . . . Yesterday morning I found out a terrible thing. I found that I was engaged —engaged *to somebody else.* I wasn't really, but I believed I was. . . . And when I made that discovery —that false discovery . . . when I realized what it meant—then all of a sudden I knew that I loved you. . . . It's strange, but I suppose that's the way of a fool. If you're a fool, you've got to have something forcibly taken away before you can realize that *without it* you can't go on. . . . Well, I'm a prize fool. There I was in my Paradise, wondering why on earth I was so happy. Suddenly my Paradise was gone. . . . And the loss opened my eyes."

" What," said Valerie slowly, " what made you think that you were engaged ? "

" I met a girl in the Park, and I recognized her. I can't tell you how or why. I just did. I remembered her, and I remembered her name."

" Yes ? "

" André."

Valerie caught her breath. Then she went very white.

" Go on," she said quietly.

" I couldn't remember where I'd met her, or anything else—except . . . except that there'd been something between us . . . *something* . . . I didn't know what. . . . Well, we spoke for a little, and I seem to have said the wrong things. It seemed absurd to tell her I'd lost my memory, because I'd remembered her. And somehow, in my efforts to get at the truth, I gave her the impression that I wanted to call back Time. . . . I only wanted to find out how I stood ; she thought I wanted to take back something I'd said or done. . . . And when we parted she thought that I loved her, and I thought that I was engaged. . . .

" Well, I had to tell you—somehow. I knew you had no idea—*knew*. You'ld never 've let me hold you and kiss your lips if you'd known that all the time I was pledged elsewhere. Some girls, perhaps . . . But you—*never*. And then, when I told you, I found that you *did* know—*had* known all along. I found that you had deceived me. I found that you, my idol, had done the most despicable thing. *You told me so*, Valerie. You never even tried to conceal it. You put your arms round my neck and told me so . . . told me you'd cheated me and let another girl down. . . .

" And I went out of your flat, picked up Patch, and tramped the streets of London till I could hardly stand. I was beside myself, partly because I'd been disillusioned, but mainly because, for all my disillusionment, I knew that I loved you still. . . ."

There was a long silence. At length—

" Why are you here ? " said Valerie.

" Because this morning I met her, and she told me the truth."

" You know . . ."

" I know enough. I know that yesterday I made a ghastly blunder. I know that I *was* engaged . . but not to her. And I know, thank God, that my hands are clean, Valerie, and that I have the right to come and ask your pardon for a mindless man's mistake."

Valerie put a hand to her head.

" You remembered her," she said. " You remembered André. And then you thought . . . I see," she added slowly. " Yes, it was natural enough." She rose and put out her hands. " I'm awfully glad you came, Anthony. Most awfully glad." He went to her quickly and took her hands in his. " But I'm awfully sorry you know about our engagement. And now "—she looked in his eyes—" for once I'm going to tell you the absolute truth. You're *not* engaged to me. You were, but you're not any more. You're free—free as the air."

" You mean . . ."

" What I say, Anthony. You are—released."

" But, Valerie, I love you ! *I love you !* Don't you—don't you love me ? "

The girl turned her head and regarded a photograph. This was framed in silver and standing upon the mantelpiece. It was a splendid likeness of Anthony Lyveden.

" I did—frightfully," she said. " I loved you so much that nothing in the world mattered—except your smile. But now . . ."

" Valerie ! Valerie ! " cried the man. " What have I done ? It wasn't my fault that I made that crackbrained mistake. And I'ld never 've dreamed you'd deceived me if you hadn't told me yourself."

" You would. You did. You asked me before I told you."

" Only because your manner gave you away."

" I know," said Valerie fretfully. " I know. It—it wasn't your fault."

" And though you'd done this thing—this dreadful thing, I loved you still. I tell you, I tramped the streets. I was nearly out of my mind. Don't you believe me ? "

" Yes."

" Then why d'you think it was ? If I hadn't loved you, Valerie, d'you think I'ld 've cared ? What made my engagement so hideous ? My love for you ! What made your deception so bitter ? My love for you. I tell you, I've come out of Hell. Don't send me back."

" I know you love me," said Valerie. " I know you do." With a sudden movement she put her arms round his neck. " No, don't kiss me. Just look me full in the eyes. There, like that. That's how you used to look, lad. . . . And now listen. I think you'll understand.

" I'm thankful this mistake's been cleared up— most thankful. In a way, it's been like a bad dream. And now I'm awake . . in a way. When you left me yesterday, I prayed for death. It—was—the— last—straw. And there have been so many . . . I don't blame you in the least. To tell you the truth, I think I should have done just the same. In fact, once upon a time I did. But that's another story. . . . And when you say you love me, I believe you do. And I'm very, very proud and very grateful. But . . ."

" You . . . don't . . . love . . . me ? "

" I want your old love, Anthony. And only the return of your memory can give me that. Perhaps I'm asking a lot, but then, you see, I'm spoiled. You've spoiled me. You can't remember doing it, but you did. And when you *do* remember, lad, then you'll understand why this new lamp—handsome and shining as it is—isn't the same."

" But, Valerie, you loved me yesterday—the day before ! You say that, when I left you, you prayed for death. That means you loved me. The new lamp was good enough then."

" I suppose it was. I don't know if it would have lasted. Perhaps it would. But now. . . ." She dropped her head upon his chest. " Oh, Anthony, can't you see? Must I tell you right out? "

The man stared over her head, frowning and seeing nothing.

After a little—

" No," he said, " I can't see. You must tell me right out."

" Well, then," said Valerie gently, " you must remember that I'm a woman. . . . And women are vain . . . proud . . . bursting with *amour propre*. It isn't your fault, I know, but—*you've remembered André*. . . ." She felt him stiffen, and lifted up her head. " And so, you see, dear," she added, with her eyes on his, " you've just *got* somehow to remember me," and the moment the words had been spoken she could have bitten out her tongue.

Her hands slipped from his shoulders and she turned away.

As she came to a window—

" I'm going into the garden," she said shakily. " Ring and tell them you want to get ready for lunch. And then come and find me—just as you used to do."

Anthony watched her pass across the terrace and down the sunlit steps.

Then he flung back his head and clapped his hands to his eyes.

*   *   *   *   *

Valerie passed down into the garden, cold with rage. She was furious with Fate, most furious with herself. She had done the unspeakable thing. She had squealed under the lash.

She had been hurt hideously, and she had shown Anthony the wound. She had lost desperately, and she had let him see that she cared. Worse. She had usurped his heart's function . . . told him the way to comfort her . . . explained in so many words that his kiss could make her well.

For two or three minutes she wallowed in the torment of mortification. Then the red mist lifted, and she examined her stripes.

Truly Fate knew how and where to lay on.

After everything—after all Anthony and she had been to each other—after all her blazing advertisement of his love—after all her secure compassion for André Strongi'th'arm, he had forgotten her and remembered André . . . remembered a girl he had only seen twice in his life. The king had forgotten his queen, but remembered the wench who had dared to aspire to the steps of *her* throne. And André—the wench—was laughing . . . hugging the truth to her breast, where it would hang *for ever*. The queen might have Anthony's love, but the wench had his remembrance. And Anthony had only seen her twice . . . only twice. . . .

Valerie stopped still and stared at a fat peacock hewn out of box.

" My God," she breathed, " what's the matter with me ? Have I no personality, no charm ? No beauty of body or soul ? No strength of character ? Have I made no impression at all—after all these months ? *None*. But André . . . in half an hour . . . How can I feel the same ? How *can* I ? How could anyone ? "

She pulled herself together and went on slowly.

He would be coming now—any moment. And she had plans to make. Things had to be determined at once. Their position had to be defined—that afternoon. She had released him, and he . . . did not desire . . . to be released. He would plead—importune her to let their engagement go on. . . . Valerie decided to let him have his way. He would want it so much, and she—she didn't care. Yes. It had come to that. *She didn't care.*

Didn't she? Was she sure? Because, if she didn't care . . .

For the life of her, Valerie could not determine whether she cared or not. Her love had been stunned. And she was turning it over, trying to ascertain whether it was quick or dead. Then, whilst she was peering, she heard Anthony call. And at the sound of his voice her love opened its eyes.

She did care, then? Yes, of course she cared. But—*in a different way.* There was something—some bar between them. Not a bar, exactly——

Again she heard him call her—quietly, with no assurance . . . like a man who is rather afraid of a Christian name.

A great wave of pity surged over Valerie's heart. She felt as though she had beaten a faithful dog. And now, for all its devotion, the dog was afraid of her, uncertain of its reception. It was pathetic. After all, it wasn't the dog's fault. He couldn't understand. . . .

He couldn't understand.

The phrase flamed. That was it. That was the bar—the shadow which lay between. Their mutual understanding had been infinite. And now it was gone. The splendid, perfect bridge had become a jetty. And while she could go the length of the jetty, Anthony must stand still upon the opposite shore—because he couldn't understand. And he couldn't understand because he couldn't remember.

Twenty-four hours ago that hadn't mattered. But then his memory was withered. Then, whole or halt, the man was still Anthony—her Anthony. Then she could have crooned over his infirmity. But now the lame had walked—*for somebody else*. . . . What hadn't mattered twenty-four hours ago had become vital.

Valerie turned to meet Lyveden, feeling curiously uncertain of herself.

Her anger was gone. Her overwhelming pity had put out that fire. Her love was in fretful attendance. One moment it was there, panting : the next, it was out of reach. It seemed to come in gusts, as the wind on a boisterous day. Now it was tearing, and now the air was dead calm.

She spent the whole of luncheon and most of the afternoon probing this mystery—a painful and bootless operation. As for Anthony, he spent the whole of his time trying to remember. This was transparently plain. Indeed, he made no secret of his endeavours. Valerie could have screamed. . . .

When luncheon was over, by his request the girl showed him the house—an uncanny business. After a little, however, she fell into her stride. . . .

" This is the library."

Anthony followed her in.

For a moment he stood, looking round. Then—

" What a very beautiful room," he said.

Valerie agreed politely. She could not tell him

that, only three months before, it had been his sanctuary : that that was his tobacco upon the table : that those were his pipes. . .

It was the same everywhere. The place bristled with memories. Real evidence of his recent habitation stood out on every side. He admired a rug he had given her, 'because it was fit for a queen.' He brushed by his own overcoat : accepted his own cigarettes. . . . Memories and evidence alike fell upon the bare rock. 'And because they had no root, they withered away.' He was pushing his way through a thicket, searching for boughs. Valerie tramped behind, and the boughs, which, of his blindness, Anthony thrust out of his way, flung back and hit her in the face.

On a sudden, desperate impulse, she took him upstairs and showed him the room in which he had lain sick of brain fever.

Anthony stared about him.

" I take it," he said slowly, " this was my room."

Valerie could only nod.

Then she stepped to the wardrobe and pulled out a drawer. It was full of collars and ties.

Together they peered at them.

" Mine ? " he whispered.

" Yes."

Presently they walked in the garden, as they had walked before—times without number. It seemed impossible that he should find the pleasaunce strange . . . hesitate at this corner, where they always turned . . . spell out the motto on the sundial, like a visitor. Yet he did all these things.

They came to the spot—the low stone seat where he had asked Valerie to be his wife. As they approached it, Valerie began to tremble. Surely this . . . The next instant they were by—safe and sound. It meant no more to him than a seat on the front at Brighton meant to her.

Later, Anthony announced that he thought she could sing.

" Not that I remember," he added hastily. The poor fellow was honest enough. " But there was a piano in the library, and I saw music about."

" I used to," said Valerie. " Would you like me to now ? "

" Oh, if you would. . . ."

Such pathetic anxiety could have but one sire.

Valerie shivered.

For half an hour, perhaps, she sang steadily. Anthony sat in a chair with his head in his hands. The airs were brutally familiar, the beautiful voice foreign. It was no good.

She gave him tea on the terrace before he left. And there, as well as they could, they thrashed things out.

" D'you want me to keep away ? " said Anthony suddenly.

Valerie regarded the toe of a little suède shoe.

" No," she said, " I don't. I love you, you know."

" But you said——"

" I know. Don't remind me of that. You don't mean to me what you did. But nothing else on earth means anything at all." She lifted her head and gazed into the park. Under the afternoon sun this made a royal picture. A Goldsmith might have caught the landscape's smile, a Boucher its dainty charm, but only a dying John of Gaunt could have heard its utterance. Valerie continued slowly, measuring her words: "You see, when I thought your memory was dead, I didn't care. The only thing that could have made me mind would have been your regret. But you didn't seem to care at all. So I didn't, either. But now—now that I know it's not dead—only asleep—perhaps because it's human to be a fool, I want it back. All of a sudden it's become a precious bit of you—a bit I can't spare. But I can't spare what's left of you, either, Anthony lad. Be sure of that."

Anthony rose to his feet and bared his head.

"I'm very rich," he said gently. "Because I was richer once, I'm not going to whine. As for my memory, if there's a God in heaven, it'll come back. And when it does—when it does, will you marry me, Valerie?"

"Yes," said Valerie, "I will."

"Till then—may we be betrothed?"

"Yes."

Anthony hesitated. Then—

"You're very good to me," he said, turning away.

In an instant the girl was on her knees at his feet.

"Anthony, Anthony," she wailed, "how can you talk like that?" She caught his hands and pressed them against her face. "You blessed, wonderful thing! I'm the very luckiest woman in all the world —and the most ungrateful. You talk about my being good. I'm wicked, graceless, cruel. 'Good to you.' I couldn't be good to you, Anthony. A priest can't be good to his god. Besides, I love you too much. D'you hear? I love you too much. It's because I love you so much that I've behaved as I have this miserable day. Yesterday was a shock—a frightful shock. I've been dazed—distracted ever since. . . ." She put her arms about him and buried her face in his coat. Anthony stood like a rock. "I won't come back this evening," she added quietly. "I want to be quite alone. But I'll come up tomorrow to stay, and if you'll ask me to dinner, I'll dine with you. Don't think I'm being nice. That's utter blasphemy. I'm just crazy about you, and that's the truth."

If ever a heart gave tongue, it did so then. If ever love was afire, that speech betrayed it.

Anthony lifted her up and kissed her mouth. . . .

It was a most natural action. Valerie herself would have been surprised, dismayed, if he had not done it. It was the acceptance of her oblation the touching and return of the cup. . . .

Yet, when she felt his touch, only by a most violent effort did she subdue a shudder. And when he kissed her, the blood froze in her veins.

Anthony noticed nothing, or, if he did, attributed it to the shaking she had had the day before. When all was said and done, he felt shaken himself—shaken and rather shy of his beautiful lady.

When it was time for him to go, she came to the steps. At the last he kissed her hand and remarked how cold it was.

"My hands were always cold," said Valerie.

Anthony read a meaning that was not there, and could have thrown up his hat. And she saw him read it, and could have burst into tears.

Then he entered the car and was whirled away. . .

Valerie almost fled to the library. Into her hands had been thrust the sleave of truth—the truth about her feeling for Anthony Lyveden. All she had to do was to unravel it. She put a match to the fire and curled herself in a chair. . .

Anthony was all her world. Whether she loved him or not, there was no one and nothing else. There never would be. That was as clear as daylight. More. Love him she did—desperately . . . more, perhaps, than ever she had loved him before, *so long as he did not love her.*

Anthony in repose she found most worshipful. She could sit all day at his feet. But the moment he became the lover, she loathed the sight of him. In a word, while she could love him, Anthony must not love her. Any protestation of love made her feel cold. A corporal expression of affection was simply revolting. Why? *Because he could not remember.*

Did she touch his hand—a million tender memories were behind that movement. Did he touch hers—he was impelled by some new motive, in which she had no share. It might be love : it might be—anything. She could take hold of Anthony, but Anthony must not respond. She could caress him, just as one clasps a casket—because of the relics it holds. She would be touching the old Anthony . . . the one she had worshipped and lost . . . the one who was dead . . dead. And the dead could not respond. If they did, it was gruesome—loathly. If they did, love was swallowed up in death—instantly. . .

Yes, there lay the truth.

She could go to him, but he could not return to her. When he tried . . .

Valerie shuddered.

As for Anthony, he was peering out of the limousine's window, marking Brooch's bulwarks and striving desperately to remember that he had seen them before.

CHAPTER VIII

STRAIGHT STREET

THE limousine sailed into the summer evening, leaving a long wash of dust to mark her passage. The cooler air suited her admirably, and there was now an effortless elasticity about her movements which set the cap of Drowsiness upon her passenger's head and then pulled it down over his eyes. This was as well, for the latter was worn out. Long ere the car reached Basingstoke, Anthony Lyveden was asleep.

The car sailed on.

Soon, with her peculiar magic, sundown set everything afire. Streams ran with golden water : meadows and dells were full of crimson light : pinewoods became the very gates of glory—peering between their bars, you saw the promise of another world : moors glowed and smouldered : peeping windows and weathercocks burst into flame : while the road itself curled in and out of sudden dusk and splendour, flashed between laughing hedgerows, dropped into sober bottoms and, now and again, swung over a solemn shoulder to march beside the pageant for a fantastic mile.

Sleeping steadily, Anthony saw none of these things. Indeed, he was deep in London before he waked, greatly refreshed and astonished that he had slumbered so long. He decided gratefully that if Nature was a good doctor, the chauffeur was an excellent nurse, and had more cause for gratitude than he imagined. If the heat of the day was over, not so its burden.

The journey was finished, Kensington Palace Gardens had been won, and Lyveden, who had just alighted, was in the act of thanking the chauffeur before he entered the house, when a taxi flung up the drive and, skidding with locked wheels to within six inches of the limousine's off fore wing, discharged its frantic passenger into an atmosphere of speechless indignation.

André Strongi'th'arm.

The girl flashed to the steps and seized Anthony by the arm.

" Quick ! " she panted, haling him to the door. " Quick ! Richard's inside. Richard—the man I'm engaged to. He's like a madman. He wouldn't hear me out, and he swore he'ld thrash Plague till he couldn't stand. I tried to stop him, but he threw me across the room and locked the door."

With a shaking hand Anthony rammed the key home. . . .

As the door yielded, a burst of passionate altercation assailed their ears. Then came a screech of fury, the sharp smack of a fist, the snarling worry of a dog, and the crash of a mighty weight meeting the floor.

Anthony hurled himself across the hall. . . .

An instant later the library's door was open, and the two were inside.

A man was standing straight in the middle of

the room—a proud, tremendous figure, with a fair, close-cut beard, thoughtfully pulling his moustache. His bearing, physique, and style were those of a ruler of men. Ears back, teeth bared, one paw raised, Patch stood at his feet, bristling with hatred, snarling up into his face—no empty threat, as the trickle of blood upon the great wrist argued. The man, however, did not appear to notice him. He was looking beyond at Sir Andrew, who, with a cut and swelling lip and one leg obviously out of action, was making violent but ineffectual endeavours to get upon his feet.

As Anthony entered, Sir Andrew beckoned him.

" Help me up," he said thickly. " Don't stand there gaping, you fool. I've hurt my knee. Help me up. He's struck me, and I'm going to break his back."

The stranger turned.

" Ah, Lyveden," he said lightly. " I'm glad to see you." He jerked his head at Plague. " Do as he says," he added. " I haven't thrashed him yet."

André flung herself upon his arm.

" Richard, Richard," she cried, " listen to me! If ever a man did you and me a good turn, it's that man there. You know me well enough. I don't beg anyone's pardon without good cause. Yet I apologized to him because——"

" Don't make it worse," said Winchester, setting her gently aside. Then he took a whip from the table. " Out of the way, Lyveden ! "

Anthony, who had helped Sir Andrew to his feet and then treacherously pushed him into a convenient chair, took no notice at all. Indeed, he had his

hands full. The knight was beside himself with
fury. That the man who struck him was alive was
bad enough : that his familiar friend should be
preserving the man's life sent him almost out of
his mind. He fought and raved fearfully. The
chair, however, was deep, and Anthony was behind,
with his hands on his shoulders. Sir Andrew could
have not risen to save his life.

" Lyveden," said Winchester again, " let him
get up."

Anthony looked him in the face.

" One at a time," he said quietly. " You must
deal with me first. And after you've dealt with
me, you shall deal with him."

" Don't be a fool," said the other ; " I've no quarrel
with you."

" You have," said Anthony. " But, if you'll
leave this house, I'll let that go."

Winchester frowned, and Sir Andrew stopped
struggling, screwed his head round and peered into
Anthony's face

After a little—

" I understand," said Winchester, " that you've
lost your memory. If you hadn't—you would remember that I mean what I say. That gentleman there "
—he pointed contemptuously to Plague—" has got
to go through the hoop. If you like to postpone
his chastisement for so long as it takes me to knock
you out, I can't prevent you. But it seems a futile
proceeding. It won't profit him and it'll damage
you."

Anthony laughed.

" Since you knew me," he said, " I've grown
whimsical." He looked down at his patron. " If

I take my hands from your shoulders, sir, will you stay still where you are?"

"No," roared Sir Andrew, "I won't! This is my show. The blackguard struck me, and I'll knock his face through his head."

"Afterwards, sir, afterwards. Let me——"

"I *won't!*" raged the knight. "I WON'T! Lemme get up, you hound!" He surged in the chair impotently. "Blast you, *lemme get up!*"

"Not till you promise to let me have first go."

The paroxysm of rage which this definite defiance provoked was truly frightful. Sir Andrew's complexion rapidly assumed the colour of a damson plum. That one or more blood-vessels must burst seemed to be beyond doubt. His secretary clung to his shoulders as a helmsman clings to a wheel in heavy weather. At last, however, the tempest blew itself out.

"All right," said Sir Andrew thickly. "An' if you don't kill him, I will. An' I'll kill you, any way," he added violently.

Anthony took out a handkerchief and wiped his face.

Then he stepped forward, smiling.

"Put down that whip," he said.

André was clinging to his arm.

"Stop, stop, Anthony! You're mad. You can't touch him. He's twice your weight, and—Richard " —she swung about—" but for these two men here, your life and mine would have been broken up. Is this your payment? Is this——"

"André," said Winchester shortly, " I've heard enough. With motives I'm not concerned. They may have been most worthy. So are the motives of the carter who breaks his horse's back. The gentleman sitting in the chair has to be taught manners "—Sir Andrew began to make a rattling noise —" has to be made to understand that, if he must bully, he should bully men. As for Lyveden, his blood's on his own fool's head. If he can't remember, I should think he could see that I'm the wrong man to cross."

"And I," said André quietly, "am the wrong woman. Give me that whip." Winchester hesitated, staring, and the girl took it out of his hand. "You prate to me of manners. Look to your own." She turned on Anthony and Plague. "And you—and you. You rotten crowd of wasters, where were you bred? Howling and slogging each other in front of me. I'm not a drab from the slums. I don't want to witness your beastly instincts. For ten solid minutes I've stood here, in this room, and been dishonoured. If I'd liked to scream, I could have had half Kensington here. But you all knew I wouldn't do that, because I should pay more dearly than any of you. So you banked on my not screaming. My teeth were drawn, and that was all that mattered. That I was alone—a woman, that I might be scared—revolted, didn't affect the case. And I am revolted. I feel literally sick. As men go, I'd thought you three weren't bad. I was wrong. You're as cheap and rank a bunch as ever I saw. There's nothing to choose between the lot of you. You're just trash: and I hope to God I never see any of you again!"

For a full minute nobody seemed to breathe. Then—

"I beg your pardon," said Anthony.

" Beg," said André, and cut him across the face.

The dog leaped at her hand, but Lyveden struck him aside and had him fast before he could leap again.

In dead silence the girl stepped to the door, opened it, and passed out.

As she crossed the hall, the chauffeur, butler, and footmen tried to make themselves scarce. They might have spared their pains. She never noticed them.

She opened the front door and left the house.

As she passed down the drive, she began to sob.

" It was the only way," she moaned, as one who has sold one treasure to save another. " The only way—to make sure. Richard won't touch him now."

This was quite true.

After an awkward silence, Winchester shook hands with Lyveden, humbly apologized to Plague, and went his way.

There was no more spirit in him. André had spiked his guns.

*   *   *   *   *

No one of those who, upon that memorable evening, assisted to transport the K.C. from his library to his bedroom will ever forget the episode. It would have lived, any way : but the invective alone, with which, as with some preserving chemical, their burden sprayed their travail, assured its incorruption.

The scene was Homeric, worthy of the Gobelins. No mere paint-brush could have caught the tremendous atmosphere. Between them, Anthony and four servants bore the injured giant as retainers their

wounded lord. A feature of the exploit, more embarrassing than traditional, was the lord's active interest
in the operation. From force of habit, the latter
directed his removal and constantly endeavoured,
during its progress, physically to correct and punish
any failure to appreciate his commands. His frantic
efforts, for instance, to reach the butler, who had
hold of his right foot, in order to inflict upon him
grievous bodily harm, threw everything into confusion—particularly the chauffeur, upon whose face his
master was depending for support in his adventure.

The steward hovered, vulture-like, about the pro-
cession, with smelling-salts and brandy. The Sealyham made an excited and distracting escort, bark-
ing until all present, except Sir Andrew, prayed
for death, circling dizzily about the *cortège* in the
open and settling down as an obstructive flank-
guard when the Narrows were reached. Indeed,
the ascent of the staircase stood out of the epic a
patch of true purple. The steward was given notice
at the foot: the footmen were sacked before the
turn was made: Anthony and the butler succumbed
in the course of the turning operation, and the chauffeur, who thought there was one more step than
in fact there was, was charged to destroy himself
that night.

Finally the bed-chamber was won: the valet
offered up a short prayer: the bearers withdrew,
and Anthony descended, sweating, to summon a
doctor.

As the steward closed the door, Sir Andrew called
him back and held out a five-pound note.

"You and your gang have earned it," he said
grimly.

The steward bowed.

"If you please, sir, I'ld—we'ld rather not. I only speak for the others, sir, when I say that we couldn't think of it. Not that we aren't most grateful, but there isn't one of us, sir, as wouldn't be proud to carry you to—to the Marble Harch, sir, if you'ld permit it."

"God forbid !" said his master.

"Oh, without doubt, sir," said the steward piously. "But——"

"I shall dine in this room," said Sir Andrew. "So will Major Lyveden. Good night."

"Good night, sir."

The doctor came and was reviled. Finding the knee sprained, he prescribed a recumbent position for seven days, and was instantly desired to go to hell for seven years. As he left the room a glass was thrown at him.

At last dinner was served.

Anthony was rent and cross-examined and rent again. Finally he was ordered to ring up Lady Touchstone and invite her to lunch the next day.

"Say it's important, and say you won't be here. Say I fell off the terrace and can't come to her. Ask what she'ld like to eat. Above all, say nothing about this evening's business."

"Very good, sir."

Five minutes later he reported that the lady would come, was deeply concerned, would like an omelet, some stewed fruit, and cheese straws, hoped very much that Sir Andrew would pass a good night.

The knight stared at the Sealyham, slumbering upon his bed.

"A discerning woman," he said. "And a better

friend to you and your runaway girl than either
of you deserve."

Anthony hesitated. Then—

"You make me a little uneasy," he said slowly.
"What are you going to say to Lady Touchstone?"

"What's that to do with you?"

"I don't know," said Lyveden. "That's just
why I'm uneasy. You see, she's Valerie's aunt.
And I couldn't bear Valerie to think that I was—
wire-pulling."

"If she knows you at all, she knows you're too
much of a fool," said Sir Andrew shortly. "Knaves
pull wires—not fools." He yawned and rang the
bell by the side of his bed. "Good night."

"Good night, sir," replied his secretary, picking
up Patch.

"And for the love of God, don't go out in the
Park to-morrow morning."

That Sir Andrew Plague, misogynist, steadfast
disbeliever in romance, should have been plunged
into the very surf of a passionate affair, sucked under-
neath, spewed up, drawn back and then sent sprawling
into the backset, was arguing Fate's belief in a rod
for the fool's back. That he should have been selected
to harness these turbulent breakers was Fate's idea
of a joke. That, having harnessed them, he was
not satisfied, but felt unaccountably impelled to still
their fret, was due to Lady Touchstone alone.

Cherchez la femme.

When a man who hates women and despises love
interferes on behalf of a lover and gets knocked out
for his pains, it might be thought that he would
kick himself with great violence, rend the particular
lover, and repair to some far country where women

are not allowed. Not so Sir Andrew. In the first place, he could not kick himself because the condition of his injured knee put any attempt at gymnastics out of the question. As we know, he rent Anthony ; but that was not so much because he was the lover as because Colonel Winchester was yet alive. Finally, he did not leave London, because a searching cross-examination of his secretary concerning the latter's relations with Valerie French had revealed that his work was not over. The 'work' of course, was nothing but a labour of love.

La femme came to lunch the next day and, having eaten and drunk, listened politely to the knight's account of his mishap. When he had finished, she observed gently enough that a man lying to a woman always reminded her of an amateur teaching a professional his job.

"Not that you're not quite good," explained her ladyship. "As one who knows, I think you shape very well. Your falsehood handicap would be about fourteen. But I'm about plus five. All women are. It's a gift, of course. We're just born liars. Never mind. I'm not a bit curious. How did Anthony get on ? "

Sir Andrew breathed very hard.

At length—

"From what I can gather," he said, " your niece sees fit to regret his loss of memory. Why the devil she should passes my comprehension. It's nothing to do with her. And, needless to say, she hasn't a leg to stand on. His present defect doesn't affect the contract. Mentally and physically the man's perfectly sound. But apparently she finds it inconvenient. Very well. Assuming she's sane, there must be something she wishes Major Lyveden to remember."

Lady Touchstone frowned.

" She probably wishes," she said, " that he remembered her."

Sir Andrew stared.

" I daresay she does," he snorted. " I wish that I could forget my age. But I don't let the fact that I can't interfere with my appetite. I repeat that, assuming she's sane, there must be something she wishes Major Lyveden to recall."

" And I," said Lady Touchstone, " repeat that that ' something ' is Valerie French. And, while I remember it, what delicious bread you gave me ! It's perfectly clear that your baker sleeps in the house. And I'm not surprised that misfortunes don't spoil your appetite. It'ld take a great deal to spoil mine if I kept a table like yours. Is it a he ? "

" I believe," said the knight, " it's a woman. Happily for us both, I've never seen her ; but when the Census was taken, her sex appeared on some paper I had to sign. We get on very well. I pay her as she likes to be paid, and she feeds me as I like to be fed. But to return to your niece. Why does she make this ridiculous stipulation ? "

" Does she ? "

" That's what it amounts to. Lyveden's a fool, of course. If he wasn't—he'ld snuff it out. But, so far as marriage is concerned, his mind's diseased. Instead of demanding performance, he desires to gratify her whim. He recognizes this caprice, dignifies it, confers upon it the rank of a condition—a condition precedent."

" Has he said so ? "

" Virtually. He fenced, of course, but his—er —his handicap's about forty-five."

Lady Touchstone laughed. Then she knitted her brow.

" Don't think too hardly of Valerie, and don't despise her squire. They're a remarkable pair. Anthony's desperately honest, and his judgment is sound. Valerie, I want you to meet. She's not only astoundingly lovely, but she has a clearer brain than almost any woman I've ever known. As for her honesty—well, she's a glaring exception to the rule. Her handicap is about the same as yours. They've both suffered most heavily by no fault of their own. They were made for each other, and if they were parted to-morrow for good and all, neither the one nor the other would ever so much as look upon anyone else. I know you mock at love, so I won't refer to it again, but I tell you we're dealing here with something which is above contracts, which no man-made canons can touch. Two perfect, gentle specimens of the human race have been brought together : as one who is interested in humanity, surely you must desire their permanent union."

" Madam," replied Sir Andrew, speaking with considerable warmth, " I do nothing of the sort. But for the fact that a marriage has been arranged, I should seek to prevent my secretary from committing an unwarrantable act of folly which he will live to regret. Since, however, the bargain has already been struck, I am ready to do what I can to compass its execution."

" Your choice of words," said Lady Touchstone, " suggests a hideous comparison. I believe you think all marriages should be solemnized upon the scaffold, and that, when sentence has been passed, some official should bawl, ' So perish all idiots.' "

Sir Andrew shifted uneasily, forgetting his injured knee. The squeal of agony with which he repaired the omission sent his guest's heart into her mouth.

" Oh, what have I said ? " she wailed. " What have I said ? I assure you——"

" Nothing ! " shouted her host. " Nothing at all. I—I beg your pardon." With a shaking finger he indicated the offending joint. " This blasted knee, madam, is enough to drive me mad. I loathe and detest inaction. I hate being girded and carried before my time. Yet if I so much as move . . ."

He let the sentence go and flung himself back in his chair like a petulant child.

Lady Touchstone was by his side, and her hand on his arm.

" I am so awfully sorry. I know so well what it means. But please try to remember that now you're in Nature's hands. Pain's her signal to stop. If you obey her orders, she treats you better and quicker than any leech alive."

The giant blinked at the slight, gloved fingers upon his sleeve and, after a little, up into the smiling face.

" You're very gracious," he said humbly.

With a heightened colour, my lady resumed her seat and, the iron being hot, presently beat out a promise that the knight would lie abed for two days.

" Of course," she concluded, " I should never have come to-day. It was very handsome of you and most unselfish. You've deliberately retarded your recovery because you were anxious to help two—two—idiots to their doom."

P

" I was anxious," replied Sir Andrew, " to have your advice. Now that I have it——"

" What counsel have I bestowed ? "

" You have advised me that Miss French is sane, that she desires to be personally remembered, that her desire is just. I honour and accept your advice."

Lady Touchstone smiled.

" It's very nice of you to accept what you do not believe."

Sir Andrew reddened.

" You are more eloquent than you think," he said huskily. " I pray you forget my outburst just now. It was the last, blind rush of the bayed boar."

Lady Touchstone caught her breath.

After a moment the giant continued, frowning.

" I have always looked upon women as an unnecessary evil. My mother I never knew. My father died when I was fourteen. In fourteen years I saw him seven times. I was reared by two aunts, neither of whom was necessary, both of whom were evil. They believed that, but for me, they would have inherited my father's fortune—and used me accordingly. At their hands I endured penal servitude for ten long years. . . . I have fought shy of women ever since.

" Things sentimental I have always scorned and eschewed. Finding life brief, I sought to eliminate such stuff as weighed nothing. Sentiment stood first upon my list. I judged it idle, an empty toy, froth. When I found it clinging to my sleeve, I tore it off and stamped it under my feet.

" It follows that the love of women seemed to me a very perilous vanity, a snare of the devil himself."

The knight paused and passed a hand across his eyes.

"Well, madam, you and Lyveden have opened my eyes. He has shown me that there is a sentiment which is not sickly, which, sired by honesty, illumines the cold severity of life. You and he have shown me that 'there are more things in heaven and earth than were dreamt of in my philosophy.'"

"I'm—I'm very glad," whispered Lady Touchstone, who was upon the edge of tears. "What——what have I shown you?"

Sir Andrew stared upon the floor.

"You?" he said. "You have shown me that women are not always unnecessary and not necessarily evil."

* * * *

One week had gone halting by.

André Strongi'th'arm had left London: Sir Andrew was walking with a stick: Lady Touchstone was looking tired; Valerie and Anthony Lyveden were the best of friends.

The sky was clear enough, but the atmosphere was unreal. The blue bird was there, but he was off colour.

Looking upon her niece and Anthony, Lady Touchstone felt inclined to scream: looking upon Lady Touchstone, Sir Andrew snorted and blew and, finally, begged her acceptance of a dozen of port.

It was this solicitude for her corporal health which stung the lady into action.

She fell upon Valerie that evening.

"A drink," she said, raising her eyes to heaven. "He actually offers me a drink. It's rather pathetic

—like a child pressing a toy upon a woman in tears."

"I hope you'll take it," said Valerie. "I'm sure——"

"I had to give up port," snapped Lady Touchstone, "before you were born. Besides, I don't want booze: I want exercise. Why am I here, in London? The streets are up, and Anthony Lyveden's found. Why on earth don't we get a move on?"

"You mean . . . ?"

"What I say. A move. I don't care what it is. But this appalling inaction is breaking my heart. The play's the thing—not the interval."

"What you really mean," said Valerie, "is that I have provided a ghastly anticlimax. Anthony's entrance was worked up into a perfect sunrise of undreamed-of ecstasy—I worked it up—and, now the millennium's here, we're talking about the weather."

"Let me at once admit," replied her aunt, "that I couldn't have put it so well. Having done that, I feel at liberty to tell you that you ought to be ashamed of yourself."

"But is it my fault, Aunt Harriet? Is it my fault?"

"That the time is out of joint? No. But you alone can reduce the dislocation." Valerie knitted her brows. "Think. What can anyone do except you? How can anyone move until you give the direction? We're all—Sir Andrew included, and Anthony most of all—afraid to breathe, for fear of upsetting the boat. I'm only speaking now because I'm desperate, because I can't sit still and watch us drift and drift. . . ."

" Whither ? "

" Who knows? That's the dreadful part of it. We can't see a yard ahead. We may be drifting on to rocks or breakers——"

" Or into harbour."

" No," said Lady Touchstone. " And that's the danger. No ship that ever was launched drifted into harbour. You've got to work to get there."

Valerie pondered awhile.

Presently—

" Shall I ask them to come to Bell Hammer ? "

" Just as you please. I can't advise you because you've got the chart. But it's a move of some sort, and I'ld rather drift at Bell Hammer than drift in Town."

" I'll ask them to-morrow," said Valerie. " I suppose they'll come."

" If they do," said Lady Touchstone, " my doom is sealed. Sir Andrew's trying to decide whether to marry me or no. And when he sees me on the terrace in my grey corduroy, finishing that jumper for Anthony, it'll be all over. But I don't think I can, can I ? "

Valerie laughed mischievously.

" I can't advise you," she said, " because you've got the chart." Lady Touchstone choked. " As an uncle, I should be very proud of him. And if, when he loses Anthony and you lose me——"

" Andrew Plague," said her aunt, leaning forward and looking into Valerie's eyes, " is a man of action." She paused. " If he decides to marry me, he will not wait upon ' I would.' And, if I were to reply that I would marry him if—when you and Anthony are wed, he would immediately withdraw his offer.

He has no use for contingencies dependent upon the whim of an inscrutable Fate. . . . Neither have I. When you told Anthony that you would marry him when he remembered you, you did a barbarous thing." Valerie started. "Yes, barbarous. He loved you passionately. He loves you passionately still. Is he to suffer because of his affliction?"

The girl looked away and down, wringing her pointed fingers. The woman lay back in her chair and shaded her eyes. After a moment, she continued to speak—very tenderly.

"The Lord gave his memory. As a little, motherless child, that wonderful spring began to well at the back of his tiny brain. First he remembered little prayers, asking God nightly to 'make him a good boy.' Then he remembered nursery rhymes—immemorial toys and jingles, sacred nonsense. Every book of those rhymes should have a rubric. 'In nurseries and places where they lisp, here followeth the Anthem.' Well, that wonderful spring has failed. That abundant, refreshing fountain, in which we go and plunge our tired minds a hundred times an hour, has been dried up. The Lord gave, and the Lord hath taken away. Don't think I'm being harsh. I understand. But, Valerie, unless you can say to yourself, 'I don't love him '——"

"I do!" wailed Valerie. "I do! But . . ."

" —unless you can say, 'I know I can't make him happy,' unless you can say, 'I believe he will make me unhappy,' it is your bounden duty, after all that has passed, to take that condition back. Think. If he had no sight, wouldn't you give him your eyes? And thank the good God for the blessed privilege? Of course you would. Then let him

share your memory. Make him free of your beautiful
fountain, and let him bathe his poor, tired brain.
When I think of that poor, dear fellow, straining
heart and soul, for love of you, to wring a favour
out of the fist of Fate——"

"Don't, don't!" cried Valerie, lifting her head.
"Don't whip me any more. I never meant to be
cruel." She fell on her knees and buried her face
in Lady Touchstone's lap. "I love every hair of
his head. I'ld give him my soul to-morrow—you
know I would. If he was ill, and it would help him,
they should bleed me white. And you know how
little I'ld care about his memory if only it—really—
was—dead."

"'Vanity of vanities,'" said Lady Touchstone
sadly. "'All is vanity.' Don't think I'm lectur-
ing. I'm crying—in the wilderness. Vanity's the
terrible freemasonry to which all women subscribe.
If I were a man, perhaps I could argue with you.
But now you've made me a sign—you've invoked
our tacit, cursed sisterhood, and, because I was
born a woman, you've shut my mouth."

Valerie looked up into the other's face.

"I'm glad," she said gently, "I'm glad you understand. . . . For now, when I marry Anthony, as
I shall—if he'll take me—within the month, it'll
be the greatest comfort in all the world to know
that you're there—at my shoulder, that you've
got a smile for me, which he can't fathom, that, no
matter what's written, you'll always be able to read
between the lines."

Lady Touchstone wept.

Presently she smiled through her tears.

"I might be your sister, Valerie."

Her niece put her arms about her neck.

"Dear Harriet," she said, and kissed her.

Lady Touchstone closed her eyes and blessed God.

*   *   *   *   *

Patch was plainly delighted to see Bell Hammer again, and when he found his log in its proper place he lifted up his voice in heartfelt gratitude.

Anthony watched his excitement with hungry eyes.

He supposed that the log was a toy and, as such, kept for the terrier in the bedroom which he had used; and the dog remembered his plaything as a matter of course, and——

Here the billet was brought and laid at Anthony's feet. Two bright, brown eyes stared up expectantly into his: a short, white tail moved slowly to and fro. Clearly the game was waiting, and he—he had forgotten the rules. . . .

Lyveden stooped and caressed the eager head.

"Not to-day, old chap," he said gently. "To-morrow, perhaps. Or—or the day after."

The man was not unhappy. At times he was radiant. After all, as lovers go, he was unearthly rich. He had been given the very fee simple of Paradise itself. True, the estate was in trust, but one day the trust would be broken and he would enter in . . one day. . . .

Till then—well, he was very lucky: he had much to be thankful for. A serious flaw in his title had been done away. He was, so to speak, in the straight. He would, of course, have liked to be able to see the post—have some sort of idea how long the straight was. Still . .

Valerie was very sweet—very. No one could have been sweeter. He was most awfully proud of her. And—and she was splendid company. . . .

Company. The word seared his brain. His wonderful, peerless shepherdess—his queen—his darling . . . was an excellent pal—*pal.* Yes, that was it —*pal.* Hell, how he loathed the word! Pal. . . . More. The bower had been rearranged—turned into a lounge, a parlour. . . . Arcadia had been converted into a recreation-ground. . . . And Love —Love had been decently clothed in a coat and trousers, with a nice, fat gag in his mouth and cuffs on his little pink wrists. . . . The exquisite master piece was gone, and a vulgar parody hung in its sacred room.

Anthony groaned.

It was not that he wanted to sit in the shade of an oak and sigh all day into a reed; it was not that he wanted to lie at the feet of Amaryllis, setting her brows to music and calling the heaven to wonder at her soft, dark hair. He wanted to take her hand and run down the dewy glades: he wanted to lift her to pick the dangling fruit—to stand with her on the hill-top and watch the sun get up, mark the breath of her nostrils upon the evening air, plunge with her into the horseplay of the wind: he wanted to hear the woods give back their laughter: he wanted to know that Love was enlarged, free— free to look out of her eyes, free to float upon her voice, free to sit upon his shoulders and flash in her smile. . . .

Lyveden pulled himself together, wrenched his mind out of this perilous groove and tried to thank his stars for providing such a nice recreation-ground.

It was vital that he should not lose heart—*vital*. So long as he did not lose heart, he had the ring on his finger . . . the magic ring which, when he had found the trick of it, would turn the recreation-ground into the Garden of Eden.

Then he sat down on his bed and racked his brain until his head ached. . . .

*   *   *   *   *

Six hours had passed by.

Valerie, her aunt, and Sir Andrew had retired, and Lyveden and Patch were sharing the library fire.

This was too good to be left.

Most of the logs had melted into a quilt of red-grey ash, and such as were still surviving had become mere rosy brands, which winked and glowed silently and, from time to time, settled peacefully into their feathery grave.

The Sealyham was lying on his side before the hearth. Anthony was sitting on a corner of the broad club-kerb, smoking lazily and remarking the silence of the country with grateful ears. He enjoyed it amazingly, this peace. To listen, with windows open, and hear no sound, save the deliberate movement of a grave-faced clock, was fascinating. . . .

A tall door opened, and Valerie came in.

Patch started up, and Anthony got upon his feet.

" And why," said the girl, advancing, " aren't you in bed ? You're tired. You admitted you were. Yet you sit up."

" It's a way children have," said Anthony. " I'm so pleased with the pretty fire my hostess gave me. And I'm not at all sure that isn't why you've come

back. I thought you looked at it longingly when
you went—to bed."

"As a matter of fact," said Valerie, stooping to
stroke the terrier, "I came to see you."

"You're a brilliant hostess," said Anthony, "but
an unjust judge. You blame me for sitting up,
and then deliberately incite me to repeat the offence."

Valerie laughed.

"It's a way women have," she said.

With that, she stepped over the Sealyham and
took her seat on the kerb. Anthony resumed his,
and, having knocked out his pipe, stretched up his
hand and set it upon the broad stone mantelpiece.
Then he folded his arms and looked at the beautiful
face four feet away.

Valerie stared, smiling, into the fire.

Miss French was one of those women who are
full of natural grace. She never took thought how
she should sit or stand, but she never assumed an
unbecoming pose. As a Naiad should sit by a fountain, so sat Valerie by that wood fire.

Her turned, down-looking head gave you her
lovely profile—straight nose, proud, sensitive mouth,
delicate chin. The column of her neck rose, white
and gleaming, from the broad mouth of her dress.
This was simple—a rich, plain purple—low-waisted,
sleeveless, admirably cut, with points touching the
ground. Black satin shoes, black stockings enhanced
the beauty they shod. She sat sideways, straight-
backed, much as a woman sits upon a horse. Her
small, firm hands were folded upon her thigh. The
toe of one little slipper rested upon the floor: the
other lay close, braced against the silk of her stock-
ing, four inches below the knee.

The form was that of a woman : the pose, the
air, those of an artless child. As for her beauty,
this was neither childish nor feminine : it was that
of the wild flower.

" D'you know," said Valerie slowly, " I'm twenty-
six ? "

The man regarded her, setting his head on one
side.

" I think I'ld 've said you were younger, but, to
tell you the truth, I've never thought of it at all.
You don't suggest years or the passing of time. In
fact, you discountenance them. When you speak
of your age, it's like a man in waders pointing out
that he's standing in water."

" Nevertheless," said Valerie. " I'm twenty-six.
And in a fortnight's time I shall be twenty-seven.
. . . Yes, in two short weeks. You see, I'm very
shrewd. I've given you just nice time to think
of a present. . . . And now, having been so con-
siderate, I'm going to spoil it all and ask you to let
me choose your present myself. . . . I'll tell you
what I want. *I want your name.*"

" Valerie ! "

As Anthony started to his feet, the girl swung
round and caught the lapels of his coat.

" Listen, lad, listen. I say, I want your name.
For the moment—that's all . . . for the moment.
. . But if you'll do me the honour to give me
that—marry me quietly here on my birthday morning—well, you'll make me wonderfully happy,
Anthony dear, and, I think, the proudest woman
in all the world."

There was a long silence.

Then—

" What is love ? " said Anthony, quietly enough. The girl started. " Don't think I'm being dramatic. I want to know. I think I love you. In a way, I think you love me. I asked you to be my wife. You've said that you will—in a way. My impulse is to dance. And yet. . . . We're young and goodly, we two. Are we in love ? "

" I think so. Use my eyes and look back. We were—passionately."

" ' Were '—yes. Have you outgrown that rapture ? "

Valerie shook her head.

" No more than you."

" You mean that it's in abeyance . . . pent up ? "

" Yes," said Valerie.

Anthony stared upon the floor.

" I wonder," he said. And then again, " I wonder."

The small, white hands slid away, and the girl slipped back to her corner of the club-kerb.

" You see," he went on presently, " I feel so much in the dark. That first day was different. The dark didn't matter at all. In fact, there was no dark. But now—now I've eaten of the tree of the knowledge of good and evil, and I can see the clouds."

" You'ld like to wait ? " said Valerie. " Well, it's natural enough. In a sense I've played with you."

" I told you my impulse was to dance. My impulse is to leap at the offer you make. I'm trying to talk dispassionately, you know. Well, my impulse is to snatch every wretched crumb I can get. My impulse is to take you in my arms, hold you as you've never been held, and then take the pins out of your glorious hair to see what it looks like when it's about

your shoulders. . . . But then you know that."
He folded his arms and laughed. " No. You say
that the return of my memory will set things right.
You're confident, persuaded of that. And I want
to be sure, for your sake, that your prophecy is sound.
You see, I want to be fair. If you marry me, you're
done. You can't go back."

" What of yourself ? " said Valerie.

Anthony shrugged his shoulders.

" I love you," he said.

" And I . . . ? "

He took his old seat upon the fender.

" That's different," he said positively. " The
squire adores his queen : the queen, her king. When
the squire becomes king——"

" Anthony, Anthony, what's the matter with
me ? You call me a queen, dress up my shame in
honourable words, turn my miserable——"

Anthony checked her with a touch.

" My queen can do no wrong."

Valerie covered her face.

" Listen," she said. " For more than a year,
now, I've loved you. The first time I ever saw you
I loved you as I do now. We never made love,
you and I. We just exchanged hearts the very
first time we met. I loved you, body and soul—as
I do now. Your smile, your laughter, your voice,
your strength and gentleness—all these things were
the breath by which I lived. When you touched
me, mirrored yourself in my eyes, kissed my hand,
I loved you most of all : and when you took me
in your arms, the world stood still. I used to long
to be married. I wanted to be with you all the
time. I wanted to wake in the night and see you

asleep by my side, bend over you, kiss your hair.
. . . I want to now." She lifted her head slowly
and met his eyes. "I've read about love. I've
seen a woman's eyes light when her man came into
the room. But I think our love was supernatural.
It was like a cord strung tighter than cords are ever
strung. A breath made it vibrate. Our understanding was infinite. Our sympathy was so deep
that it was almost absurd. We weren't lovesick.
We never pawed one another. We never had to be
together all day long. Some of our happiest moments
were spent apart—*apart*, Anthony. . . Sometimes,
in those last weeks before you disappeared, you—
you used to go to Town just for the day. Well,
those days gave us a chance of focusing our love.
It was like standing back from a picture to see it
in its true light. I told you so once, and you laughed
and said you agreed and that, since we both felt
the same, we'd better remain single : and then you
picked me up and put me on this mantelpiece and
asked what it looked like from there. And the
Pleydells came into the room before I was down,
and Boy put up Adèle to keep me company, and
Berry stood between us and said he was a cuckoo-
clock." She broke off with a half-laugh, half-sob
which tore Anthony's heart. The next instant she
had herself in hand. "Well, there you are. I'm
getting away from the point. We shared everything, you and I. *Everything*. Every slightest
emotion. I can't explain why or how. It was a
miracle : and yet it seemed the most natural thing
on earth. . . .

"And now—there's something, Anthony, that we
can't share. It's not a chance sensation—I could

bear that. It is that very miracle that I've been speaking of. Source, stream and sea—every shining inch that was our heritage, is mine alone. You can't inherit it . . . till you remember . . ."

His head bowed, Anthony sat very still.

The girl went on—fiercely.

"Why should that matter so terribly—make such a difference? I can't explain. There's something I can't control. Perhaps I love you too much. Perhaps the cord's too tight—too sensitive. Perhaps it is that miracles go their own way—override instinct. . . . But I can't pretend, dear, because that's blasphemy. We're treading holy ground. . . . I love you. I love to be with you. I love to do what you do—share your life. But there's a gap in our relations that only your memory can fill. Your sympathy is strange: your understanding a substitute. I ask you for bread, Anthony, and you give me a stone. . . . It's not your fault, lad, it's not your fault. And God knows—God knows it isn't mine. And when—when you remember. . . ." She fell on her knees beside him and put her arms about his neck. "Anthony, Anthony, I love you! 'Love'? The word's useless. You're the only thing in all the world that matters. I'm just mad about you, my darling, but you mustn't be mad about me."

Anthony looked into the deep blue eyes.

"I think," he said slowly, "I think I see what you mean. I've forgotten our precious masonry, and yet I'm using the signs. When I kiss you, I'm speaking a language which I don't understand. You don't know what prompts me to do it: you only know that its motive is foreign to you—doesn't spring from that heritage which once was ours. And that heritage—that masonry is something you can't renounce. Whether you would or no, the gods won't let you. . . . Yes, my dear, I see, I understand. . . . And I'm easy now. Your prophecy is sound. When my memory returns, it—it'll set things right." He looked away suddenly. " I'm sure it will return," he added. " I'm sure it will. But . . . Supposing—supposing it shouldn't, Valerie . . ."

" It will, my Anthony, it will."

" It—it mightn't."

" It will," breathed Valerie. " It will."

He turned his head again and looked again into her eyes. The stars were there now, and her whole face was alight with love and eagerness. Her proud lips were parted, and the warm perfume of her breath beat fast upon his chin. And her arms were about his neck. . . .

" Yes," he said shakily, " it will."

Then for the second time he turned away.

The arms slipped from his neck, and Valerie rose to her feet.

Anthony stood up and put his hands behind him.

" So the queen," he said gently, " cast her bread upon the waters and married her squire. And she never regretted this because, while others looked upon her as the squire's lady, the squire never forgot that she was his queen."

Valerie took his head between her cool palms.

" She was a very lucky woman," she said tremulously.

Then she drew down his head and kissed his eyes.

CHAPTER IX

THE SWINE'S SNOUT

A CARDINAL laid down his pen and sat back in his chair. For the last three days he had wished for tidings from England, and wished in vain. And now another postman had passed and had left no letters. . . .

His Eminence rose to his feet and started to pace the room, with his chin in his hand. For all his simple faith, John, Cardinal Forest, was growing uneasy.

A servant entered the chamber, salver in hand.

" The postman returned, Monseigneur. He had overlooked this dispatch."

The prelate ripped open the letter with an impatient forefinger.

Bell Hammer,
New Forest.

Dear John,   *Sept. 24th.*

The weather is improving, and the glass is slowly going up. That stifling, thunderous atmosphere has been done away, so far as I was concerned, in the very nick of time. I tell you, I was being choked. But now, upon the seventh day of October, Valerie and Anthony Lyveden are to be wed, and I can breathe again. I know this will bring you to England, and the thought exhilarates me. If the Vatican refused you leave, I should wire to the Pope. Our little crowd is huddled about the gate of Paradise, knocking and ringing and staring between the bars. But the porter will hear you. . . .

To Anthony his loss of memory means nothing at all : to Valerie it means—everything. It meant nothing to her, either, till he remembered André Strongi'th'arm. . . . Yet it is not just vanity. Valerie is not like that. There is vanity there, but there is something else. So long as his memory was dead, it was out of the question—like the moon. Then, suddenly, the moon was available. Somebody else had had it—for half an hour. . . . There is nothing like potential possession for making a thing desirable. No collector covets the Venus of Milo, because she is not for sale. But if the Louvre were " To be Sold, Furnished," half the rich men in America would be licking their lips. I am, of course, discreetly begging the question. Already your shrewd forefinger has found the flaw in my plea, which is that I am valuing his memory at more than it is worth. It is, you will rightly say, not to be compared with Venuses or moons. I cannot help that. Neither can Valerie. You know that she is not whimsical. You know it, John. Yet she craves to be remembered. She smothers her craving as much as ever she can ; but it is there, in her heart. And Anthony knows this, and would readily sell his soul to give her her heart's desire. . . .

That is the sum of my trouble—trouble which no outsider would ever suspect. Valerie seems radiant ; Anthony the happiest of men. The Pleydells dined with us last night ; the Alisons arrived after dinner ;

they all danced in the gallery, and at two o'clock this morning I felt twenty-six. I confess that six hours later I felt four score, but, then, the flesh is weak. Oh, the glass is rising without a shadow of doubt.

When they are married, they will go abroad for some months ; certainly they will visit Rome and sit at your feet, so you must come quickly and give them just cause for veneration. As you know, they will be provocatively rich. Anthony's place in Dorsetshire is very fine ; the house is warm and red, and was designed by Inigo Jones ; its staircase makes my mouth water. The estate itself is considerable and very lovely. His town house is a convenient luxury ; six tiled bathrooms and a passenger lift. He has bought a new Rolls, as he says, to assert his opulence, and we all four float about the country with the smug superiority of profiteers. ' All four,' I say . . .

Andrew Plague, whom, if I have done him justice in other letters, you must be itching to meet, is a tower of sanity and strength. I have never met anyone whose contributions to every kind of conversation were so consistently invaluable. His reputation is unspeakable, but Anthony or I stumbled upon the rich vein of humour which underlies his nature and has never been exploited before. Its yield is amazing. This is as well, for I am to be his wife. I am indeed. When you come, you will see why. For one thing, there are some honours too high to be declined ; for another, his personality is most compelling—I simply dared not refuse ; finally, I love children—and he is nothing but a great child that has never been understood. He insists that he does not love me—is most emphatic upon this point. He has, he declares, the greatest regard for me—delights in my company, but that is all. After all, it is a child's prerogative to lay down the laws of the game. I play it gravely—at times with tears in my eyes. He reminds me of Samson's lion. 'Out of the strong came forth sweetness.' How wild the lion would have been, could he have foreseen his posthumous philanthropy!

He will go on with his work—for a while, at any rate. At the moment he is on holiday—his first for twenty-five years. He likes it so well that his clerk is at his wits' end. The finest mill at the Bar, the only mill which never, never stopped, has at last come to rest. Solicitors can't get their grist ground. They won't go elsewhere, but keep on demanding their meal. And Andrew sits on the terrace and gloats placidly over the consternation he is causing. Not all the time, of course. I won't allow that. Yesterday we made him help Anthony to change a wheel. He protested violently, but I reminded him of Mucius Scævola and dissolved his wrath in a posset of toothsome wit which he brewed at my expense. I meant Cincinnatus, of course. Now he is most interested in cars and is to learn to drive. I told you he was a child.

And so, you see, our spikenard is exquisite stuff. So clear and exquisite, John, that it shows up that speck of a fly which I have dealt with. If it were cruder ointment, the fly would pass.

Affectionately yours,

HARRIET TOUCHSTONE.

P.S.—Yes, of course, I am hoping most desperately that he'll remember you. If you were here with them, you'ld be catching at straws. Besides, he might—easily.

His Eminence picked up a diary and knitted his brows. . . .

That evening he made his arrangements.

He left for the county of Hampshire the following day.

*   *   *   *   *

"The almanac's out," said Lady Touchstone. "The calendar's lost its place. To-morrow's October, and here's another midsummer's day." She turned to the sideboard. "And mushrooms and all."

"Let me put on the lid," laughed Valerie. "Or can't you bear it?"

"My dear," said her aunt, "my cup is bottomless. And don't talk of lids. It hasn't got one."

"Uncle John's on his way."

Lady Touchstone clasped her hands.

"I shall go to Church this morning," she announced tremulously, "whether there's a service or not. It's —it's only decent."

Sir Andrew looked up from his letters and into the park.

"Will you drive me to Brooch after breakfast?" he said, quietly enough.

"I will," said Anthony.

The women heard the request and wondered, but not for long. After all, the K.C.'s affairs were high matters, and Lyveden was still in his confidence, if not in his pay.

The meal proceeded cheerfully.

Sir Andrew had no desire to be driven to Brooch —and, for the matter of that, no intention, either. But he was extremely anxious to talk with Lyveden undisturbed.

Let us see why.

The moment the knight had appreciated that the curing of Anthony's defect was seriously desired, he had appreciated also that there was only one way to go about it. Whether even that way would lead to success, no one on earth could tell. But there was no other way at all. What exasperated Sir Andrew was his knowledge that the way in question was barred—barred by a flimsy rail, only meet, to his mind, to be trodden under foot. This was the Rail of Sentiment.

Valerie French was desiring that Lyveden's memory should return. Very well. It *had* returned once . . . once only . . . for a moment of time. And that was at the instance of André Strongi'th'arm. . . . Reason suggested bluntly that *the latter should try again.* There was a chance—a good sporting chance that she could develop her success, that she would be able to coax the capricious truant back into its cage. The devil of it was that the lady could not be employed. . . .

Why? Because, forsooth, fruit of her picking would lose its flavour. Miss Valerie French was nice—*nice.* So she had the grapes what did it matter whose fingers reached them down? Such fastidiousness was grotesque—sickening. . . .

However, care as he might, Sir Andrew was so sure that André's agency would be unwelcome that he had not so much as hinted at such a venture even to his affianced wife. Instinctively he knew that to do so would be to waste his time. The flimsy rail, in her eyes, was a five-barred gate—which it was sacrilege to approach. These women. . . .

For all that, an honest firm of detectives had not lost sight of the girl. The knight, for what it was worth, received a report of her movements every morning . . . for what it was worth. . . .

It was the latest report, delivered by hand at breakfast, which made Sir Andrew so anxious to talk with Lyveden.

Hitherto the road had been closed—by a rail or a gate. Now it was about to be obliterated. In less than thirty-six hours it would have ceased to exist.

I have, I suppose, a weakness for letting things speak for themselves. Five minutes ago I thrust an original document into your hands. And now, sirs, here is another. In a sense, I am avoiding my duty. Yet this I do, not of laziness, but in a belief that evidence at first-hand is preferred to secondary, however tricked out and garnished the latter may be.

PRIVATE AND CONFIDENTIAL.

Sept. 29th.

Sir,

We beg to enclose a copy of the further information, regarding Miss S., obtained by our agent, and received by us this evening at eleven o'clock.

Your obedient servants,

LACKLESS AND CO.

MISS S.

Thursday, September 29th.

This lady left Chipping Norton for London to-day. She was met at Paddington by Col. Winchester, and proceeded to the Berkeley Hotel.

They lunched in the restaurant, and left the hotel together at 2 p.m.

Miss S. returned alone at 6.45 p.m.

At 8 p.m. she proceeded to the Carlton Grill, where she was joined by Col. Winchester.

Shortly before 9.30 p.m. Col. Winchester escorted her back to the Berkeley Hotel, leaving her at the door. She did not go out again.

Observation concluded at 10.30 p.m.

I have ascertained that :—

(a) Two passages have been taken in the names of Col. and Mrs. Winchester on the Castle Rising, *which leaves Southampton for Cape Town on Saturday next.*

(b) Col. Winchester and Miss S. are to be married to-morrow (Friday) before the registrar.

(c) Immediately after their marriage the lady will proceed alone to Southampton, where rooms have been reserved for to-morrow (Friday) night at the Grand Hotel.

(d) Col. Winchester will proceed to Southampton on Saturday next by the boat-train which will be run in connection with the Castle Rising.

By a quarter-past ten Sir Andrew, Anthony, and Patch were in the Rolls, and the latter was stealing down the long avenue into a flashing wonderland of green and silver.

The forest keeps the road from Bell Hammer to Brooch, walls it with bracken, wards it with beech-woods, screens it with sentinel firs, honours it with the majesty of reverend oaks. And in due season, this side of Napery Green, a certain pride of maples will find for it a sovereign's escort, gorgeous and brilliant beyond belief. Your progress, sirs, may be royal, any day of the week. But drench all these champions with dew and then clap the gay sunshine on to their trappings. . . . Sirs, you shall see a parade which will beggar Bravery itself. More. The cool, fresh atmosphere is charged with the bouquet of a forgotten wine—wine that was trodden by Romance, bottled by History. You shall, if you please, snuff the very perfume of dreams. On either side, magnificence of green, laced all with silver, stands up and peers or nods its dazzling plumes; the yellow road becomes a scented gallery driven through laughing magic, raised by some Oberon to please his queen; and every sunlit glade leads to some Castle Peerless, each hollow hides the splendid fret of chargers, and every glistering brake stifles the echoes of some haunting call.

When they had gone, perhaps, three-quarters of a mile, Sir Andrew touched Anthony upon the arm.

" We're coming to a road on the right—a private road. I marked it the other day."

" I know," said Anthony. " There's a gate."

" That's right. I want to go that way."

" Right," said Lyveden. " I don't know where it leads, but——"

" I assume it leads to privacy. That's what I want."

The gate appeared, and Anthony slowed down.

" I'll get out," he said, " and you drive her through. It's all practice. Put her in first and——"

" Another time," said Sir Andrew, opening his door. " I want to get on now—to where we can talk "

He alighted and opened the gate.

Wondering what was afoot, Anthony passed through. . . .

Two minutes later the highway was out of sight, and the car had dropped into a little dell, with a fair greensward on either side and a whispering splash before. Thick screens of foliage turned the spot into a natural court. Indeed, but for the alleys letting the narrow road, the close, green walls stood

snug and flawless. Luck was with the two men.
They had stumbled upon the very parlour of Seclusion
itself.

Anthony slowed to a standstill without a word.
Then he stopped the engine and opened his door.
Patch leaped out excitedly and stared about him.

The dog regarded the car as a magic carpet. Its
function was to carry him to pleasant places. If
during a run he was not permitted to alight, the
carpet had not come off. . . .

After a moment's inspection of his surroundings,
he decided that this morning the carpet had done
very well. The sward was sweet and might have
been laid—probably had been laid—for him to gambol
on. As for the brook . . .

He made for the brown water, panting, going upon
three legs.

Sir Andrew lighted a cigar and tilted his hat over
his eyes. Anthony proceeded quietly to fill a pipe.

" Circumstances," said the knight slowly, " have
forced my hand. I have formed a certain opinion.
I formed it some time ago. I proposed, however,
to keep that opinion to myself, because, obviously
rational though it is, I anticipated that it would be
rejected, if not offensively, at least with all the horror
of uplifted hands. Ugh ! " He paused, drew at his
cigar and then let the smoke make its own way out of
his mouth. " This morning I learned that in some
thirty hours' time all opportunity of action upon
this rational opinion will be definitely withdrawn. I
therefore count it my duty at least to put this opinion
at your disposal. You will decide whether you will
use it or no."

Anthony smoked solemnly, looking straight ahead

and listening with all his might. A dripping Patch inspected a crevice in the brown brook's bank with every circumstance of suspicion. . . .

Sir Andrew continued slowly.

" You want your memory back. Very good. *You've had it back once.*" The other started. " That girl in the Park revived it. . . . There's a chance that what she did once she can do again. There's a chance that she can do more. She lighted the fire. It went out because it was neglected. Other bigger things intervened. The point is, *she* lighted it, while no one and nothing else has been able to strike a spark."

" Yes ? " said Anthony. " Yes ? "

Sir Andrew frowned.

" Whether she can relight it and, having done so, fan the flicker into a steady flame, no one can tell. It's a chance, of course—no more. Personally, I think it's a good one, but that's neither here nor there. But what I *know*—not because I'm a wizard, but because I've a brain in my head—is that it's too good a chance to miss." He thrust his cigar into his mouth and sucked it savagely. Presently he proceeded explosively. " If you want to miss it, you can. It's easy enough. But if you don't want to, well—you'd better look sharp. She's sailing for Cape Town to-morrow afternoon."

There was a long silence.

The frenzied sculpture of the Sealyham, who was trying to dislodge a stone, was clearly audible.

At length—

" How," said Anthony, " do you know ? "

Sir Andrew produced the report and gave it into his hand.

The other stared at the sheets.

" You—you've had her watched ? "

" I have," said the knight.

" In case I might want to try."

" Yes."

Anthony sighed.

" You're a friend in a million," he said quietly.

" That be damned," said Sir Andrew. " Besides, it remains to be seen. And now don't maunder. Read. Read what those serpents say."

Anthony read.

Then he lowered the papers and stared at the dash.

" I think you're right," he said. " I believe that girl could bring my memory back. But—I'm awfully sorry, sir, but I'ld rather not try."

Sir Andrew raised his eyes and ground his teeth.

Then he dabbed at the paper with a shaking hand.

" You see what they say ? " he cried. " You see what they say ? *Southampton — alone — to-night.* Southampton. Not Dover, or Plymouth, or Liverpool, or any other damned port. Southampton—*half an hour's run from here, where we're sitting now.* And to-morrow that girl, who can bring your memory back, ceases to be available. . . ."

Anthony laid a hand upon his arm.

" Don't think me ungrateful," he said. " I'm not. I——"

The giant cut him short.

" Curse your gratitude. I was moved to do what I've done by a sense of duty—a crazy, distorted sense, which a month ago I should have rendered to the devil from whom it came. But now I'm bewitched. . . Be that as it may, I've set my hand to the plough. The share's pasteboard, the soil rubbish. Never mind. What I've done I've done from a sense of duty towards my neighbour."

"As you please," said Anthony. "Let the gratitude go. I want to explain. Of course, your opinion's rational. It's devilish sound. And I firmly believe that girl could do the trick—which is a galling reflection, because she's the one person living to whom I can't apply." Sir Andrew let out a squeal and clapped his hands to his head. The other proceeded imperturbably. "You see, sir——"

"I don't. I can't. I haven't a beam in my eye. If I had—if I was a slobbering idiot with straws in my hair, I might be able to appreciate this maudlin diffidence. Don't dare to tell me I see. It's—it's slanderous."

"How can I apply to her? She's messed up everything once. It wasn't her fault, but she did. But for her, I shouldn't be in this plight. But for that girl——"

"I know, I know," raged the knight. "Why, that's the core of the matter, you frightening fool. You've got the stick of truth by the dirty end. That wretched girl is the witch of this damned fairy tale. She's turned you into a scapegoat, and *she's* the only being can change you back."

"She can't, sir, she can't. That girl's my evil genius. She can't undo what she's done, because she's evil. She's done grave harm already. If she recovered my memory, she'd tear the whole thing up. My case is bad, but not desperate. I've only got to remember, to pull it round. But if through *her* I got my memory back, my case would be finished —dead. The only chance I have of pulling it round would have gone—been sold for a shadow. It'ld be lost for ever."

Sir Andrew smote with his hand upon the arm of his seat.

"You're mad," he groaned, "mad. The girl's not evil. What she did once she did by accident. What she would do to-night she'ld do by design—honest, faithful design. If you and she are faithful, where's the harm? Together you're weaving a garland to lay at Silvia's feet. So the flowers are pulled in honesty, what does it matter to Silvia whence they come?"

"It matters much," said Anthony. "She's a woman. She wants the garland—longs for it. But if André Strongi'th'arm showed me the way to make it, she'ld have no use for it at all."

"And you," screeched Sir Andrew, "you're to pander to this indecent whim—humour this queasy wish-wash—muck and be mucked. . . . Goats and monkeys!" he wailed. "Aren't you a man? What if the weaker vessel does fret and toss upon the flood? Isn't it your proud office to bear her up? Are you to play the part of the hungry Greek—following, fawning, cringing, a mindless slave? Because she finds it warm, are you to sweat? Are you to shiver because she finds it cold? You shake your head. . . . Then take the line you should. Lift up your eyes and look. God made you honest and gave you common sense—talents worth having. Why chuck them into the draught? Use them. Do as they say. They never as yet led any man off the path. The Will-o'-the-Wisp's this cursed Sentiment. *That's* the false prophet. 'Go up and prosper,' it spouts. 'Go up and prosper'—with its lying tongue in its cheek."

He snatched out his watch and slapped the shining dial. " In thirty—twenty-four hours—your chance will be gone. Miss it, and you'll repent your folly all the days that you live. I know what I'm talking about. I've seen something of life. Fortune doesn't press favours on us poor fools. If we decline them, she smiles and goes her way. You may shout till you're black in the face, but she'll never turn back."

He stuffed the watch into his pocket, threw himself back in his seat, and mopped his face.

Anthony sat very still, staring upon the terrier, who had abandoned the water and was rolling luxuriously upon the sward.

At length—

" I can't," he said. " I daren't. It isn't sentiment that prevents me—I promise you that. It's understanding, sir. I know how Valerie feels, for I'ld feel the same. I shan't regret my decision. If I never get back my memory, I shan't regret it. For me my memory is above price. Yet to buy it like this would be paying far more than it's worth. What's the use of a poison which'll heal a withered arm ? "

Sir Andrew wrenched open his door and descended violently upon the sward.

" So be it ! " he roared. " Sit in my lady's chamber and drift to hell. Be played with. Worship each fleeting vanity. Leap at each maggoty whim. First it's a white blackbird, then it's the way it's snared. Next it'll be the colour of your hair or the set of the nose on your face. I've warned you. I've done what I can. But you're besotted . . . *drunk—blind drunk* . . . soaked with that sickly poison the devil keeps for fools. . . . *Love ?* Invalid port ! Snake-sweat ! "

With the laugh of a maniac, the giant flung up the road and presently pounded out of sight. Not out of earshot, though. For a long time Lyveden could hear him alternately laughing and yelling like one possessed.

As for Patch, he was deeply disturbed. The dog had seen many tempests, but never one like this. For a while he stood still, staring in the direction in which Sir Andrew had gone. Then he ran to his master, whining tremulously. The latter made him free of what comfort he had.

*   *   *   *   *

The train tore through a station and plunged into the countryside.

Mrs. Winchester folded the map which she had been studying, tossed it into her dressing-case, swung her feet on to the seat and lighted a cigarette.

" One last splash," she murmured, regarding two admirable legs, " and then, ever after, the loyal and dutiful wife. One last run with *la grande passion*, and then—finish. It's perfectly monstrous, of course— far the worst thing of all the many I've done. Aunt Charlotte would become unconscious if she knew. She'd probably die—shock to the pious system. But, then, she won't know. With luck, nobody'll know—except Mrs. Richard Winchester and Major Lyveden." She caught her underlip between her teeth and bit it feverishly. " God knows how I'm to manage it, but it must be done. I'm twelve miles away, and I've got about eighteen hours. If, after getting so far, I can't scrape home, I ought to be shot." Moodily she regarded the end of her cigarette. " As a matter of fact," she muttered, " I ought to be shot any

way. Bluffing Richard into staying in Town to-night
was the rottenest thing a woman ever did. But I'll
mend it—I swear I will. I'll make him the finest
wife a man ever had. . . . But I must see Anthony
again—I *must* take back that blow."

André was nervous.

Who goes hungry, but resolute, is said to tighten
his belt. The idea, I imagine, is to make belief that
his belly is full—the pressure of the belt suggesting
the recent consumption of a square meal. By talking
aloud and defiantly, André was ' tightening her belt.'
In a word, she was making belief that she saw nothing
to fear.

At eleven o'clock that morning she had been law-
fully wed. Already her husband was sixty miles away ;
very soon he would be distant some seventy-two.
She had arranged this deliberately in order that that
evening she might visit another girl's man. Her
husband must not know this, neither must the other
girl—obviously. Nor, indeed, must anyone. ' Fraud,'
' desertion,' and ' trespass ' were not nice words.
Coupled with the name of a bride not twenty-four
hours old, they were positively ugly. Indubitably,
no one must know.

Irrationally and somewhat half-heartedly she argued
that she could not leave England without asking
Lyveden's pardon for striking his face. This was, of
course, a fiction. André had a large heart. She
loved her husband, she loved Lyveden, and she loved
herself. Of the three, her love for her husband was
the most stable, and her love for Lyveden the most
hot. Still, mad as she surely was to see him again,
to do the girl justice, the very recklessness of the
adventure considerably enhanced its • charm. The

idea of one last scandalous escapade was most appealing. That time and tide were against her but whetted her will. To be able to look back later from the more or less peaceful *fauteuil* of married life and see the notch she had cut upon the wall of Scandal, feet—yards higher than that of anyone else, was an alluring prospect. Again, it was live melodrama, and André liked playing the heroine very much. I do not mean that if she and her husband had perceived Anthony Lyveden upon the other side of the street, and Winchester had urged her to go and speak with him, André would not have done so with an eager heart. She would have leaped at the chance. But to filch the chance out of the very strong-box of Decorum —that was to turn an act into an exploit. André and d'Artagnan would have agreed together.

The train slid into Southampton at set of sun, and ten minutes later Mrs. Winchester was following a page to her sitting-room upon the first floor of the Grand Hotel.

As the boy opened the door, a priest, who was sitting by the window, started to his feet.

The boy exclaimed, André, who had been upon the point of entering, recoiled, and the door was hurriedly and apologetically closed, only to be reopened an instant later.

The occupant of the room stood before them.

He was a handsome man, tall and fresh-faced, silver-haired. His air was gentle and dignified; his clear, blue eyes declared him honest and kind; his mouth was firm, yet humorous. He was clearly a prelate of consequence, but certainly a man in a million.

"I apologize profoundly," he said. "I've no

doubt that this is your room. It is not mine. Mine's
opposite. I asked to be allowed to telephone, and
as there was no instrument in my room, they showed
me in here. Pray——"

The rest of the sentence was lost in the sudden
stammer of the telephone-bell.

Instinctively the prelate turned. . . .

" That's your call," said André.

" It's of no consequence. I can speak downstairs."

He sought to pass. . . .

" Of course not," said André, detaining him.
" Please speak here. Why on earth should I mind ? "
She turned to the page. " Which is my bedroom ? "

" I cannot make use of your room at the expense
of your convenience."

" All right," laughed André, passing into the room.
" And now, do answer, or they'll cut you off."

The man smiled his thanks and stepped to the
instrument.

" Yes ? " he said gently. " Yes ? . . . That's
right." André slid into a chair and took out a cigarette-
case. " Hullo . . . Is that Bell Hammer ? " The
girl started violently, and the case slipped from her
hand. " Can I speak to Miss French ? . . . Oh . . .
Is Lady Touchstone there ? . . . Cardinal Forest.
. . . Cardinal Forest. . . . Yes." There was a pause,
during which His Eminence stared out of the window,
and André, with shaking fingers, contrived to light
a cigarette. At length : " Is that you, Harriet ?
It's John. . . . Yes, I'm speaking from Southampton
—the Grand. I've just arrived. . . . No, but it
seemed easier this way. . . . Listen, Harriet. Will
you send for me, or shall I get a car ? . . . Very

well. . . . Wait a minute." He looked at his watch.
" Ten minutes to six. . . . But if they won't be back
before half-past, hadn't I better . . . Very well. . . .
But, Harriet. . . Let her come alone—I mean,
without him. . . I'ld like a word with her first.
. . . All right, about seven, then. . . . Good-bye."

The cardinal replaced the receiver and turned to
his hostess.

" I am so very much obliged. I think few people
would have been so nice about such an intrusion."

André tried not to tremble and managed to laugh.

" You have nothing," she said uncertainly, " to
thank me for."

His Eminence bowed and passed out.

Fifteen minutes later Mrs. Winchester was in a
hired car, hammering over the road to Napery Green.

Luck was with her, manifestly.

By an extraordinary accident she had been apprised
of the enemy's orders of the day.

For an hour from half-past six, while Anthony
would be at Bell Hammer, Valerie would be out of
the way . . . for an hour. . . .

Feverishly she consulted her wrist-watch for the
fiftieth time. . . .

If it took half an hour to get from Bell Hammer
to Southampton, it presumably took half an hour
to get from Southampton to Bell Hammer. She
would be there, then, by twenty-five minutes to
seven. Very good. But before she approached the
house, she must be certain that Valerie French had
left. With luck—more luck, she would pass her
upon the road. . . .

She put her head out of a window and cried to
the young mechanic not to drive so fast.

Bell Hammer stood back from the road. So much
the map said. How far back, she could not tell.
But she could not drive up to the house. Lady
Touchstone was there, and Plague. . . She would
have to leave the car and walk from the road. And
if the house stood well back, that would take time.
She had known drives a mile long. . . .

André thrust out her head and told the young
mechanic to increase his pace.

The light was failing now. Two days ago summer
time had come to an untoward end. But the evening
was warm and dry, and the air was as soft as silk.

The car snarled through a village, and André peered
at the map. By holding this close to the window,
she could just identify her road. She decided that
the echoing hamlet was Blue Sleeves. And Blue
Sleeves lay four miles from Napery Green. . . .

André put up the map and kept her eyes glued to
the shadowy road ahead.

At Napery Green they would have to turn to the
left. Then, if the map was honest, Bell Hammer
was standing about a mile away—a mile and a half,
perhaps. . . .

André determined to inquire at Napery Green.

As they ran into the village, she peered at her
watch.

Half-past six.

The driver slowed up for instructions, and André
got out.

She was back in a moment.

" There's a lodge on the left of the road about
a mile farther on. Don't drive in. Drive past—
about twenty yards."

The mechanic nodded.

Hitherto, since leaving Southampton, the roads had been theirs; but now they were on the highway which runs from Brooch to Bloodstock and carries its share of traffic on summer afternoons.

Three char-à-bancs went raving—lumbering arks of wassail, noisy, affectionate; a racing car stole by, muttering thunder; bicyclists flitted like ghosts; and presently a landaulette passed. But the chauffeur was smoking. Valerie was not there. . . .

The tall gates were open, and there was a light in the lodge.

André descended and told the man to wait.

"Pull up a little more. A car may be coming out. I shan't be long—about a quarter of an hour."

The youth glanced at his watch. Then—

"Or right," he said sulkily. "A quartervanour."

André hesitated.

Then she opened her bag. By the light of a lamp she picked out a five-pound note.

"I might be longer than I think. But, whatever happens, stay here until I come." She folded the note and tore it clean in two. "There's half a fiver. If you want the other half, do as I say."

She left the fellow staring and stepped to the tall gates. For a second she stood peering. Then she flashed by the lodge and into the drive.

It was dark indeed now, and she could not see ahead. The avenue might have been endless. She sped up the smooth roadway, impatient for a view of her goal. . . .

Suddenly the beam of a searchlight shot out of the darkness in front of her, raking the park on her right, swinging her way. In an instant she was

bathed in brilliance—blinded. . . Then the beam
swung on past and away.

For a moment the girl stood spellbound, watching
the unearthly shaft sweep, like some fatal, ruthless
blade, over the sleeping pastures, stripping the night
naked. . . .

Then the pulse of an engine fell upon her
ears.

A car was coming. Plainly the drive went curling
up to the house, and the car had been rounding a
bend. Its headlights . . .

Valerie! It was she, of course. It was Valerie
leaving for Southampton to——

With a shock, André remembered that the car
was coming her way. And she was full in its path.
Any second that merciless beam would betray her as
surely no poacher was ever betrayed before. She
darted behind an elm not an instant too soon.

The shaft of light swung round, and the car with
it. In a moment the avenue had become a blazing,
sonorous choir.

Her back pressed close against the sheltering trunk,
the girl felt dazed, terrified. . . . The narrowness
of her escape, the abrupt rout of that darkness on
which she leaned, the sudden overthrow of silence,
rammed home the villainy of her adventure. She was
lurking—a thief in the night. Her plunging senses
snatched at the parable. That fearful, resonant
glare was Doom, approaching his prey. She had
thought to avoid it, but now it had altered its course.
It was coming straight for her. She could hear—
feel its advance. In a second it would crash into her
elm. She awaited the shock dully. . . .

Then the squall passed, and she was left sick and

shaken, leaning against her bulwark with her knees sagging and her chin on her breast. . . .

After a minute or two she lifted her head.

Then she stood upright and wiped the sweat from her brow.

" Of all the painful fools," she muttered, with a tremulous laugh. " If I'm going to get cold feet, I'd better clear out." She dabbed her face with a handkerchief and felt for her puff. " Heavens alive, what have I got to fear ? Besides, my nerve's the only thing I've got. Without it, I'm done. With it . . ." She powdered her face thoughtfully. " Well, I've got away with a lot since I was foaled."

The storm had cleared the air.

André felt better than she had felt for hours.

When she stepped back into the roadway, the thief had slunk out of sight. In his stead, a cool-headed musketeer smiled, tilted his chin and presently cocked his extremely expensive hat.

Had André known that the car which had just swept by was carrying two people, whose names she had never heard—Captain and Mrs. Pleydell, friends of the house—that Valerie, who had returned un-expectedly early, had used a road which was not shown on her map, that Cardinal Forest and his niece were at that very moment shaking the dust of Southamp-ton off their tires, I doubt if her nerve would have responded so handsomely to the spur of her will. What is quite certain is that she would not have wasted a valuable ten minutes upon a deliberate reconnais-sance of the curtilage of the mansion.

Be that as it may, the stable-clock was striking the hour of seven when the girl glided on to the terrace at the back of the house.

A window was open here—open wide. From the garden below you could look right into the room. This was a library—you could see the books ranged orderly upon the walls. More. There was some one there. Some one was sitting, smoking, in a deep chair. . . . They seemed to be reading. . . .

The other windows were black. Only upon the first floor a faint radiance about the sides of two rectangles argued drawn curtains with a light behind.

André stole over the flags, holding her breath. . . .

Three yards from the library window her foot struck some object which moved—went rolling and making a dull sound. It was a terrier's toy—a piece of rubber cast in the shape of a bone.

Instantly came the scuttle of paws upon parquet, and André fell back against the wall.

Patch appeared upon the terrace, prick-eared, suspicious. For a full minute he stood, staring out into the night, listening, motionless. Then he turned slowly and re-entered the room. . . .

With a hammering heart, André crept very close. She could hear the fire now—the soft hiss of logs and the lick and flutter of flame.

As she bent forward, a page flicked.

"Come in, Mrs. Winchester," said Plague, quietly enough.

André's heart gave one tremendous bound.

Then she stepped forward and over the window-sill.

The dog started to meet her, but the knight never moved. The latter's back was turned and he was at ease in a chair, with a cigar in his mouth and an open book upon his knee. By his shoulder a delicate pillar of bronze was distributing the light of three lamps hung from its capital.

After a cursory inspection of the girl, the terrier turned away. He knew who it was.

For a moment André stood still, finger to lip.

Then—

" How did you know ? " she breathed.

" I heard you a moment ago. They telephoned just now to say you were on your way."

" Who ? "

" Agents in my employ. As you've had Lyveden watched, so I've watched you. What are you here for ? "

" I want to see him again."

Sir Andrew frowned. Then he laid down his book and rose to his feet.

" You can't do that," he said firmly. " There are "—he swallowed vehemently—" most powerful reasons why you and he should not meet."

André stared.

" What are they ? If you mean I'm married— well, that's my affair. If you mean that he's engaged——"

" I don't," said Plague shortly. " As reasons go, those two are pretty sound. But mine are sounder still. I'm sorry," he added kindly. " If I could have stopped you coming, I would have done so."

" You like me," said André suddenly. " Why ? "

Sir Andrew blinked thoughtfully.

Then—

" You're bold and downright," he said. " That may or may not be why. But I like you well enough to wish you, at least, no ill. Therefore go as you came. You can't see Lyveden, and you mustn't be found. I shall say nothing."

André took her seat upon the arm of a chair.

" I want to see him," she said.

Sir Andrew's face took on a darker shade.

"Don't be a fool," he snapped. "I may like courage, but bravado I loathe. You're out of order. I'm trying to get you back."

"Listen," said André. "That night, at your house, I struck him. I cursed him for an outsider, and then, when he begged my pardon, I slashed him across the face. You're wise. I expect you know why I did those things. . . . But he doesn't look for motives which don't appear. He thinks me a howling cad, and I—I don't like that."

"If that's why you came," said Plague, "I'll put that right. You know and can trust me. I say, I'll put that right. And now take an old man's counsel and go your way. You mayn't 've won so much, but you haven't lost. And that's as well, for you can't afford to lose."

"You forget I'm out to win," was the cool reply. "Let me see him, and I'll go."

The knight stamped upon the floor. Then he hurled his cigar into the grate and set his teeth.

"Can you appreciate," he hissed, "that you are not in a position to dictate? That this is Miss French's house? That you have not been admitted, but have 'gained admission' thereto? That I can ring that bell and have you shown out? That scandal and ignominy are preparing to spring upon your shoulders?"

"I came to see Major Lyveden. If he refuses to see me, I'll go like a lamb. I was foolish to come like this. I ought to have gone to the door and rung the bell."

"So should burglars. But they don't—for obvious reasons."

The girl rose to her feet.

"You think," she said coldly, "that——"

"I *know*," said Plague. "Why bandy words with me?"

"Then ring that bell," flashed André. "Send word to Major Lyveden that I am here. If he declines to see me, I'll go as I came."

With a frightful effort, the giant controlled his voice.

"Madam," he said, taking his watch from his pocket. "I give you two minutes in which to leave this house. If when that time has expired you are still here, I shall write to your husband to-night, relating this visit of yours and requesting him to restrain you from molesting Major Lyveden again."

André went very white.

"Write and be damned," she said. "And now will you ring that bell?"

In a way the request was needless, for here the door was opened, and Valerie French and the Cardinal entered the room.

Valerie was speaking.

"Don't thank me, Uncle John. I'm in your debt. The smell of that air! I'll bet that's something Italy hasn't got. Nemi must be very lovely, but the breath of the New Forest"—here she perceived Mrs. Winchester, and paused—"is the scent Time uses when he wants to pretend he's young. Let me introduce my uncle, Cardinal Forest—Miss Strongi'th'arm —Sir Andrew Plague."

Her self-command took every one by the throat.

Sir Andrew, whose nerve was his pride, felt like a private-schoolboy and almost stood upon one leg. His Eminence, for whom the name "Strongi'th'arm" had been like an evil spirit besetting his darling's sleep, put a hand to his head and, with a fumbling brain, strove to accept the reports which his eyes and ears were offering. As for André, the feeling of inferiority which Valerie always inspired became positively painful. A meek lady-in-waiting, whom the queen had surprised in the act of trying on the crown, would have been less discomfited.

Before the silence could settle, Valerie put out her hand.

" I'd no idea you were coming," she said, with a quiet smile. " Of course you'll stay to dinner, if not the night. Now that I come to think of it, I saw a car by the lodge." She turned to the men. " Uncle John, you know your room. Sir Andrew, it's time to dress. André and I are not going to change to-night, so we'll give you twenty minutes' start."

The Cardinal girt up his loins and turned to the knight.

" It sounds as if we weren't wanted," he said, with a grave smile. " She doesn't mean it, of course. For one thing, we're too decorative. But let's go—just to teach her a lesson."

" *Non docent, sed discunt*," said Plague, and followed him out—unsteadily.

Patch, who had run to greet Valerie, watched the retiring lawyer and then returned to the hearth.

As the door closed, Valerie touched the other upon the arm.

" Come and sit down by the fire."

André shivered. Then she lifted her head.

" I must go," she said abruptly, holding her eyes upon the ground. " I beg your pardon, and—I'm much obliged."

" What for ? "

" For covering my retreat. It's not a thing the—the enemy often does."

She turned to the window.

" Am I your enemy ? " said Valerie.

" You have no choice. I'm an outlaw. I've been—warned off."

" Why do you talk like this—like an escaped convict ? And if you were, you know I'ld harbour you, as you would me. You've never let me down."

" That's not my fault," said André, facing about. " It's Andrew Plague's. Three weeks ago he stopped me, and he's stopped me to-night. I should hang on to him," she added, with a bitter laugh. " He's a dog in a million. A thief doesn't stand an earthly when he's around."

" What," said Valerie, " do you mean ? "

" Why d'you think," said André, " I left my car in the road ? Because I didn't want your household to know I was here. I didn't come in by the door, you know. Thieves don't. I came in by the window. And I knew you were out. To be frank, I never dreamed you'ld be back so soon. . . . And then, having ' effected my entrance,' I met the dog. I was doing my best to bluff him when you arrived." She spread out her hands and set her head on one side. " So, you see, you're perfectly right—I've not let you down. I've done my level best to, and I'd got a jolly long way, when that excellent dog chipped in and cramped my style."

" I wish to Heaven," said Valerie, " I had your pluck." The other started. " If I were a man, I think I should be mad about you. Your courage is dazzling. You set it above pride, above safety, above success. And, because you do, all these things, as they say, are added unto you. And always will be. . . ." She turned to the grate and spread her hands to the blaze. " What did you come for ? "

" What do thieves come for ? "

" To steal, I suppose," said Valerie.

" That's right. I came to steal. I came to see him."

" I don't call that stealing," said Valerie, ringing the bell by her side. " If I wanted to see Richard Winchester, I shouldn't ask you."

André laughed.

" You won't strike, will you ? " she said. " I've bared my shoulders and put the whip in your hand. I've done it before. But you won't strike. I suppose I'm too rotten—too low . . . even for that . . . leprous."

A servant entered, and Valerie turned her head.

" Ask Major Lyveden to come here "

The man bowed and withdrew.

" What are you doing ? " cried André, hoarsely, panic-stricken.

" I'm pleasing myself. Don't go. You came un-asked. Now I request you to stay. I have the right, I think. You've given it me." She glanced at a clock. " Dinner's at eight—in thirty-five minutes' time."

With that, she smiled very steadily, stepped to the door and passed out.

Only the great can do great things as great things should be done. But then Valerie French was a great lady.

As for André, the girl felt rather cheaper and much more frightened than she had ever felt in her life.

That she did not there and then make good her escape shows, I think, that Valerie's personality, like the Cheshire cat's grin, was surviving her presence in the flesh. The steady, blue eyes were gone, but the look of them was still there. Before it, as a sheep before her shearers, André was dumb.

She stood as Valerie had left her, leaning against a table, with her lips parted and her beautiful head thrown back. . . .

Stretched upon the hearth, his nose between his paws, the Sealyham regarded her silently.

Anthony came in swiftly, dressed for dinner.

" You want me, Valerie ? I——"

He saw who it was, and stopped dead.

André never moved.

Only the dog jumped up and ran to his lord.

" What's the matter ? " said Anthony. " Are you ill ? "

" No," breathed André, " I'm not. I wish I was. I wish I was dead."

There was a pause.

" I don't know why you say that," said Lyveden awkwardly. " But I don't know what's happened. I'd no idea you were here. Of course, Plague had no right to ask you to come."

A faint frown gathered on André's brow.

Then she lifted her head and turned to the man.

" Plague—ask me to come ? What do you mean ? "

Anthony stared.

" Didn't he get you here ? "

" Plague ? "

" Yes."

" I don't understand," said André. " Why should Plague get me here ? "

s

" We quarrelled about it this morning," said Anthony
" He wanted me to see you, and I refused."

" Why did he want us to meet ? "

" Because he believes that you could bring my
memory back."

" And why," said André slowly, " did you refuse ? "
The man hesitated. " Don't you want it back ? "

" Yes, yes, I do."

" Then why did you refuse ? "

" I want it for Valerie. She wants my memory
back. And—and I don't think she'ld care about it,
if it came through another girl."

A curious gleam leapt into André's eyes—almost a
glitter. She veiled it instantly.

" No," she said slowly, " I don't suppose she would.
I shouldn't either." An odd strained note slid into
her voice. " It would be a sort of stigma—suggesting
that, however you and she felt, down at the bottom
of things, the—*the other girl had meant more.*"

" That's right," cried Anthony eagerly. " You've
got it in one. I couldn't make Plague see it. Of
course, the suggestion would be false——"

" Of course. ' False as—as dicers' oaths.' "

The irony of the quotation, the hysterical mockery
in her tone, fell upon deaf ears.

The man continued excitedly.

" Exactly. But what—what'ld make it so ghastly
is that, *so long as she and I lived, the stigma would stay.*
Once my memory's back, it's back for good. The
mischief'ld be irreparable. It'ld last——."

The look in the big, brown eyes cut short the sentence. Tense, burning, desirous, it bored its way
into his brain. Dumbly the man stared back—fasci-
nated, paralysed. . . .

He was snared—netted—*limed* . . . caught in the very toils which he had been teaching his enemy to spread. . . .

Already something was stirring at the back of his brain . . . something . . . .

"Till death," breathed André. "It'ld last . . . till death. . . ."

The room seemed to grow smaller—the walls were closing in : the scene—my God, the scene was changing ! André was in evening dress—with a great fur coat, flung open, and a throat and chest like snow. Where the light caught it, her wonderful, auburn hair burst into flame. Behind her gaped a huge fire-place, and the breathless silence of Night in the grip of Frost hung like a pall. . . .

Suddenly the girl recoiled and clapped her hands to her mouth. The burning look in her eyes changed to a bright stare of horror.

"Don't !" she shrieked. "*Don't !* Think what you're doing, man ! My God, d'you want——"

Quick as lightning she turned and struck at the elegant lamp-stand with all her might

The pillar fell with a crash. . . .

Wrapped in the sudden darkness, neither she nor Lyveden could see where the other stood. Gradually the glow of the fire silhouetted two shadowy forms. . .

André was whispering hoarsely.

"Where—did you—meet me—before ? "

There was a dreadful silence.

At length—

" I—I don't know," faltered the man. " I—I can't remember."

A sigh . . . the brush of a dress . . . a footfall . . . .

When Anthony pulled himself together, groped
his way to the door and turned a switch, the room
was empty.

Only the Sealyham stood by the broken pillar,
with his ears back, tentatively wagging his tail. . . .

CHAPTER X

UNTIL THE DAY BREAK

HERE is matter, sirs, which neither you nor I were ever intended to see—a human document, penned by a girl in her bedroom, night after night, while her husband sleeps or wakes upon the other side of the wall.

November 7th.—We were married a month ago to-day. I cannot realize it yet. I'm rather happier, because I have him all the time. But that is all—*all*. Strange, how, from childhood on, one stares at one's marriage as at an elephant, finger in mouth. The nearer it comes, the more curiously excited one gets. Every one tells you you're going to begin a new life: and you thank them nervously and get all ready to be reincarnated. Your entrance into wedlock becomes a soul-shaking event. Sometimes it looms, and you're afraid. The step is invested with such tremendous, immemorial traditions, that it ranks with Death itself. The Prayer Book, in fact, does the two equal honour. By the time the day is here, you fully believe you are going to be transferred to another plane—take on a new shape, or something. And then . . . nothing happens— *nothing*. You're just exactly the same. So's everything. The momentous words have been spoken, the charm has been uttered, the wand waved, but the miracle has not come off. If you've taken a step, there's no sign of it. You've certainly changed your name, but you can do that in *The Times*. I never was so disillusioned—and relieved. At least, it reduces Death to the level of a sea voyage, which one just doesn't want to take. I suppose one does take it. I daren't assume anything now. . . .

I like Cairo. Who wouldn't? It's like a dramatic version of Æsop, done in the stalls. You brush against fables or parables at every turn. I saw a camel to-day, its body completely hidden under its load of hay. It looked like a moving stack. It just swayed philosophically along, blinking. A man with a goat-skin of water on his back was selling it outside Shepheard's. Inside, Martinis were being mixed. As we were driving home, we fell in with a funeral. Just then the traffic was stopped, and for a moment or two our eight-cylinder cabriolet marched with a trolley of professional wailers. We got in so late last night that we took it easy to-day. We went to the Bazaar and, later, to the Citadel, to see the sun go down. To-morrow . . .

Anthony remembers nothing. He knows what the places are like and tells me what to expect. Cairo, like Port Said, is familiar : but he cannot *remember* having been here before. A curious thing happened. We were wondering which on earth of the hundreds of cigarette-shops sold the best cigarettes. Presently, he picked out one, saying he liked its style. The moment he went inside, the people recognized him. That was the shop he had chosen when he was here before. . . But that's not memory. If it is, it's unconscious and amounts to a glorified instinct. He can remember nothing.

With it all, he's just splendid. I hope and believe he's happy. I know I'm—happy. He's a magnificent squire. . . . I'm minded to cross out those words, because, reading them over, I feel hot with shame. But I won't. I'll let them stand, and read them over every night and beg his pardon for daring to set them down. He's not a squire at all. He's the finest, most perfect lord that ever a woman had. And, to do his wretched wife honour, he's playing the squire. And she lets him . . . *lets* him. .   It's lucky for me I live in the twentieth century   A hundred years ago I should have met with a very short shrift. I wonder if he's asleep. If I was sure, I'ld go in and put his clothes straight and look at his blessed face. But I'd better not.

November 8th.—I feel very small. So does Anthony. This morning we looked upon the face of the Pharaoh ' which knew not Joseph.' It is a hard, proud face. One understands why he was so harsh about the bricks. A live statue of the overseer of the building of the Great Pyramid was also most illuminating. With unlimited labour and that man's ' drive ' behind the work, the stones simply had to go up. This afternoon we saw what that ' drive ' had done. . . . We both agreed that you can't appreciate it at once : so to-morrow we move to Mena. I repeat, we feel very small. That Abraham was probably taken to see it, just as we've been taken to-day, is too big a thought for my brain. The poor thing recoils, like a puppy that has been sent to round up a mammoth. And Abraham stared upon it from much the same distance in time as we stare upon the Coliseum. . . . Such antiquity surely can put one in one's place. In its presence I feel a ragamuffin puppet, striking attitudes in a giants' council-chamber. My ' sea of troubles' sinks to an insignificant puddle : my joys, to a child's scratches in the sand. And yet . . . Cheops and Abraham and Rameses were puppets too. They had their puddles and scratches. And, when they told themselves ' It's all the same in a hundred years,' it didn't do any good. It didn't dry up their puddles. They're dry now, of course. Mine'll be dry—when I'm dead. . . . I wonder if his memory *is* coming back. If it isn't, what *are* we to do ? What is to become of us ? I can't sit down and tell him the story of our love. I can't. For one thing, it won't go into words. It was the most precious ritual that ever was used. And we never learned it. It just came natural, like instinct. How can you teach a miracle ? You can't. If you do, it becomes a conjuring-trick. Why do I care ? Why does it matter so terribly ? God knows. I suppose, because he remembered André. I suppose so. At least it's founded on that. That started the mill. Jealousy. . . . Yet, I'm not jealous of her—now. The point is, what are we going to do ? We might go on like this for ever, if we weren't in love. But we are, passionately. Both of us. Only, I'm in love with the original, while the reproduction's in love with me. . . . At present we're drifting amicably—most amicably—in the hope of picking up a tow. Which means that *we're going the wrong way.* Presently, he'll get tired of playing the squire. He'll go to the Club . . . hunt six days a week to my three . . . work. . And, one of these days, he'll go. Anthony, my Anthony will go. I'm asking for it, of course. And yet . . .

November 9th.—He is wonderful. So gentle, so easy, so natural, so handsome in all he does. Except that he doesn't call me ' Ma'am,' I might be a queen, and he my dearest equerry. He calls me ' Valerie ' —never ' darling ' or ' dear,' but ' Valerie ' always. He just rules Sentiment right out. He gave his word and he is determined to keep it up to the hilt. I try to make his path smooth, and my wretched efforts show what an infinitely inferior creature I am. I trip and blunder and fall over myself. He walks steadily, with bleeding feet. More. As often as I stumble and am like to pull us both down, it is he that holds me up. To-day my shoes got full of sand. He made me sit down, untied the laces, took off the shoes, emptied them and put them on again, talking evenly all the time about Andrew Plague and Patch. He was flushed and his hands were shaking, but he never touched me. Now, most unobtrusively, he avoids, when he can, the loose sand. I see it, because I'm a fool and would rush in. But he is an angel. . . . I kiss him, of course. I began without thinking and I can't give it up. I didn't, one morning. He just looked at me. " Listen, Valerie. If I wanted to kiss an image, I should. I should please myself. ' Eyes have they, but they see not.' The porridge, I may add, is beneath contempt. You know. Lumpy. Still, this sea air is so imperious . . ." He not only sinks his feelings, but he spares mine. ' Spares ' ? He considers— waits upon them. He is a king, who has put a slave's collar about his neck. He has tried to turn himself into an image, and he has become an idol—my blessed idol. ' He that shall humble himself, shall be exalted.' And I—I suffer it. I suffer this monstrous Saturnalia

to prevail. . . . I broke down to-night. We had
walked to the Great Pyramid and stared at it under
the moon. Coming home, I broke down—suddenly.
Anthony stopped, took off his coat and spread it upon
the sand. I sat down, and he sat down by my side.
I put my head in his lap and cried like a child. He
talked quietly, in a steady tone. " It will come
back, Valerie. Don't lose heart. Together, we can
do anything. It will come back. . . ." After a
while, I put up my face and kissed him. Cold as it
was, his face was wet with sweat. . . . I believe
I have married a god. Yet, a god would not kneel.
No. I have married the finest man God ever made
—whose love for me is wonderful. As we got up,
I asked him, " How can you love me ? " " How
can I help it ? " he said. " There's no one like you
and never has been, in all the rolling world." I
could not say anything. I cannot say anything
now. Such devotion, such respect for such a cause
leaves me dumb.

November 10th.—I have realized that I am a married
woman. I realized it to-day. We had driven to
Cairo for luncheon at Shepheard's Grill. Afterwards, I was sitting in the lounge, and Anthony
left me to speak to a clerk at the bureau. As he
was coming back, I saw a man stop him and speak.
The two stood talking for a moment, and I watched
them impersonally, casually, as one regards other
people in an hotel. Suddenly, out of the blue, it
occurred to me that one of those men was mine—
my husband. . . . That tall, handsome man, with
the dark hair and the cigarette in his hand, was *my
husband.* . . . A thousand times I had looked on
husbands and wives and thought no more of the

relation than I had of their size in gloves. ' What's Hecuba to him ? ' And now, I was a wife : and that, standing there, was my husband. We were married, joined for all time. I had failed, hitherto, to see the wood, for the trees : with the result that I had almost unconsciously passed over into that state which I had always regarded so distantly, with so detached —so mild an interest. . . . I was still tingling with the excitement of realization, when the two came across and Anthony introduced the man. They had been gunners together, so the man said. His name was Toby Redruth. He seemed very nice and delighted to see Anthony again. He said he wasn't sure of him at first—*he looked so much older.* And, when Anthony looked straight at him and took no notice, he thought he was wrong. Then he became positive. . . . He was clearly swept off his feet by Anthony's loss. He couldn't get hold of it at all. His naïve bewilderment made us both laugh. It seems the last time they were together was here, at Shepheard's Hotel. And then one went east, and the other—Anthony —west. Redruth is English, but has a job in Australia. I liked him a lot, and, just as we were going, he fairly won my heart. He'd begun to recover by then. He was walking with us to the door, when he stopped and touched Anthony upon the arm. " There's just one thing which you really ought to know. You actually saw it happen, and it's a thing that half the Army would have given their teeth to see." Then he told how a subaltern in France had got the guns away out of the very jaws of the German infantry. Anthony and I listened, spell-bound. " And I saw that with my eyes," concluded Redruth. " He ought to have had the V.C. with a couple

of bars : but you know how these honours go." " Did
he get *nothing* ? " cried Anthony. Redruth smiled
very tenderly. Then he turned to me and put out
his hand. " And that," he said simply, " is why your
husband was given the D.S.O." I could have kissed
his honest face. But for him, I might never have
known . . . never . . . what *my husband* had
done. . . .

November 11th.—I have done it. I have been in,
while he slept. I have seen my husband, my Anthony,
fast asleep. The room was full of moonlight—this
wonderful Egyptian moon. I stole in, like a ghost,
barefoot. I was afraid to breathe. Then, when
I saw him, I forgot my fear. I didn't want to wake
him, because it would have been a crime : but that
was all. He looked like some picture I've seen—I
can't think where. ' A Shepherd Asleep,' or something. His precious lips were parted, and there was
a smile on his glorious face. His sleeve had slipped
back, and his head was resting on his bare, brown
arm. His hair was rumpled, and his colour was
high. His coat, open at the neck. He looked so
young and happy . . . so free from care. . . . For
a moment, I couldn't grasp it, and then—I understood. He was relaxed . . . at play. The strong,
resolute look had disappeared. He was a child again,
a care-free child, that has no need of resolution,
because the World's smiling and Life's a game. *No
need of resolution.* . . . That eager, happy look
cut me like a knife. It was the most terrible rebuke
that ever a woman had. He must sleep, to be at
ease. My darling must go to sleep, before he can
put off care. All day he is on duty—goes armed. His
eyes are always vigilant, his jaw set, his nerves taut,

his soul patiently possessed. Only, when sleep comes, does the soldier disappear and the boy come out to play. Poor boy. Poor pit-pony, that toils so patiently day after labouring day, and never scampers in the meadows—never, save in his dreams. . . . He was dreaming, I think. I think he must have been. He looked so happy. . . .

I stole out, as I stole in. And here I am writing now, while he is dreaming. I feel dazed. I never realized that I was committing crime. I never should have realized, if I had not been in and seen the boy at play. He is a thousand times more splendid than I had ever dreamed. I have married some sylvan deity, some laughing-eyed Daphnis, who, for love of me, stamps on his springing nature, shoulders outrageous burdens he never was meant to bear, grows old and serious before his time . . . for love of me. And he does it all with such grace, that I never dreamed that at heart he was just a child. Even in the old days, he never looked like that. Once, yes. Once. Before Gramarye : before I sent him away. One morning, at the meet, after he knew that we were meant for each other, stand in the way what might. . . . I wonder what he was dreaming of. Golden days of some sort—blessed, breathless moments, when the blood sang in his veins and his heart danced to the tune that Life was piping . . . forgotten days and moments. . . . *Forgotten ?* My God, is it possible ? Is it possible that *he is remembering in his sleep ?* Or was he smiling at some fantasy of an unharnessed brain ? Supposing—supposing he *was* remembering. . . . Supposing that at night, when he sleeps, his memory returns . . . the fugitive, the wandering spirit comes back, like a shy, wild thing stealing out of the woods to visit its empty cage . . . starting at every rustle, vanishing always at dawn. . . . I am a fool. He might have been dreaming of anything—of yesterday turned upside down, of Sir Andrew teaching Abraham to drive, of any nonsense you like, spun by some Puck out of the action of the last three months. And yet . . . I cannot forget that look upon his face. It was so happy.

I didn't kiss him. He might have waked. And I have crime enough upon my soul.

November 12th.—I am sitting, waiting, till I think it is safe to go in. . . .

To-day we rode to Sakkara and saw the Step Pyramid. It actually looks older than those at Mena. Anthony rides very well. Really, we are very happy. We settled all we shall do when we get home. First, the season. We've decided to go the whole hog—Ascot, Lord's, Hurlingham, dances, theatres, night-clubs—just to find out what we like : and then, next year, we can choose. Week-ends at Bell Hammer, of course. After that, Dorset. Then abroad for a month, and back to Bell Hammer for the fall. I can't miss that two years running. Then to Dorset for hunting, with odd days and nights in Town. We shall see. . . I told him of Gramarye to-day. All things considered, it seemed a wise thing to do. He took it quietly enough. " Winchester's right-hand man, was I ? And you couldn't get me away ? What a queer thing. You have had a time with me, Valerie. . . ." Then : " I wonder who the poor fellow was they buried instead of me. I'ld like to put up a memorial, when we get back— a cross or something. The pitiful dead, you know.

And it might have been me, easily. 'The one shall be taken, and the other left.'" We rode back in the afternoon, and the sun was going down as we got in. The desert has seasons of extraordinary beauty. Sundown is one of them. Night is another. By day it is rather too brilliant, too hard, like a frozen smile. One feels that it would smile just as brightly —has smiled just as brightly, while men's throats were cracking with thirst. Thinking it over, I can see the cruel glitter behind a lot of the *Rubáiyát.*

I was right. By night, his memory returns. He has been talking in his sleep—*talking of the old days.* I can hardly believe it, and I am so excited I can hardly set the facts down. I knelt by his side and heard it—heard with my ears. . . *Patch*—that's nothing, of course, because Patch has survived, but wait—*Gramarye*—true, I'd told him of that this morning, but wait, wait—*the Bumbles, the War, The Leather Bottel, The Dogs' Home. ME.* . . Snatches, shreds only, but *I* knew where they belonged, where they came from. *He's just had distemper, sir. . . . Oak's the best. It's hard to work, but . . Valerie, I quite forgot. The kiss I gave you that day . . . You take the parade, Toby. . . . I couldn't help it, Patch. She — seemed — so — sweet. . . . Try and free your right arm. . . . I feel like a king, Valerie. You . . . Colonel Winchester wants the roan at a quarter to eight.* . . . To the world, incoherent nonsense : to me, the most blessed discourse that ever a woman heard.

Two solid hours I've been there, straining my ears. Sometimes, he never spoke for a quarter of an hour. Then he'ld whisper something so low I could hardly hear. The scene kept changing. I never knew where he was. His memory was back at work, and his brain was stepping from incident to incident in that queer, haphazard way it does, when you're letting your thoughts carry you where they will. It was back . . . in his blessed head. It flies, when he wakes, of course : but it must be very near. Perhaps . . . if, in the morning, he remembered a dream. . . . Supposing something were to wake him—suddenly . . . when he was talking in his sleep . . . *something* . . . a kiss, perhaps. . . .

November 13th.—Fate is a mocker. This morning, at breakfast, Anthony quietly said, " I had a queer dream last night." I think my heart stopped still. " I dreamed that you and I were over the edge of a cliff. And I was hanging on to the branch of a tree, holding you up. I can't remember what happened, but Patch was there. It was amazingly vivid." As soon as I could speak, " It wasn't a dream," I cried. " At least, not fiction. I can show you the cliff we fell over. The earth gave way, while we were sitting there, and you saved both our lives." He gave me a half-frightened look. " Did I *remember* it, then ? " " Yes, yes. Don't you remember it *now* ? " He looked away, and presently covered his eyes. I sat watching him, with my heart in my mouth. At last : " No," he said slowly, " I don't. I only remember the dream." I couldn't take that. I was frantic. I strove, I fought like a maniac to drag his memory back. I knelt by his side and made him go over the ground, inch by inch. I guided, I led, I encouraged, I pointed the way—I made a fool of myself and I badgered him. . . . Worse. I showed what a terrible value I set upon his memory, and drove a desperate, hunted look into his darling eyes. . . .

It spoiled our day, of course. God knows how many days it's spoiled. When we rode out after breakfast, the desert's brilliant smile cut me like a whip.

I haven't the heart to write very much to-night.

I've lost heavily to-day. I never realized at the time how much I was standing to lose. I only saw the fortune I stood to win. And I didn't win, and I've lost a lot of ground. We're farther apart, he and I, than we have been for weeks. The gulf that is fixed between us, was losing its formidable look. It seemed to be shrinking a little in width and depth. Sweet-smelling flowers—*new memories*—were blooming about its sides, and little, tender leaves were masking its grim, raw edges. . . . This morning I tore the blossoms and leaves away. I showed him the gulf, stark and gaping and black. I forced him to face its harshness. I rammed its threat down his throat— the threat that it will never be bridged. . . .

November 14th.—A man told me once that the first time he saw the Sphinx was by moonlight and that he had much ado not to burst into tears. Perhaps because of this introduction, I found the Sphinx less impressive than other things. But now it is growing familiar, and familiarity is breeding regard. Its steady, imperturbable stare is beginning to attract my attention—stick in my mind. It has stared like that, always. When the War came and Europe was bubbling like a pot, the Sphinx stared just as peacefully as ever. Whilst Anthony and I were hanging over that cliff, with Death whispering in our ears and the birds screaming below, the Sphinx was here, staring steadily into the distance. While men were hauling the Wooden Horse into Troy, the Sphinx was staring placidly across the ages. It will stare

T

like that upon the Day of Judgment. At what is it staring so fixedly ? What has it seen, so fascinating, that holds its eyes for ever ? Eternity, perhaps. Thousands of years ago, it saw eternity coming, and it has never shifted its gaze. . . . I am coming to like the Sphinx. It is not fenced with awe, like its companions. Venerable as it is, it doesn't make me feel small. I think, if it could talk, it would be very civil. I am not sure that it has not a sense of humour.

Anthony certainly has. But, then, my husband is a wonderful man. To-day, by sheer force of will, he has won back for us both all the ground that I lost yesterday morning. He made me race my pony against his : he told me stories of Andrew Plague and Patch : he pictured the dismay of the Magicians in Ordinary upon finding that the enchantment for making lice was not in their books. With it all, he never grated. " The art of life, Valerie, is to bear up. We'll lunch in Cairo and drink such a cup as Jamshyd never dreamed of. Afterwards, we'll go and be stung in the Muski. We'll give a thief-treat. You know. Apparently aged rugs. There's nothing like spending money to buck you up. Hang it, we've much to be thankful for. There's you and there's me, and there mightn't be either. And what about Hamlet Patch ? Supposing my name had been ' Buggins.' . . . You just couldn't 've married me. To become ' Mrs. Albert Buggins ' would have been too thick. And people would have said, ' There go the Bugginses.' " I had to laugh. . . . The tambourine was rolling : he kept it rolling, magically. We tore back to Mena in the evening, along that long straight road, chattering like two children. . . .

After dinner, we visited the Sphinx. I am beginning to perceive its mystery. Standing before it, you feel that you are in a presence—the presence of something immeasurably wiser than you. I know it is only a graven image, but I cannot help that. The feeling is not to be denied. And, though the Something is wiser, it is not less human. I am sure the Sphinx would be very decent.

I wonder what it cost him to do what he did to-day. I wonder what it cost Daphnis to laugh and dance and sing, with a heavy heart. A week or two more of this, and the boy will disappear. I shall have broken his heart. Only the tired soldier will be left. . . . A time must come when the pit-pony dreams no more of the green meadows and the kiss of the cool grass upon his aching heels. What happens to people who rob a pit-pony of his dreams? Surely, ' it were better for him that a millstone were hanged about his neck. . . .' *I am afraid.* My God, I am afraid to go in—in case that happy look shall have disappeared. And this boy, whose happy heart I am breaking, is *my beloved.* The little one I am offending is *my darling Anthony.* . . . How hideously Irony can grin—how *maddeningly !* And with a word I can dash the grin from its face . . . with a word and a look. I've only to call the squire and set the crown on his head. And why shouldn't I ? I love him. I'm mad about him. Why shouldn't I make him king? My God. . . . There are two reasons why. First, though I can crown him, I can't make him king. Then, if he were crowned, he'ld play the king—and I . . . I couldn't bear that. . . . Irony's grin would be replaced by a leer.

I cannot sleep. How can any murderess ? I

am going to dress and go out . . . to see the Sphinx

November 15*th.*—A strange thing happened last night. I went out alone, about eleven o'clock, and walked to the Sphinx. Its stare had faded into a dreaming gaze, and it looked extraordinarily majestic. The fanatics who tried to spoil it, lost their labour. All they did was to give it a chance of demonstrating that it is above battery. You cannot disfigure personality. I found it almost impossible to remember that it was only an image. The impression of humanity was ridiculously strong. I found myself wishing idiotically that it could speak. I don't know why. I had no questions to ask. But I felt intuitively that, if it spoke, its words would be worth hearing. All of a sudden, it occurred to me that *the man who lay buried at Girdle was Peter Every.* Girdle was miles from my thoughts. For no reason whatever, the idea just burst into my brain : and, the moment it occurred to me, I knew it was true. Its truth was manifest—glaring. Peter was last seen at Girdle. He had been at Gramarye for me. The world had been scoured for news of him in vain. More. Everybody would have *known* that the body was his, if every one hadn't been certain that it was Anthony's. As it was . . . Poor, poor Peter. Somehow—in some shocking way, he had met his death *in my service.* Instantly, the thought flashed that *it wasn't my fault.* I fobbed it off. It returned forcibly. I *knew* that I wasn't to blame. I *knew* . . . I felt that, for some mysterious reason, Peter was not to be mourned . . . that he had been devoted—dedicate. . . .

I went back to my hotel in a dream, turning my secret over and wondering whence it came. Was

It coincidence? Or had the Sphinx twitched the scales from my eyes. Perhaps, they just fell. Still, I imagine, if you sit at the feet of Wisdom . . .

This morning the Sphinx was staring as fixedly as ever.

I have said nothing to Anthony, but I am going again to-night . . to sit at its feet. I am so impatient to get there that I am going now

* * * * *

There. We have looked over Beauty's shoulder long enough, down past the bloom on her cheek and her sweet-smelling hair. Besides, my lady must change her slippers for something less exquisite : she cannot go walking the desert in those little dancing-shoes. Satin and sand will not agree together. She must choose a coat, too, out of her wardrobe, for the breath of Winter is stealing into the almanac, emerging like a grey wolf, after the great Sun has run his course. And though I should like to squire her with all my heart, I cannot afford the time. Besides, it is not my place. Wherefore, come with me, sirs, into her lord's chamber and see how he is faring, while Valerie puts off her slippers and chooses a coat.

* * * * *

Leaning against a jamb of his bedroom window, Lyveden looked out into the night. This was luminous. The moon was not up, but the brilliant stars were issuing a definite radiance, which lightened the darkness mystically. It would have been strange if the clusters with which the heaven was laden, had not asserted themselves. By some trick of atmosphere, they seemed monstrously low and lambent, ten times as innumerably numerous as ever before. Indeed, in places, the violet dome, from which they appeared to depend, was almost blotted out—there, to the right, a thousand million acres of the firmament were lacquered with a sea of silver-gilded worlds, all fretting and shimmering and rolling to Eternity's will.

For a while, the man stood, smoking, contemplating his lot.

He was, of course, immensely proud of his wife. To be known for the lord of such a dazzling creature, was a delicious vanity. So often as he considered that they were man and wife, his heart glowed. When he saw her coming to him in a public place, the cynosure of eyes, the thought that she was his lady, that that glorious smile was for him, that he had the right to rise and declare their relation, exhilarated him wildly. When chance acquaintances commended her by word or deed, he flushed with delight. He was also as deep in love as a man may be. He found her kind as she was fair, most loving and, most of all, natural. The easy, unconscious friendliness of a child, the quiet, steady understanding of a twin, the fresh, eager *bien être* of a wild creature—*tria juncta in uno*, made her most worshipful. Here was a wise head, of singular beauty, upon shoulders which were not only young, but white, shapely, supple, fit for the back of Artemis. Valerie could run like a deer. She could also enter a restaurant and stand waiting for a table to fall vacant with as much pleasing unconcern as most people use in church during the singing of a psalm. She could so decline a proposal, that the man who had made it felt idiotically rich.

With it all, the pride of her turned everything she touched to gold. Swains, servants, strangers—every one was conscious of her dignity, except herself.

Anthony knew that he was a most fortunate man . . . most fortunate . . . blessed. . . . And yet— what had he of Valerie that Toby Redruth might not have had, had he but stayed in Egypt? Her love, indubitably. For him, the easy friendliness crept closer, the quiet understanding beat more tenderly than for other men. He had his lady's love—a jewel fit for a god's treasury. The trouble was that Anthony was not a god. . . .

Man is a hunter, first of all.

The friendliness glowed like a fire on a snowy night. The hunter warmed himself luxuriously.

The understanding was straight out of heaven. The hunter doffed his cap and thanked God.

But the wild thing was yet in the forest, shy, spirited, waiting. . . . A distant, yearning look slid into the hunter's eyes.

With a sigh, the man turned from the pageant and, after looking listlessly about the room, took his pipe from his mouth and frowned upon the bowl.

Then he sat down at a table and, taking up a letter, proceeded to read it over, before he answered it.

45 *Kensington Palace Gardens,*

W.

DEAR LYVEDEN,

I am obliged for your letter, addressed to me from Rome. I think it improbable that I shall visit that city. The relics of an admirable efficiency, lying beside those of the vile immoderation which eventually broke its back, must be a melancholy spectacle. In this con-

nection, I was not engaged by your somewhat sickly rhapsody upon the Coliseum, which, after all, was nothing but an abattoir *capable of accommodating several frightened brutes and some eighty thousand idle ones.*

Which makes me conscious of a beam in my eye. I do not work as I did. I have tasted the blood of leisure. Besides, Lady Touchstone makes lawful demands upon my time—demands which I delight to respect. Consequently, I now go to Chambers but five days in the week, and no work is sent to the house.

Our marriage will be solemnized towards the end of next month, when we shall leave for the South of France —a movement which I regard with some uneasiness. Except for a visit, paid many years ago, to Boulogne, I have never before left Great Britain, but the memories of that hideous excursion still provoke my indignation. I found the French, if possible, more brainless than my own countrymen. Almost as soon as I had landed, I had the maddening privilege of watching my portmanteau, first, so placed in a luggage-net that it must inevitably fall out, and, then, fall out into the strip of water separating the ship from the quay. By way of consolation, it was presently explained to me that this was a frequent occurrence. My letter reserving rooms at the hotel had been ignored, and, since the town was inexplicably crowded, I had the greatest difficulty in procuring a lodging. I was continually embarrassed by the unaccountable inability of such of the inhabitants as I was compelled to address, to comprehend their own tongue, while the imbecility, vanity and indecency of the manners and customs, to which I was expected to subscribe, made my gorge rise. Lady Touchstone, however, assures me that all this is changed, and that Nice is a pleasant place, where English is freely spoken and English habits have superseded French practices.

On our return to England, we shall reside here for a while. I have asked Lady Touchstone to indicate what alterations she desires, but, except for the decoration of her rooms, she will hear of none being made. She will bring two bed-women, and the other servants will remain.

The dog is in excellent health.

It is right that you should know that a few days ago he was seized with a sudden sickness in the library. I regret to say that the manners of the first veterinary surgeon who arrived left much to be desired. I therefore ordered his removal and sent for another. The second at least condescended to sell me such skill as he possessed. The dog's temperature was taken and found to be normal, when the surgeon declared that his seizure was probably due to a passing indigestion, due in its turn to eating too fast. The fact that he has appeared perfectly well ever since corroborates this diagnosis. However, I have arranged for the man to call every morning, until further notice, to see that the dog is in health, for, as you know, my opinion regarding his physical condition is of no value.

He is bathed once a week under my supervision. I fear he dislikes this, for his demeanour is dejected and he frequently attempts to leave the bath during the operation. Upon being lifted out, however, his spirits immediately revive and, by the time he has been dried, his exuberance is conspicuous.

I shall be glad to see you again. I do very well without you, but I had, I suppose, contracted a habit of reserving for your ears matters which I wished to discuss, and so I notice your absence. Possibly, in the future, if our wives continue to agree, we may conveniently see something of one another.

I heard from Forest yesterday, promising to attend our wedding and speaking highly of you and of his niece. I would do much for that man, who does much to redeem for me the painful impression created by certain other divines.

I hope that you are well and do not regret what you have done. There is nothing which I can usefully say of your predicament, so I shall hold my peace. Lady Touchstone and I speak frequently of you both and wish you very well.

Should you write to me from Egypt, I beg that you will not dilate upon the Pyramids, which, though commonly accounted one of the wonders of the world, only commemorate the blockish mentality of the scene-shifters who ordered their construction. They are not decorative and serve no purpose. Their erection certainly entailed more labour, blood and tears than any building that ever was set up : and they are probably the most idiotically useless things that ever cumbered the earth.

Give my regards to Mrs. Lyveden.

Faithfully yours,

ANDREW PLAGUE.

Lyveden picked up a pen and made ready to write. His thoughts, however, were mutinous.

After a minute or two, he rose and crossed to the window, to knock out his pipe.

As he leaned over the sill, Valerie passed out of the hotel—a delicate, dark-haired ghost, silent, fleeting.

For an instant the man stood still, taken and held by surprise. The next moment, he was fighting his way into a pair of tennis-shoes. . . .

That Valerie should be abroad, unattended, by night, was not to be thought of. Plainly, she wished to be alone. He would respect her desire. She should go and do as she pleased. But, though she should not know it, the squire would be within call. It was his job.

In a flash, he was downstairs and out in the sable road.

There he stood, hatless, peering into the shadows, straining his eyes and ears, to know which way she had gone.

The sons of Nature seemed to have conspired to thwart his senses. The silence, which she had shaken, lay still as death. The jewellery of heaven was shedding a lesser light. A wandering breeze lisped, to smother her footfalls.

Then, fifty paces away, something flickered against the black of the way . . . something . . .

A moment later, Lyveden was following a pale figure, steadily flitting into the wilderness.

That the figure was that of an Egyptian, and not that of his wife, rather naturally never entered his head. Both were dark-headed, grey-clad, spectral. But this was of no consequence. The Egyptian was following the lady.

The three proceeded Sphinxward, Valerie setting the pace—blind leading the blind. . .

The girl was curiously excited. Mystery was in the air. She was persuaded that, naturally or unnaturally, in the presence of the Sphinx the field of her intelligence expanded and its focus became more sharp.

It is probable that her persuasion was sound. There was, to my mind, no mystery. Plainly, the monument inspired her. Her identification of the dead the night before was an inspiration.

It was, however, most natural that the girl should smell magic. Others, wiser than she, have done so, with less excuse. Darkness, silence, the wilderness, tradition, an age so old as passeth all understanding —if such a pasture will not draw Magic, then will no pasture. Be that as it may, the magic she smelled made her the more receptive. By the time she had sighted the Sphinx, Valerie was quite prepared to be among the prophets.

The Egyptian's emotions were at once less fine and more hazy.

Perceiving a white woman passing alone into desert places, he had followed her of instinct. Here was something superior to and feebler than himself, an opportunity to overpower which with impunity was being offered him. Not to avail himself of such an invitation would have been indecent. His forbears would have turned in their graves. He had no intent, save violence ; no plan of action, save surprise. Instinct was his conductor, and brutal instinct would tell him what to do.

The beast was evil and would have been hanged long ago, but for the love he bore his own skin— an inconvenient affection, which had spoiled more sport than he could remember. To-night, however, he could junket without a qualm. Retribution was asleep. The mists of insult, robbery, murder wreathed themselves glittering before his protruding eyes Gliding behind his quarry, he began to feel extraordinarily brave. It was only with an effort that he mastered an inclination to expectorate contemptuously.

Anthony went thoughtfully, his eyes riveted upon the splash of grey ahead. He was sure, of course, that Valerie was for the Sphinx. He feared that she was unhappy . . . was sleeping ill. He wondered if she had ever gone out by night before, decided that she probably had, sweated to think of the perils she had invited. The reflection that now all danger was overpast, he found most comfortable. The thought that she would never be aware of his vigilance, that night after night, perhaps, she would go forth, unconscious alike of peril and wardship, that his darling would be under his government, though his darling would never know, gave him an exhilarating sense of seigniory—a feeling not to be found in the prescribed equipment of squires. He kept his distance carefully, with a grateful heart.

That upon her beholding the Sphinx and presently contemplating the monster as dispassionately as she could, nothing, which could, by any stretch of imagination, be construed as a revelation was vouchsafed to Valerie, is not surprising. Divers commonplace thoughts wandered casually into her head—to be pounced upon, sifted and scrutinized in vain. Here was no gold. Presently, naturally enough, she thought of what had happened the night before—as luck would have it, a fatal exercise. Her mind fell upon the memory and refused to let go. She hauled it away and drove it elsewhither. Always, it eluded her goad and came pelting back. To see what would happen, she allowed it to have its way. It swallowed the memory whole, and then settled comfortably down to chew the cud. . . .

A feeling of disappointment began to edge its way into Valerie's heart. Apparently, the oracle was not

to work to-night. After all, it could not be expected
to function regularly. Still, she had hoped—felt . .

She did not know what she had hoped. There was
no communication which she at all desired. That
which had been made her the night before, she did not
especially value. It was, after all, of no use. Still . .

She had a ridiculous feeling that the Sphinx was
interested. To-morrow, perhaps . .

Valerie rose to her feet.

The moon would be rising soon. Very soon, the
gentle fuller of the firmament would be about her
business. Any moment now, her exquisite craft would
come stealing over the desert, slashing Night's
doublet with silver, furbishing a dull world.

Her thoughts slid back to a night a year ago, when
she had stood, as now, looking upon a landscape
which was smiling in its sleep: on the terrace . . .
at home . . . at Bell Hammer . . . with Anthony
at her side. . . . And he had wrapped his love in
a fairy tale—a tale of a frog and a princess. The
princess had kissed the frog, because—' because it
pleased her to kiss him,' and—nothing had happened.
The frog had loved her so much and had hoped so
very hard, and then—nothing had happened. Poor
frog. . . .

With a sigh, the girl turned, to meet the Egyptian
face to face.

She started violently, and then stood still as death.
The look in the creature's eyes told her her hour
was come. There was no hope.

In a flash, her folly stood out in all its nakedness.

She must have been out of her mind to leave the
hotel. Even in England, it would have been unwise.
In Egypt . . . She must have been mad . . . be-

witched. Her wretched, idiot fancy that the Sphinx had power to—*Power?* My God! *This was its power . . . this . . .*

How clear it was, now. How simple. 'Those whom the gods will destroy, they first send mad.' She had asked to be shown the mystery, and her prayer had been heard. She had sat at the feet of the Sphinx, and the Sphinx had shown her the way to dig her own grave. She had thought herself so clever, because she had found its secret—counted herself one of the elect, because she had felt its spell . . and, all the time, the Sphinx was luring her on . . . all the time she was strutting up to her doom.

And, now, the comedy was over—all but the last short scene. And Anthony, in whose presence every hair of her head was safe, was sleeping peacefully . . with a happy look on his face. . . .

She wondered dully whether the Sphinx ever smiled.

Surely, if ever it did, it was smiling now . leering and staring, as this thing before her was leering and staring horribly . . . gloating . . . with a trickle of spittle running down over its chin.

Valerie felt very sick, suddenly.

The Egyptian began to mow and gibber in an ecstasy of hate. . . . A filthy breath beat upon her face. . . Instinctively, the girl shrank. Instantly, a hand like a clumsy claw fell shaking upon her shoulder. . . .

It was at this moment that Anthony took her assailant by the throat.

To be exact, he took him by the sides of the neck, standing directly behind him, with his thumbs braced against his backbone and his powerful fingers pressing upon his windpipe. For a first attempt at garroting, it was extremely good.

The Egyptian fought like a beast that will stave off Death, without the slightest result. The inexorable grip grew slowly tighter and tighter. The pain in his spine became an agony, which no manner of screams could express. What was so frightful was that he could not scream—because he could not breathe. The pressure upon his windpipe was preventing him. Here he perceived that it was necessary that he should fill his lungs. It had been necessary for a long, long time. It was becoming vital—*vital*. He must breathe, instantly—or die. His head was bursting, like a skin that is stretched too tight. The blood was heaving, pounding against the back of his eyes. His lungs were delivering an ultimatum. The agony in his spine was not consistent with life. Something warm was running out of his ears. The inside of his head had fetched loose and was flapping like canvas in the wind, and the wind was roaring. The stars had slipped and were rushing earthward in a mad swirl . . .

Anthony, who had always understood that compression of the windpipe induced insensibility, was beginning to wonder whether Egyptians were abnormally built, when his victim's knees sagged and he collapsed upon the sand.

Anthony stepped over the body and up to Valerie's side.

The girl stared at the huddle with frightened eyes.

" Dead ? " she whispered.

Anthony shook his head.

" To-morrow," he said, " Douglas will have a stiff neck. Possibly, his throat will be sore. And, if he identifies me, he'll want to enter my service at a nominal wage. But I don't think we'll have him."

Valerie tried to laugh, and burst into tears. . .

As they were nearing the hotel—

" You do everything well," she said.

" Even violence ? "

" Yes, everything. You always did. Gods do, I suppose."

" Valerie, Valerie."

The girl turned and caught him by the arm.

" I take it back," she said. " You're not a god. If you were, you wouldn't love me. That's your only fault. That you can waste your time on a—No. Don't stop me, lad. I want you to know how I feel. I want you to know that I realize that we're playing parts—that I'm playing the part of a queen, in a pasteboard crown, while you're playing the part of my *man*, to do me pleasure. You're my lord, really. You know you are. But if you don't know it, I do. The first time I ever saw you, you were my lord. The royalty in you just crooked its finger, and I had to come. I masked it as best I could, because I'm a woman. But I had to come. . . . I'd seen you, and that was enough. I was your slave." She lifted her eyes and looked at the rising moon. " So I am now. It is my glory. . . . I lost my balance once, and trod it under my feet. I might as well have kicked against a marble wall. I was your slave. . . . How d'you think a slave feels, when her lord makes much of her ? I'll tell you. It makes her very happy and very proud, and it turns her love into an adoration. But how d'you think a slave feels, when her lord kneels at

U

her feet . . . humbles himself to do her honour . . gives up his titles and estate, because he will not use what she has not ? I'll tell you, because I know. She feels as though her heart would break, Anthony . . . and, sometimes, she wishes to God that they had never met. . . ."

There was a long silence.

At length the girl sighed and lowered her eyes. The cold, searching wind of self-reproach had died down. When she spoke again, the wild note in her voice had become wistful.

" I don't know why I keep thinking of old times to-night. But you and I stood like this once, together . . . one perfect night . . . my birthday, a year ago. You told me a fairy tale . . . a tale of a frog, poor fellow, who was in love with a princess. . . ."

" I take it, I was the frog," said Anthony.

" That's right. And he thought that, if the princess were to kiss him, he'ld turn into a prince."

" That wasn't very original," said Anthony. " The idea of Beauty bracing herself to kiss a repulsive Beast has almost the standing of a proverb."

As he spoke the words, the girl's brain plunged. *Beauty bracing herself. . . .*

The cap fitted. It was her very plight.

The curious persistence with which the fairy tale had thrust into her mind was suddenly explained, its moral immeasurably reinforced. The Sphinx— *the oracle had spoken,* just as the night before—— It occurred to Valerie that she had done the creature wrong. The evil that had befallen her was not its fault. Besides, no evil had befallen her. She had been miraculously preserved. . . . Indubitably, she had been right. Her first impression had been right.

The Sphinx *was* interested. *And—it—had—pointed her—the way.* . . .

Anthony was speaking—from a great way off. His voice was sounding ridiculously minute.

"What happened?" he was saying. "Did the princess eventually kiss him?"

"Yes," said Valerie faintly. "And—*and he turned into a prince.*"

*   *   *   *   *

An hour had gone by—the happiest hour that Anthony had ever known.

Fearful lest her recent experience should prey upon her mind, the man had laid himself out, cost what it might, to lift up his lady's heart. He had his reward. Before he knew where he was, her heart had caught his and lifted it clean into Paradise.

The two sat in her room, talking familiarly of bygone days. He could not remember them. *It did not matter.* She made him free of her memory, invited his curiosity, rallied his eagerness.

For the first time since their compact, they had exchanged *rôles*. The man was natural, and the woman was playing a part. Valerie was pretending that she did not care. . . .

Perched sideways upon a table, the slim white fingers of one hand resting upon her hip, those of the other keeping a cigarette, her back straight as an arrow, the girl was a sight to make the angels shout. Every precious bit of her was remembering Nature. The sun and the rain might have dressed her wonderful hair, berries have bled the scarlet of her mouth, violets and stars conjured the magic of her eyes. Her voice was birds' music; the smell of her, the faint scent of blossoms upon a summer's night. Fresh, lithe, glowing, she was embodying most exquisitely that very nonesuch of quality, that precious offset to decay, seldom of this world, never of any other, red, quivering vitality itself. The spring of her movement, the course of the blood in her veins, the clean breath of her body—these unseen mysteries were patent as the day. The wild thing was out of the forest : Eve was in Eden.

Sitting there, on the table, pausing now and again to shudder over a sip of brandy and soda—medicine, which he had prescribed—Valerie gave the impression of a wild thing that knew no fear. Once, she burst into song—flung out a snatch of a lullaby, which he had used to love. . . .

Little wonder that, looking upon her, the man's heart burned within him. The queen had put off her crown.

If the queen had put off her crown, the soldier was not upon parade.

Seated on the arm of a chair, his pipe between his white teeth, Anthony Lyveden was looking like a young god, refreshed—some god of the woods and streams, whom a man might take for a shepherd of high degree. The light of laughter hung in his fine, grey eyes. His firm well-shaped mouth had taken a happy curve. The eager tilt of his chin, his heightened colour, the fresh brilliance of his tone told that the porter had laid aside his pack. Care had slipped down from his pillion. The pony was out of the pit.

Valerie saw this, and the sight gladdened her eyes. She began to forget that she was playing a part. Pretence slid into Reality. If Reason flung out an arm, Nature brushed it aside. That blessed, happy look was worth anything—*anything*. Besides, she—*she did not care . . . any more*. At least . . . How *could* she care, when *the boy had come out to play?* At the thought that it was she who had coaxed him, a smile of unutterable tenderness swept into her face. . . .

Anthony saw it and, smiling, praised God.

An overwhelming desire to do more came flooding into Valerie's heart. She was giving, doing nothing—*nothing*, and he deserved so much. She wanted to honour her darling, to whom honour was due. She wanted to exalt her lover, as no man had ever been exalted before. Before his excellence, words failed her. She felt inarticulate. Yet, express herself somehow, she must. She must make him realize how incredibly dear he was. Her king had no idea —no conception how much he meant. The impulse to open his eyes became irresistible. Her ecstasy, his merit simply had to be expressed.

Valerie slipped off the table, fell on her knees and put her arms round his neck. . . .

Instantly, the happy look faded.

Before her horrified gaze, the quiet, resolute mien stole into place.

In a flash, the boy was gone, and the soldier was on parade.

The strain had come back.

For a second, the girl peered at him, wide-eyed, speechless with dismay.

Then the dam burst, and her heart lifted up its voice.

"Anthony! Don't go back! My sweet, my darling, don't be on guard any more! I've seen you relaxed,

my precious, I've seen you relaxed. I've seen you
at ease—off duty, and I can't let you go. I never
knew—never realized what it meant to you, and
I hadn't the faintest notion of what it meant to me.
It means everything, Anthony—everything in the
world. What's your memory to me? *Nothing!*
D'you hear? D'you understand? *Nothing!* I think
I must have been mad to want it back. It's you, I
want, my darling, you, you, *you!* When I see you
happy like that, I simply don't care. I couldn't care
if your memory *never* came back. The present's so
dazzling that the past pales by its side—fades into
insignificance. All these wretched weeks I've wrestled
and fought with a shadow—a rotten ghost. And
because you've loved me with a love I don't deserve,
you've wrestled and fought, too. And now the ghost's
laid. Smashed—broken for ever. It can't ever rise
again. I don't know whether to laugh or cry when I
see what a fool I've been. And you must try and
forgive me, darling lad. They say Love's blind,
and that's been the trouble with me. But now I
can see. You've shown me. You've come off duty
and shown me your blessed self. Oh, Anthony,
Anthony, smile as you did just now. Look into
my eyes and smile. Show me you know it's true
that your memory doesn't count. Don't think I'm
acting. I'm not. I mean what I say. If I were
acting, how could I talk like this? I tell you, it
doesn't count, darling. It'll never count any more.
I don't care what you remember or what you forget.
If you want to make me happy, do as I say. Smile—
look—be as you were just now. Remember the
barrier's gone, and that you and I are together, overlooking the rolling world. Look back at the last

half-hour and see how happy I've been. I broke
into song just now. Why d'you think I did that?
Because I just had to sing—out of pure joy. Does
that look as if I was caring about your memory?
Oh, Anthony, my darling, my heart, blot out the
last two months, and start again. Forget that they've
ever been—except the last half-hour. Not that you
haven't been wonderful, because you have. You've
played the squire as it's never been played before.
But now you've spoiled it all and shown me the
king . . . my king . . . my glorious, happy boy,
with a crown on his head and a look in his blessed
eyes that I can't do without, my darling . . . that I
can't do without any more."

Breathless, panting, she stopped—with her heart in
her mouth.

*The resolute look was fading. The boy—the boy was
coming . . . coming back . . . tentatively . . . venturing out to play.*

Spellbound, she watched the wonder steal into his
eyes.

Hardly daring to breathe, she watched him trying
to realize that his dream was true.

The thing seemed too big for him.

A half-perplexed, half-frightened look displaced
the wonder . . . He put a hand to his head. . . .
Then, the wonder returned, stronger and clearer
than before. The boy was beginning to smile. . .
Little by little, that blessed, happy look was coming
back. . . .

Suddenly, he seemed to hesitate.

Then, very gently, he put up a boyish hand and
touched her hair.

Valerie thrilled to her core. . . .

Again, for a moment, he hesitated.

Then, with a shy smile, he began to take out the pins. . . .

Valerie could have burst into tears of pure joy. Her cup was full. She had beaten the fairy tale. The frog had become a prince.

With a leaping heart, she bowed her beautiful head and suffered his gentle fingers . . .

When her glorious hair was all loosened, Valerie lifted her head and shook her fragrant treasure about her shoulders.

The boy gazed at it with rapture : the king was beholding his kingdom : the hunter was on his knees.

" I always wanted to see it down," he whispered, " always. The first time I ever saw you—in the door of *The Leather Bottel*, you had no hat on. I remember thinking, then, how much I'ld love to see it tumbled about your shoulders. . . . And now, my dream's come true."

His eyes turned from the glory to meet his wife's. Valerie was staring at him, with parted lips.

The light in her wonderful eyes was supernatural. Anthony started.

" What is it, Valerie ? What have I said ? What——"

He stopped short and clapped a hand to his mouth. . . .

Presently, he stood up and lifted her to her feet. With his arms about her, he smiled into her eyes.

" ' For you shall find it,' " he whispered, " ' after many days.' "

THE END